MOVING JACK

BOOK ONE OF THE LOVE WARS SERIES

MICHELLE MARS

Enjoy!!

Cover design by Jacqueline Sweet Design

Edited by Jen Graybeal

❀ Created with Vellum

DEDICATION

Sometimes we have opportunities to explore new paths/facets of ourselves. We can choose to explore them or not. I've been an avid reader for many years, but never felt I could pursue writing. Then I did, and with help, I jumped into a new adventure. It's no surprise that my first heroine is, therefore, given a chance to travel a new path and must choose to risk what is known for what could be.

This book is dedicated to everyone who finds themselves at a crossroads. Consider this the push to take a risk on something new that completes you.

And, to my loving family, my friends who pushed me, my early readers whose support and feedback were invaluable, my editor, my mentor, and the romance writing community, you all strengthened me through those doubting days.

TABLE OF CONTENTS

Adventures of a Supernatural Geek Girl

April 8, 2020

Dear Reader,

Coming to you straight from the heart of Silicon Valley. First entries can be so challenging. What can I write to break the ice and get people reading my blog? And how... when... do I mention I'm a vampire? Do I just throw it out there, have an interesting lead in, hint at it but don't come right out and say it? Or talk around it until it's a dead fish and move on?

Now that I've sautéed that sucker, let's get this blog on a roll.

Since I've mentioned it, I'm sure you've got some questions. So did I! I was killed two months ago, accidentally killed my maker, came back to life, and had to figure out vampirism all by my lonesome. My questions started with, "What the fuck? Why am I so hungry? Am I really a vampire now? What the fuck?" Once I got past that newbie-in-shock awkward stage, my questions were, "Who am I now? What can kill me? Am I the undead, the walking dead, the glittery kind, the altered-DNA kind, or something else entirely?

1

Do I have to drink blood and if so, how much and from what source? Is there a *Vampire for Dummies* I can download? Really though, WHAT THE FUCK?"

Luckily, I had the means to find answers. You see, I'm also a hacker. I scoured the internet for true knowledge instead of myths. Myths get you killed. Eventually, I ran across a well-hidden book. At first, I was sure it was a work of fiction. It contained a vampire origin story and a set of rules. The snarky sounding rules made me think I was looking at myth but since I enjoy good snark, I chose to test them out anyway. Goldmine! Hence, I'm still here.

You may ask yourself, why would a vampire start a blog? Good question. You see, I was bad with social situations before I became a vampire. Now I'm a walking double whammy of social dysfunction. I'm hoping with this blog I can bring other vampires useful information and, in the meantime, form a community. Isn't it ironic as a science and tech buff I always believed in aliens and not the things that go bump in the night and yet, here I am… Never did meet an alien. So. Here's your first vampire…

Fun Facts:
Vampires are all environmentalists. Who knew? Right? This is because we're intimately connected to the Earth. Goes back to that origin story I mentioned before. I was always environmentally concerned, because you're just being a douche if you don't care at all, but as a vampire I'm a total bitch when it comes to mother Earth. If I see you don't recycle something, I may just go fang on your ass. Not really, but #TakeCareOfOurMother.

Hugs and bites!
iByte

[1]

SEE JACK RUN

Adventures of a Supernatural Geek Girl

September 30, 2025
Dear Reader,

Over the last five and a half years of blog entries, an alien invasion, and the rise of the resistance, I feel like we've really gotten to know each other. Lately, some of you have brought it to my attention that I never discuss my dating life. I'd think with the aliens' relocation plans looming, you'd have more important things to think about, but apparently I'd be wrong.

I would *like* to say I don't discuss it because I'm busy being a rebel. ¡Viva la revolución! I would *like* to say it's because I'm too busy with an overly full dating life. I almost choked on writing that. I would also *like* to say it's because a lady never kisses and tells but this vampire would totally kiss and tell. You see, dear followers, before I can report said kisses, said kisses would have to happen. <sigh>

In my pre-vampire imaginings of vampires, they were all sexy and having sex all the time. Dating gods! Am I right? When I became one, I kinda assumed, it was like a fairy godmother waving her wand and making me the ultra-datable. Turns out, you can make the girl a vampire but you can't teach her to flirt, or dress, or be less awkward. I still get along better with my computer than with the general population. I can help lead a resistance but don't ask me to hold a conversation with a guy I'm interested in.

Don't get me wrong, I'm not completely innocent. I'm a vampire, not a zombie, not that I'm saying those exist. Moving on. Let's just say my dating life has been nothing to write home about and few and far between.

I've come to accept that I'm not the kind of girl who has guys chasing after her. If anything ever changes, you'll be the first to know.

Flashback Fun Facts:

Vampires can be out in the sunlight, just not for prolonged exposures. We have an internal turkey popper that tells us when we're nearing our exposure limit. I could be sitting right next to you at the beach. (Just not for too long. That could get messy.)

Hugs and bites!
iByte

Redwood Grove, Los Altos, CA, USA, Earth

October 1, 2025

Jack Daniels nervously looked up from her wrist phone, tapped the implant in her ear, and whispered, "Hal, off." Hal was her personal assistant link (PAL). The PAL program had been her baby before the aliens had arrived. Now, her baby was at a standstill, and she had one of the few PALs left in existence. It was thoroughly disheartening to think she'd just been using Hal to scroll through the latest comments posted to her blog entry. What a waste of a good PAL. Still, Hal definitely made it easier to multitask and keep up with her readers.

She'd been in the middle of getting offended that one commenter offered to date her in exchange for immortality—the nerve of some people—when she heard figures approaching her location, and went radio silent. She stood stock still in the clearing off of one of the beautiful Redwood Grove hiking trails. She wasn't sure why the aliens had stuck a terminal out here except maybe they liked nature. Or maybe the location was to calm the humans as they registered for relocation? After all, who could be unhappy surrounded by tall trees, deer, and the sound of water? The answer to that last question is, she could, because she couldn't afford to be caught by the wrong people and especially not by the aliens.

Whoever was approaching, was still some distance away, and she couldn't tell yet, how many were approaching, but her multitasking time was up. Hal testily, but neurologically, answered her, "You could be nicer when turning me off, you know. Rude, much?" She detected a huff from him before he shut himself down, but couldn't remember when she programmed a neurological huff into his code. At least once out of every two interactions with Hal, she found herself reconsidering the PAL personality profile. That is, if she was ever able to return to working on it. Not any time soon, with how things were going.

Focus!

"Come on. Come on. Come on. Download faster." She

anxiously whispered at the aliens' computer terminal, keeping her other senses trained around her. She had zero intention of getting caught.

Ugh, you're talking to inanimate objects again, Jack. Isn't it bad enough you talk to yourself a lot? You know… like you're doing right now? Maybe she needed to spend more time with her friends when she got back to base. At least she still had her sense of humor.

The sound through the trees grew progressively louder, closer. A human would even be able to hear something soon. Anxiety clawed through her, making her feel like a heart attack was imminent, but that was impossible seeing as her heart no longer pumped blood and hadn't for over five years. Not since becoming a vampire. Instead, when anxious or excited, she experienced an energy elevation that made her body thrum and tingle. And boy, was she thrumming and tingling now.

The smart thing to do was to listen to the feeling and take action. Yeah. That was unlikely. She was pretty sure she didn't have a functioning survival instinct.

Since making the right choice was off the table, she continued to stand around waiting for the download to finish. Tapping her foot. Gnawing her lip. She was likely to get herself caught, and with her luck, this particular terminal would only connect her to Staraban recipes and gardening tips. Of course, if the aliens had their way, those things might just prove useful. So yeah.

The Staraban had arrived on Earth eight months earlier freaking all the humans the fuck out, even with their peacenik approach. "We come in peace and are here to save you."

They even came bearing pamphlets. Who knew first contact would involve a freaking pamphlet? In said pamphlet, they claimed Earth was a dying planet and humans were getting relocated to a shiny new habitable alternative. Right! Who believed that? As far as Jack was concerned, when something sounds too good to be true, you shove it right back into outer space.

Focusing back on the task at hand, she was quite sure she was stuck with the slowest computer in the galaxy. She had excellent hacker skills but even she couldn't change the speed of the alien processor. Apparently, the aliens could travel through space but couldn't figure out how to make a computer download quicker than a turtle's speed. *Ladies and gentlemen, this is the insurmountable issue for all sentient beings. Space travel, no big deal. Lasers for weapons, sure. Food replicators, yep. A faster operating system, nope. Sheesh! Who knew?*

Her vampiric senses went on full alert as she picked up more information about the approaching parties. She could now tell that there were two teams of aliens and they seemed unaware of her presence, since they weren't covering their approach nor running at her. It'd be hard for them to pick up her presence anyway, for now, since as a vampire, she didn't need to breathe and didn't have a heartbeat, so she easily kept under the radar. Vampire perks. Of course, if she was still here when they made it to the clearing, she'd be pretty hard to miss.

Still listening for any sign of alarm, all she heard was slow gait, easy breathing, and relaxed conversation. She guessed they were here on pleasure not business and definitely, luckily, were still unaware of her. Since Staraban physiology included having two hearts, she could also deduce that two aliens were approaching from the south, since she caught four heartbeats, and three aliens were approaching from the east, with six heartbeats. If they stuck to their current pace, she calculated that they'd reach her location in about two minutes.

If they'd been human, she could have taken all five of them in a fight, but the Staraban were strong and fierce warriors. She hadn't had to battle with them, yet, but she had seen news coverage of them quelling some of the riots that occurred when humans first learned they weren't alone in the universe. One Staraban in a fight, would be a challenge, though she still thought she could win, but all five, no way. *Come on, Jack! Get this show on the road already!*

Another minute passed, her anxiety clawed even deeper into her, and the computer finally, *finally*, finished downloading the information she needed. Since no one was around to see her do her vampire thing, she moved at a blurring speed, grabbed her drive, shut down the terminal and kept blurring into the tree line to the northwest. *Yep. That's me. Captain Blur. Like the Flash, but not.* She silently chuckled. At least she could amuse herself before getting caught.

She began heading directly back to the Humans Against Relocation Movement (HARM) HQ, but her lack of survival instinct reared its head again. *Who needs sound decision making anyway?* She paused, gauged her distance, and jumped into a tall tree about a quarter mile away. Curiosity may have killed the cat, but the vampire? *Nah. Observation is a form of information gathering, which is why I'm here. Right?*

Jack stopped her imitated breathing as the aliens entered the clearing. It always amazed her just how similar they were in form to humans. In fact, they could sing along to "Head, Shoulders, Knees, and Toes" if they were so inclined. She silently giggled at that thought, picturing the mighty warrior aliens participating in the silly children's song. *Still amusing myself.*

What wasn't the same, besides the whole two heart thing, was that the aliens were also taller and more muscular than most humans. The four males and one female in the clearing were prime examples of this. Jack was five-foot-eight and yet, the aliens were much taller. The males all looked like extras from the movie *300*. Ripped and ready to fight. *I bet they all have a six pack. Or maybe even an eight pack?* The alien female was sleeker but still muscular and tall. Their skin also had a marked golden look to it. Not tan exactly, but not yellow either. It was definitely distinct.

She was loath to admit it, but secretly, she had always found something alluring about them. Jack knew better than to be deceived by their beauty, though. As a vampire, she had run across her fair share of both friendly and cruel vampires and yet they were all beautiful. Well… maybe not her, but all the other vampires. Still, something always drew her to the Staraban. Perhaps because they were such an enigma and she'd never met a puzzle she didn't have to solve.

As far as she could tell, they weren't the Borg nor the Empire. They didn't opt for assimilation or destruction, but instead they seemed to always look for a peaceful solution before going for the beat down. They *seemed* to actually believe they were helping the poor, idiot Earthlings who couldn't be trusted with big decisions like where to live.

She found it hard to remain unmoved while observing their friendly and affectionate demeanor with each other. It was obvious that they were all close. *Friends? Family? Lovers? Do they take more than one lover? How do they even make love? Why the hell am I thinking about this?*

She wished she could hate them. It would make this rebellion so much simpler. Instead of being that boyfriend you *know* is an asshole, they behaved like the irritating one who was generally a good guy but thought you needed his mansplaining to get you through life. *Yeah, right. No man or alien is going to tell me what to do!*

It took her a bit, but she suddenly realized her gaze kept returning back to one specific alien. There was something about him that kept her *riveted*. He had wavy black hair that hung loosely around his head. She couldn't discern his eye color at this distance, but there was an intensity of purpose, an awareness of his surroundings that set him apart. He seemed a man with intense control. Of himself? Of others? Maybe. He just didn't seem as relaxed as those around him. He wasn't classically handsome, though thinking that about an alien was ridiculous anyway, but still, his features were severe with a firm jaw line, wide nose, and slanting brows. No softness that she could tell. A shiver of awareness ran down her back. It was cold, or something. He looked absolutely scrumptious in the alien one piece, form fitting, tan uniform which hugged him like a glove, much like Jack suddenly wished to be doing. *Oh Shit!* Her growing arousal as she stared at him, tripped her vampire switch and her fangs elongated. Blood-hunger and sexual hunger often triggered the same physiological reactions.

She tried to get a grip on her libido. *They're probably just like that TV show V, the original one, not the new one, where it's all good on the outside but you unzip them and, wham, behind door number one is a lizard man!* Unfortunately, desire continued to course through her. As Jack's hunger flooded her veins and pooled in her core, she pictured leading him away and having her way wi—

She tensed. Instinct made her go completely and utterly still.

Tarc wandered into the clearing with his brother, best friend, and second in command, Bren, at his side. He enjoyed every moment he could spend out in nature and took every opportunity to get away from base to do just that. It saddened him to think that Earth, which was a truly beautiful and naturally diverse planet, was dying. For this outing, he and Bren planned to meet up with their youngest brother, Drei, who was set to leave Earth that evening, their beautiful sister, Caran, and their close family friend since childhood and head of security, Nial. They had chosen a stunning wooded area near an outpost they had set up a few months back when they had relocated the humans around it.

"This area is quite lovely." Caran, scientifically brilliant since she was little, studied the trees nearby. "I will need to grab some samples before we leave the area. I want to further study the flora an—"

"Looks like we have lost your sister already." Nial laughed and slapped Bren on the back.

"Yes. Always a risk when encountering any new plants, flowers, dirt, species… basically anything classified as new and organic is fair game for little sis." Bren teased and winked at Caran.

"Similar to your need to study anything classified as female, compatible, and willing. But of course, your study is rather shallow since it lasts for only a night." Caran countered.

Everyone laughed and Bren shrugged. "It is not my fault the females love me. I do not want to hinder peaceful accords."

Drei, a delegate of the All Alien Alliance, coughed. "Brother, you leave so many angry females behind you, I am surprised you are allowed anywhere near a negotiation."

Bren looked a bit sheepish but with a glint of humor in his eyes. In classic Bren form, he responded, "I am always up front in what is happening, it is not my fault my charm makes them want more than one night."

Caran groaned. "I know I brought it up, but now I regret it. Could we stop talking about my brother's bedroom exploits?"

Nial gave Caran's nose a brotherly tweak which she swatted

away irritably. "Just think of it in scientific terms. A study of the male in his natural habitat."

Caran rolled her eyes. "You would know all about that, too. I would rather study the plants around here." She turned to Drei. "Are you ready for your trip back to the Alliance?"

As the others joked and began checking in about their day, Tarc did not participate. His siblings were often amusing to observe, but he did not often join in with their jokes. He never quite knew how to drop his cloak of control, of being in charge, of being responsible. Right now, though, he had another reason he did not participate. Since walking into the clearing his senses had gone on alert. He had tensed, aware of everything. He could not pinpoint the cause of the unease, but something was not right. Something. Something. As he took another breath, he noticed a distinct scent in the air. He let his inner predator take over and breathed a little more deeply to understand where the scent was coming from. There was an abundance of it near the registration terminal but that was starting to dissipate. What he was not prepared for, was how intoxicating he found the scent. He closed his eyes and let it infuse his system. It appeared the strongest was heading into the tree line to the northwest.

He scanned the trees in that general direction. As he did, he could not shake the effect of the smell nor the sure feeling that they were being observed. Then he saw it. No. He saw her. At this distance, there was no way to be sure the person in the tree was a female, but the scent and his gut told him she was. He watched as the figure went unnaturally still. She must have realized he was staring at her.

He took barely a moment to tell his family and friend that he needed the area searched. That he had reason to believe there may be others around. He sent them to the south, east, and west, while he headed directly towards the figure. He ground his teeth as she dropped down from the tree. He picked up his pace, almost running. The words were out of his mouth before he could think better of them. "Do not run, female! I will not harm you!"

That went about as well as he expected and he cringed as her pace increased. His did too and his inner predator shifted all of his attention to tracking his prey.

An hour later, his inner predator was hissing and biting at the bit. Catching her would have been simple, if he had directed the others to help him, but her smell had been so damn enticing. He had wanted her all to himself. Of course, now that he had chased that same smell for so long, through neighborhoods and shopping districts, it was quickly losing its appeal. That was a lie. It was just as intoxicating. He was just tired of trying to hunt her down. He felt both a grudging respect for and a deep frustration with the female.

One thing was for sure, he needed to find her. Her scent had been near the terminal and he wanted to know why. Also, in theory, he was tracking a human female, but he was not so sure about the human part. Her agility, silent movement, and speed hinted at something *more*. He wanted, no, needed to know for sure. Was there another, more dangerous, species on Earth that they needed to be aware of?

He nearly growled out loud when he saw that she had circled him back to the relocated neighborhood near the park where the chase began. He continued to follow her scent, though, which surprisingly led into the abandoned library. He listened intently. A musty smell permeated the air, but her scent... her scent was now very strong and all around where he stood. His muscles went on full alert, ready for action. *She is here.*

"*Fash!*" The Staraban curse flew out of his mouth as he flew forward. He used the momentum to whirl around. Considering the strength of the hit, he gaped at his would-be attacker. Something did not equate.

Crouched in a battle stance was a woman with pale skin, who looked to be in her mid-twenties, by human years. She was only as tall as his chest with a curvy, sensual body. She was wearing the Earth clothing black boots, black jeans, and a tight, black shirt with the words "People are Interesting. Books are Better." Her dark brown hair with red stripes weaving throughout was pulled back in a ponytail. Her eyes were the color of one of his new favorite Earth foods, chocolate, and shown with a brilliant fire, and her lips... He could not take his eyes off her lips. He knew he should say something, but before he could think of what, she lunged at him again. *Fast.*

He dodged her attack. *Since when can humans move like that?* "Stop! Now." He demanded. Instead, she attacked him, again. He narrowly avoided her.

"Stop following me." she snarled. "I don't want to hurt you, but I will if you make me."

He snorted.

That was a mistake. His little prey narrowed her eyes at him and attacked ferociously. He blocked a few of her hits, but grunted when one landed squarely on his chest, staggering him back. He fisted his hands. *That actually fashing hurt.* He did *not* want to hurt her and so he maintained his position, "I just want to talk, little human."

"Little? You know what... never mind. I meant what I said. Stop following me and leave me alone. In fact, better yet, get you and all your big alien buddies back on your spaceship and go home like E.T."

He had no idea who this eee tee was but he could not miss that her tone dripped with sarcasm. Irritation flitted up his body. He was not going anywhere. "We are here to help yo—"

"Off of this dying planet," she interrupted in a mocking voice. She put her hand on her hip and in her regular voice, added, "Save it. I don't believe you. Want to try again?"

He glared at her. "Are you questioning our honor? We do not lie. *I*, do not lie."

Her answer? She lunged at him again hitting his chest and knocking him even further back.

Different emotions were fighting for supremacy. Anger that this human female dared to question his honor. Annoyance that she was able to land so many hard blows. Curiosity to figure out what she was. Desire. *Desire? Damn, he was horny.* He had always admired a strong, fearless female. There was no fear in this one. Only fight.

As they squared off with each other, he imagined what it would be like to lift her up in his arms, have her wrap those strong legs around his hips, and drive himself right into all of her power and beauty. He was so hard, his cock was trying to punch a hole through his well-maintained uniform. He saw her sniff the air in confusion. *Do humans do that?* Her gaze veered directly towards his painfully hard member and then slowly, seemingly cataloguing his body parts, back up into his eyes with such heat, a growl escaped him.

That was when she pounced again, pushed him hard in the chest, propelling him backward into the wall. He was about to defend himself, when he realized that this time, she had not jumped away. No. This time she was pressed right up against him, kissing his throat as she started clawing at the clasps on the front of his uniform. Some small part of him warned that this was reckless and not like him, but his body stopped listening to that part when he felt her lips on his skin and her hands on his chest. More insistent was the need to get his hands on her too. Both of their lustful scents were now swirling and combining around them in their own mating ritual. It was like being enclosed in an aphrodisiac.

He threaded his fingers into her hair and yanked her head back for a kiss running his tongue along the seam of her mouth until she opened on a sigh. His tongue delved in, tasting her and sparing with her tongue. There was nothing sweet about this kiss. It was either a fight for supremacy or a race to a mutually pleasurable conclusion, he could not tell which, and he did not care. He was operating on pure instinct. He was pretty sure the same was true for the ball of fury and lust in his arms. And that thought just made him even hotter. Harder.

Her hands fumbled with the fastenings and she growled into his mouth, so he pushed her hands out of the way, and undid them all in a few deft moves. She took over and pushed the material off his shoulders. She had the material most of the way down his chest when she broke from his mouth and started kissing his neck again. Tarc ran his hands from her hair down the length of her back. He could feel the muscles that ran along her body shifting and tensing as she began to kiss her way down his chest. He was not used to giving up control in these types of situations, but there was no way he was going to stop her right then. "You feel amazing."

Their combined scents utterly engulfed him. She was spicy and rich and sweet and it blended perfectly with his own masculine scent. All of his senses were fully tuned in to her. Smell, touch, beauty, taste, and the sounds she was making deep in her throat. The combination was driving him out of his mind and uncomfortably, out of control. The thought, *she is mine,* was on repeat in his head and he could not understand why. Still, he did not have the capacity to question it at that moment.

She fumbled with the clasps at his waist, and once again, he pushed her hands out of the way, and undid them for her. When he finished, he moved his hands up the front of her body, inch by inch until he cupped her perfectly rounded breasts. They filled his hands completely. He wanted to feel them with no clothes between them, so he pushed her shirt up even while she was tugging his uniform down. He lifted her shirt over her breasts and saw she wore a lacy black Earth undergarment underneath. His fingers teased at her nipples poking at the material and she whimpered. He pushed the material down releasing her breasts and felt the weight of them with his palms. She whimpered again and arched her back. He could not stop feeling her and rubbing his thumb back and forth over her very erect, hard nipples.

Her hands, which had stopped moving while he fondled her, now moved to the front of his uniform and gripped his throbbing member. He grunted. "Yes. Feel me." She pulled away from his hands and once again pushed down on his uniform. This time she got it past his erection and even further pooling at his ankles. She came back up, palmed his hard shaft and kissed her way back up his chest. "Your hand on me feels so, so good." His hands went back to tweaking the hard buds of her nipples and he could not wait to get his mouth on them. He was just about to lean down to do just that, when she planted a kiss on his throat and he felt a sharp pain. *"Fash!"*

Before he could register what had happened, she was gone. Left behind was her apology on the wind and her scent still surrounding him. *What the fash just happened? And damn she moves fast.* He considered chasing her again but since his pants were down around his ankles, he knew she would be long gone by the time he could.

He reached up and felt something wet on his neck. He looked at his fingers and saw blood. Anger vied with unfulfilled lust but ultimately, neither won out. He yanked his pants up and re-clasped everything, doubly frustrated, and wondered how he would find his blood-thirsty vixen. *I cannot believe I fell for her seduction. Was it all just a ruse to get away? Thank the goddess that Bren was not here or else he would torment me endlessly for this.*

She may have drawn first blood, but Tarc planned to capture her, find out what she was doing in the clearing, and then... then he would make sure they finished what they just started. *Only this time, I will be in control and she will be begging for me.* First, he needed to find her.

He walked back toward the clearing where it all began and found his brother Bren and sister Caran waiting for him.

"Where have you been? We were about to send out a search squad." Bren scolded. "We had to send Drei with Nial back to base so Drei could prepare for his departure."

Caran looked at him inquisitively. His sister's mind was always working. "Does it have something to do with the female scent in this area that is now all over you?" She raised an eyebrow at him.

He groaned. Of course he would not be able to hide this from his observant sister. "I chased her down. She attacked me." He tried to shrug it off.

Bren smirked and punched Tarc in the shoulder. "She attacked you? Is that what you are calling it now? You know we can smell what you guys were doing, right?"

He did know and flushed with embarrassment and frustration. The embarrassment not from the sexual scent, but from remembering how she had left him. Actually, the frustration was from that too. "It is none of your business. All you need to know is that she got away and I am devising a way to trap her so I can interrogate her. I do not think she was here without purpose."

He headed to the terminal. It was still functional. He tapped on the terminal a few times and found what he thought he would. The terminal had been accessed recently. "I believe she accessed our network through this terminal. Apparently, she has learned our technology language enough to connect to it."

"Is there anything that she could access that would be an issue?" Caran came up alongside him looking concerned.

Bren answered, "Depends on how good she is at digging through data. In theory, the top layer information should not be a problem, but our information is all connected on some level. If she was able to dig deep enough, she could find ship schematics, weapons information, deployment records, basically anything and everything. Tarc, whatever happened between you, you have to find this human female and make sure to stop her."

"Oh. I definitely plan to find her. Do not worry there, brother." He silently added, *and then, she will be mine.*

Jack still couldn't believe what she'd done. Since when did she try to pull off the whole sex kitten routine? Worse. Since when did she acciden- tally bite someone? Oh. I'm sorry. Did my unusually sharp teeth trip and fall into your carotid artery? My mistake! She groaned inwardly.

At least my sexy alien, no, not MY, THE sexy alien, ugh, I mean THE ALIEN hadn't chased me. Of course, I literally left him with his pants around his ankles. She had to giggle at that.

Jack studied her surroundings and her humor died. It always saddened her to travel from relocated, empty areas like Los Altos into populated, functional areas like Mountain View. There was still life here. *As it should be. As it would be.* Her mission was always clear in her mind.

She detoured on her way back to stop at what used to be termed Whole Paycheck grocery. Even though it was old slang, she still enjoyed calling it that. Tonight was going to require at least two to five pints of organic, free-range ice cream. She picked up a bottle of fair-trade, sustainably farmed, organic wine, scanned all the items with her wrist phone and checked out. It was a good thing Gobble paid well, because as supplies dwindled these luxury items were getting more and more expensive. She stuffed everything into her Bag-in-a-Pocket and was on her way towards HQ again.

Jack was always amused how easy it was to hide HARM HQ in plain sight. Four years before, Gobble, one of the biggest tech companies in the world, opened up Gobble Neighborhood, a mixture of multi-family and dorm-like buildings located on the north side of their campus. Top executives from Gobble and many other Silicon Valley giants of industry didn't believe the claims the aliens were making regarding Earth dying in the next ten to twenty years. Sure, there were problems with global warming, but they didn't believe that the planet itself was that close to the brink. So they set aside one of the dorm buildings to be used as HARM head-quarters, diverted some of their top talent in programming as well as scientists from many fields, to figure out if there was any validity to the aliens' claims and if there was anything that could be done to stop relocation.

As she made her way onto the Gobble campus, she pressed behind her ear. "Hal, call his majesty."

"I'm sorry Jack, your sarcasm is getting in the way of your productivity again. Whom do you want me to call?"

Jack smiled. "Hal, are you actually criticizing my sarcasm with sarcasm? Well done, but we both know you know exactly who I mean."

Hal quipped back. "Are you talking about his eminence and your rebellion-leading better half, Will?"

She snorted. "My better half? Ha. Well. Okay. That's fair. Yes, I mean him."

"Connecting you now."

A deep, aggravated voice answered. "Are you alive?"

Oh how to answer that? I haven't been really alive for five years but I'm still not really dead. "I'm calling you from the great beyond. I always promised that I would haunt you."

"If I believed in that nonsense, I might worry. As it stands, any useful information from the other side?"

Jack laughed, "None that I know of. In other news, I'm fine, back on campus and heading to base. How are things there?"

Will sighed. "I'm in charge of the worst resistance in the history of rebellions. Programmers and code breakers want a constant stream of pizza, soda, and chips. Of course, to counter all those bad decisions, they also just applied for me to set up a gym on the lower level. A gym. This isn't a fucking spa. It's a re-bell-ion. If one more of them applies for an arcade room, I may just volunteer someone to go off planet."

"Well… Um… Okay, then. How about I just see you when I get there."

"No. No. Tell me. How did it go? Were you able to hack into their system?"

"Yours truly is a hacking goddess, as you know, and yes, I hacked the shit out of their system." Jack was not going to talk about what happened afterwards. "I downloaded something, now it's just a matter of seeing what it is. Alien porn maybe? Their version of cat videos?"

Will scoffed. "I can't think of anything I want to see less than alien porn. I can't imagine nor do I want to, what these aliens do in the bedroom. Nope. Not thinking about it. Just get your ass back here. I think they are out there arguing over the Stranger Things series finale. Again!" A long-suffering sigh made its way across the air waves.

The aliens seem to do what we do in the bedroom. She kept to herself. "Try not to kill anyone and my ass, as well as the rest of me, will be there soon. Bye! Hal, end call."

"You could be more understanding of his position." Hal said irritably.

"Are you kidding me?"

"Well. You could. Dealing with the running of the base while you go gallivanting around kissing aliens…"

Jack stopped dead in her tracks and her jaw dropped. "You were aware of that?" She was utterly horrified. "I don't remember turning you on."

"You were too busy being turned on yourself to notice that I was connected. You never have read through the team manual. What kind of programmer doesn't read about what their team members are doing? My protocols are to turn myself on when I sense you may be in danger; i.e., when you are in a fight. If that's what you'd call what you were doing."

Jack felt her energy thrum with annoyance. "You... will... never... talk about that incident again or I will have to permanently disconnect you. I put up with your deeply inappropriate obsession with Will but bringing this up would be grounds for your extinction."

"May be worth it." He paused. She waited. "Okay. I won't mention it, but I bet you bring it up with Rory in less than twenty-four hours."

"Not a chance." Jack came around the corner of one of the other dormitories. "Hal, off."

"Hey gorgeous! Why don't you bring your pretty ass over here and we have a systems integration meeting?" That comment came from the mouth of a medium height man sporting a bro-beard, a leering stare, and a really unpleasant smell.

Jack rolled her eyes, wondered what everyone's fascination was with the location of her ass, shrugged her shoulders, and pointed to a hidden corner.

Creep-bro's eyes grew wide in shock and then he excitedly followed her.

As soon as he entered the dark corner, Jack stared him directly in the eyes and issued forth her power. "Come here, turn around, and lean your head to the right." Glamoured, the creep-bro complied. "Thank you for providing me lunch, asshole. You won't feel this nor remember ever meeting me." She bit down and drank. Only eating from those that deserve it makes drinking a chore. The blood tastes good because its blood, and bad because its blood from someone usually pretty disgust-worthy.

When she was finished, she cringed at having to lick at the puncture holes to close them, but she couldn't leave him with holes in his neck. After biting some jerk, Jack always felt like she wanted to wash her mouth out with soap or acid. This time was no different. It was better than biting unsuspecting good people, though. That was a rare occasion, one borne out of desperation. She turned her lunch around, and reinforced his sudden amnesia.

As she made her way down the last path to the dorm, Jack felt sated for blood, but prayed her ice cream hadn't melted because she really, really, needed some frozen reinforcement. She couldn't excavate the alien's blue eyes and hard body from her mind. She would have to figure out a solution to the programmers' series finale dilemma but after that she would head straight into a very, *very* cold shower.

Her hands made their way to her wet breasts. She stared into his blue eyes. She knew from the interaction in the library they were the clearest blue. Those blue eyes were blazing while she massaged the mounds and tweaked her nipples. The heat in his eyes, the lust, drove her forward. Her right hand continued to play with her breast but her left made its way down her water-slicked belly. Her fingers found her pussy and teased the folds there. Her breathing sped up as he moved his hand down his own body, fisting and pumping his long, hard, beautiful erection. She threw her head back, fingers playing with her clit. Slow circles to start but then she delved her fingers into her center and fucked in and out. Then back to pressing on her clit until she couldn't stand the pressure anymore, she came, moaning loudly.

Jack opened her eyes and smiled in satisfaction. That had to be the best bout of self-care she had ever had. Of course, her initial intention for the cold shower had been to put that damn alien out of her mind. That was an epic fail or win depending on your perspective. *Damn girl. Why him?*

She shut the shower off, stepped out, and looked in the mirror as she dried herself. Flashes of their fight and aftermath played through her mind. *Okay. You indulged. Now it's time to get back to work. You are trying to get rid of the aliens. Remember that. No. Seriously. Remember it. Just do it. Great. Now you sound like Dora the Explorer.*

After getting herself dressed in jeans and a new shirt that read,

"I'd circle around for pi," Jack sat with a pint of ice cream, a glass of wine, and her laptop. Having taken care of the programmer arguments earlier, diverting them with a nacho party, Jack retreated to the sanctuary of her personal apartment, had her, ahem, cold shower, and was ready to begin.

She put her watch on and tapped behind her ear, "Okay, Hal. I assume you've been reviewing the upload of our downloaded information? Find anything useful yet?"

"Well, hello to you too, Jack. How are you doing Hal? I'm good thanks, and you? Good? Great. Oh. You don't have to thank me for all my hard work. Oh wait. You didn't."

"Hal. You realize I did do all the work on PAL emotional responses. I can turn those off with just a little bit of code," she returned dryly.

"Har. Har. Two words for you Jack: Anger. Management. Okay fine. I translated all of the files from the alien Standard Economic Language (SEL) to English for you. You can skip over file folders one and two. Those are assorted bits of information you can come back to regarding the planet they are moving humans to. File folder three has all the files regarding the humans that have been processed through that terminal. File folder four has random emails regarding family members' well-being, recipe sharing, and some love letters, the last might be fun to read for kicks. Otherwise, you will want to start scanning in file folder number five and on. I haven't sorted those yet."

"Thanks, Hal. You are organized as usual. Good work."

Sounding sarcastic and shocked, "Was that an actual complement?"

Jack ignored him. She scanned memo after memo resembling your basic business operations and procedures. Boring in any language and, apparently, on any planet. Into her second pint of pumpkin pie ice cream, second glass of wine, and bored to tears, Jack was about to give up when an alien version of an email-style communication caught her attention. She read through the thread.

"Bingo. Hal, transfer currently open files to my Gobble watch. I need some real food and to talk to Will and Rory."

[2]
DON'T KNOW JACK

Adventures of a Supernatural Geek Girl

October 1, 2025
Dear Reader,

You might wonder after my last entry, how the hell this dating-defunct rebel vampire found herself face to kissy face with an alien. Good question. Really fucking good question. Hell if I know, seems to be the best answer.

One minute I'm doing the whole hacky-hack the alien computer outpost thing and the next I'm running from one of them, fighting him, and then um... getting a bit intimate with him. Then doing something so embarrassing, and well, let's just say I got away. Even more sad, that's probably the best date I've had in years. Definitely the hottest, but that's beside the point. The point is, I should never have made the dating post. I totally set myself up for this to happen. It's like that classic book, *The Secret*. You know. Where you think about what you want and draw it to you. Well, I didn't mean an alien universe! That is never happening again.

And really, what self-respecting vampire can't control her damn fangs?

Flashback Fun Facts:

Vampires do have a reflection. A vampire a long time ago convinced his townsfolk that "no reflection" was a thing because he didn't want to get killed. Once he started the rumor, he was able to "prove" he wasn't a vampire. So many myths started like that. Just someone trying to survive or messing with the locals. Heh!

No hugs and bites from me this time. Just one frustrated and embarrassed vampire.
iByte

HARM Base, Mountain View, CA, USA, Earth

October 1, 2025

Jack walked into the shared eating hall and headed over to grab a plate of food. Having Gobble as a benefactor definitely didn't suck. Today's dinner was a Thai theme. Spring rolls, tofu vegetable Pad Thai, shaking beef salad, chicken curry with coconut rice, and a mango sorbet for dessert. Everything smelled heavenly, but when presented with pad thai, Jack only had eyes for the peanut sauce. Heaping a large portion onto her plate and adding a spring roll for good measure, she headed over to grab a green tea. Food in one hand and tea in the other, Jack turned and scanned the crowd. Over near the far wall, she spotted what she was looking for and strode in that direction.

Rory, full name Aurora Espinoza, was animatedly waving her hands as she spoke. She was all of five-foot-four, but when Rory walked into a room, and especially when she started talking, the space would vibrate with her enthusiastic and energetic approach to just about everything. On top of that, she was stunning. Like a mural of Penélope Cruz and Priyanka Chopra's best features. Her thick, dark-brown hair, hazel-brown eyes, and curvaceous, muscular figure caused every head to turn her way.

As she approached, Jack overheard Rory telling the story of how one time she and Jack had accidentally wandered into the middle of a paintball war while out hiking. Lucky for them, one of the teams had extra firearms so they were able to join in and give as much as they got. *That was a good time.*

Jack tried to tip-toe up behind Rory. It was a game they liked to play. Jack might be extra stealthy but Rory had extra-sharp senses.

Just as Jack thought she had made it, Rory's voice changed tones and she spoke over her shoulder. "You finally joined us, chica. I've been dying to learn everything you found out. You did find something out, sí? Did you run into any trouble? How long did it take you to break into their system? I bet you were fast. Sit. Sit. Tell us everything." She scooted over just a bit to make extra room for Jack to take a seat. She slid the gun she'd been tinkering with over, too.

Jack smiled warmly at her best friend, took the seat she offered, and began to eat. After over five years of friendship, she was well-used to the firing squad of questions she and Rory often shared. That was how they became friends, after all.

Five years earlier…

Jack had been a new vampire and had gone too long without feeding. She was truly ravenous but couldn't find any bad guys around her to use. Her energy was almost completely depleted. She had to feed. She had been near a dance club when it truly hit her and so she waited in the alleyway for some guy who was hopefully at least a jerk to come pee on a wall there. They always do that and so deserve to be dinner for defacing the property.

Unfortunately, or fortunately, no guys-a-peeing had showed up. Instead a young, striking woman appeared. She looked like she needed some fresh air, though she also could have been drunk. It hadn't mattered. Jack was too far gone and so approached the girl and tried her Jedi mind tricks on her. "You will not remember this. You are safe and all is well. Now please tilt your head to the side and remain silent."

Rory had stared her directly in the eyes in response and then angrily began, "No way. You keep your fangs to yourself. You were going to lean on in like I'm some kind of delicious enchilada—which of course I am—and take my blood without asking? The least you could do is ask. I require I give consent every time someone is eating me out no matter what part they are eating. No blood for you!" Jack figured she must have looked as pathetic as well as confused as she felt because the girl then kept going. "It's not fair for you to look like a little puppy getting kicked. Listen, I know that you need to feed. We all need to eat, but really, you should ask me. I am no one's all-you-can-eat-buffet."

Jack was shocked to a standstill. "You know what I am? You

don't mind if I feed from you? How is it that my powers didn't mesmerize you? Who are you? What are you?"

Rory had calmly answered, "Claro que sí. Vampire. No, if asked that is. I can't be mesmerized. Aurora. I could tell you but then I would have to kill you."

Jack had laughed at that last line since she used it often as well. A painful clench gripped her insides and she grew quite serious as she was brought right back to what was most important. "Aurora, will you please let me feed from you? I have gone too long without, and now I am quite frankly a hot mess."

"Chica, you passed hot mess a long time ago, now you are just a mess mess. Come here."

Jack rushed over to Aurora. They looked each other in the eyes, something passed between them, some shared otherness, loneliness, and then Aurora tilted her head and pointed at her neck. Jack bit down gently and fed.

When she was finished drinking and lightly licked the wound shut, Aurora took charge. "You now owe me dinner. Come. There is a diner two streets over and I am in the mood for a juicy hamburger. I have a feeling you and I are going to be friends, so you may as well start calling me Rory and what do I call you?"

"Jack. My name is Jack."

Jack munched her way out of her musings.

"I did find something out. I also did run into some trouble." *Literally!* She kept eating between responses. "Breaking into their system was a breeze but the download took forever. I thought the machine was going to start showing me a spinning rainbow circle."

"Trouble? What happened? Are you okay? Why didn't you mention it when we talked earlier? Dammit!" Will Jackson sat across from them looking quite irritated. Gorgeous but definitely irritated. He had beautiful dark-brown skin, black eyes, and a stunning white-toothed smile, when he chose to flash it, which was definitely not now. His firm build and shaved head made him look like quite the formidable figure, and he was. Having come from the special forces, the man could fight. If he couldn't, he wouldn't have been able to co-lead the resistance, but at his core he was a scientist. He was a genius at some form of geologic science. They had worked for different departments of Gobble before coming together to form HARM. They swiftly grew into their co-leader roles and learned to rely on each other. At this point, she would count him a friend and they made an effective team.

"It wasn't a lot of trouble and I'm fine. I'll explain about that soon, but first let me show you what I found." Jack pushed her tray off to the side, tapped the glass table to turn it on, and synced her phone to it. She tapped behind her ear to bring Hal back into the mix. "Hal? You with me?"

She winced as Hal's loud, exuberant greeting came through. "Will! It is so nice to be in your presence as usual. Anything I can do for you? Need me to order you anything? Can I look something up for you? That is a great shirt."

Will groaned but then smiled in amusement. "Hi Hal. It's nice to hear from you as always." Amused or not, he drummed his fingers on the table with growing impatience.

She couldn't decide if she should get on with the information sharing or if she should drag this out and see if she could cause Will to blow a gasket. Decisions. Decisions.

Practically and necessity won out.

"Hal. When you are done flirting with Will, please pull up, to the table, the communications we found."

"Fine. Hal do this. Hal do that. You are so bossy."

"Damn straight. Now pull them up."

The first had been sent three days earlier and read:

All Alien Communication
    Qisto,

Earth's relocation is more challenging than expected. The Vrolan assessment of the humans' creativity and ingenuity was accurate but their ability to accept our presence and their relocation was not. Perhaps

28

they are not worth the effort and cost? We believe this operation will take much longer than anticipated. We are also deeply concerned the conflict and resulting deaths or injuries are not in line with our company mission. We will have to ask for an extended contract and payment to complete the relocation since we are forced to handle the humans slowly and with care.
Tarc - Commander
Alien Relocation Cooperative

All Alien Communication
Tarc,

Mission stays as contracted even though resistance at this level was unexpected. Still a worthy endeavor and we plan to extend the contract and payments accordingly.
Qisto

All Alien Communication
Qisto,
Bren will send a new agreement, shortly.
Tarc - Commander
Alien Relocation Cooperative

Will tapped his fingers on the table even harder, creating a background rhythm to their mutual disquiet. "There seems to be more than one group involved in our relocation. Who are the Vrolan? Anything else from the terminal?"

Jack shook her head. "Nothing useful unless you want to start a gossip column featuring alien love letters."

Will's look was pure aggravation. It was too easy to needle the tense man.

Rory jumped in. "I wonder who this Tarc is. If he is the commander, then I'm guessing he might be el jefe of the cooperative. I don't remember seeing anyone named that or Bren on any of the broadcasts or pamphlets. Curioso. It seems only the PR team is known to us. Of course, they can't actually make any decisions.

Maybe if we approached this Tarc and were able to convince him to leave Earth alone, they would?" She continued tinkering with the gun as she spoke.

"My thoughts exactly." Jack was super excited by where this could lead. Any lead would be great, really.

"Well, we always do think alike."

"Except that time at the Dark Beat dance club."

Rory shuddered. "We will not discuss that night. ¡Silencio!"

Jack nudged her friend and winked. "That night is just our secret." She looked back towards Will. "Your thoughts?"

Their antics finally got mister grumpy pants to look amused. "One of these days, I'll have to extract that story from you guys. For now, we need to find out more about this Tarc. If we want them to leave and avoid conflict, we will need to convince him they do not want this contract." He seemed briefly lost in thought and then his eyes turned like laser beams toward her. "And the problems you ran into?"

Gulp.

"Oh. She definitely ran into a problem—"

"Hal! Quiet." To Will. "It was not a big deal. Some Staraban came to the spot I had been working in. I escaped before they arrived but then one got a whiff of me and he chased me through Los Altos and into the library. I attacked him, he mostly stood there and told me to stop, I didn't listen, and then I got away. See? No problem."

Will looked at her skeptically and shifted forward in his seat. "And how exactly did you get away?"

"I distracted him, made sure to trip him up if he tried to follow, and ran away. I don't think he wanted to hurt the little human female and so he underestimated me." Jack looked back as innocently as she could. Will, unlike Rory, still had no idea she wasn't human.

"Did you learn anything from him? Will he be able to track you here? Should I double the guards?"

"She learned a lot about—"

"Nope. Hal. Go to sleep."

30

"Humph. You can't appreciate a good PAL. I'll see you later, Will. Have a nice night."

"I learned that he was a really good tracker and that they have an exceptional sense of smell. That is all. You know, I really should replace Hal, but I just don't have the heart to get rid of the oaf."

"No extra guards then?"

"No. I don't think it will be necessary. I got away clean."

He looked at her in contemplation for bit longer and it took a lot for her not to squirm uncomfortably under his assessing gaze. Finally, he said, "Okay. I'm off to read and pretend I won't be surrounded by these crazy programmers tomorrow. I'll consider what we have learned and if there is anything we can do with it. Let me know if you find anything else. Nice work."

Will cracked one of his heart stopping smiles as he walked away and she and Rory both sighed, looked at each other, and giggled like schoolgirls.

Once they were alone, Rory looked at her again and the interrogation began in earnest. "Spill it. He may not know you very well, pero yo sí. What happened? Did the alien hurt you? Did he say something that made you anxious? Hal may be a pain in the ass, but he also doesn't usually lie. You will tell me eventually, so just spill it now and save us both time."

Jack flushed with embarrassment and couldn't meet Rory's eyes. She didn't know how to explain what had happened. "You know how you're really good with guys and I'm horrible with them? Well…my awkwardness with men apparently extends to this alien that chased me."

She'd tried so hard to contain it all, but now that she was talking, the words poured out like Niagara Falls. "You see, he was this super-hot alien. I was observing his hotness from a tree and then my teeth popped out and I was like, what the fuck? You know? And then he chased me and we fought and while we were fighting I guess he had some dirty thoughts or something because his scent changed and it smelled hella amazing and next thing I knew I had pressed him against a wall, um, using all of my body and I was trying to take his clothes off as quickly as possible. And damn he could kiss. Like

31

knee-meltingly good kisser. And he tasted and smelled so, so good and after undoing his pants, as they fell down and I was gearing up to ride him like a horse was when my damn teeth popped completely out and nicked him on the neck. He yelled in pain and I zoomed away. He probably didn't chase me because I left him with his pants around his ankles. And I was soooo tempted to go back because I wanted more, more, more. I tried and failed at a cold shower—it ended in masturbation—two pints of ice cream, wine, and work and I'm still horny as hell."

Jack finally paused to catch her breath—she may not need to breathe but you can't make sounds without air and it can be quite habitual—and looked at her friend. She thought she would see revulsion or confusion at her actions. Nope. Rory *was* red in the face but it looked like it was from strain. And sure enough, she apparently couldn't contain it anymore, she started laughing and laughing. Jack grimaced. "Not the reaction I was looking for." She scowled.

"Amiga, it is just…just…so very you. Good kisser you say? Maybe I need me an alien lover, too. I could play Mata Hari and collect intel while collecting—"

"Get serious! That's the problem. It is soooo *not* me. I felt completely out of control. I'm never out of control sexually. I'm too analytical for that kind of behavior. Stumbling words and being weird around a hunky male I could see, but this? This is wrong on so many levels, including but not limited to the fact that I still lust for him. Luckily, I will probably never see him again, so it won't matter."

"Told you, you would tell Rory in less than twenty-four hours. I really should have made it a bet like if I win, you transfer me to be Will's PAL."

"Hal!"

"You told me to go to sleep, you didn't tell me to turn myself off. Sleep is interpretive."

Rory was still laughing, but not quite as hard. That was something. Jack's shoulders slumped as the weight of all she'd done and experienced today struck her. She needed time to process and achieve some equilibrium again. "Hal. Please just go away. I really don't want to deal with this anymore."

She must have sounded as defeated as she felt, because Hal's voice sounded very serious suddenly. "Okay Jack. I understand. Let me know if you need anything else from me. I'm here if you do." In his interpretation of a sexy voice he added, "I'm here for Will if he needs anything too." Then he swiftly added, "Shutting down now."

Rory sobered immediately. "Chica, I'm sorry. I didn't mean to laugh so much. Well, maybe I did, but not if it really bothers you. Why don't we have some more of that wine and talk this through."

"Thank you, but I think I just need to be done for the day. Some quiet, some sleep, and I'm sure the embarrassment will be easier to manage tomorrow. Perhaps if I write about it in my blog, I'll be able to unload it before bed. You know?"

"I know. Let me know if you need me. Estoy aquí para ti siempre, hermana."

They both leaned over and hugged. "I know you are always here for me, my sister. I'll let you know if or when I'm ready to talk. I need time for it to marinate."

"I think I'll go invent more ways to blow things up and finish my adjustments on the altered gun I've been working on, before bed. Or maybe, after hearing your story, instead of bed I'll go find that new doctor that was hired on. Have you seen him? ¡Caliente! I'll see you in the morning for breakfast. Buenas noches." Rory was an amazing electrical engineer brought on to help adjust munitions to become better and more effective against the alien invasion. She had always worked for a division of Gobble dedicated to technological advancements that only the department and the government knew about. She was good at keeping secrets. Jack was pretty sure she would make a great Mata Hari if she so chose.

"It's a deal. See you then. Good night."

Jack got up and made her way back to her room. She spent a couple of hours tying up loose ends, writing a blog about her encounter, checking her comments section, and choosing another abandoned terminal to hit. Then she pulled off her clothes and spent a thoroughly restless night fantasizing about blue eyes, a firm jaw, and hungry lips.

October 2, 2025

Her instincts woke Jack up to the realization that she was no longer alone. Before opening her eyes, she took stock of what she knew.

After breakfast, she'd come to another abandoned area in the heart of Sunnyvale and hacked into the terminal near a park. The area had been abandoned since the humans who used to live and shop here were either relocated, awaiting relocation, or had moved to an area not yet scheduled for relocation. She had set up her connection to the aliens' version of The Cloud and started her download. This time her search had been more specific. She hoped to get more information about Qisto or Tarc and to understand what was really behind the relocation of Earth.

Utterly exhausted from spending most of the previous night agitated by her fantasies about a certain alien male and from having had a lot of sun exposure the day before, Jack had sought the refuge and shade from a nearby tree and she must have fallen asleep. *Oh Shit!*

She listened intently gathering information about who was there. Two heartbeats right in front of her. About ten feet away. *Two humans? Unlikely. Damn. An alien.* She listened more broadly and couldn't find anyone else for at least half a mile in any direction. They were alone.

Okay. I can handle this. Maybe they didn't notice my download. I just need to subdue one alien, collect my data, and get my ass out of here.

She took a whiff of the air and was absolutely sure she couldn't have smelled what she smelled. *No way!* She opened her eyes and found herself looking into the same blue eyes that had haunted her all night long. She gasped and took her first full inhale since waking up and his intoxicating scent flooded her system. *How?*

Tarc waited patiently. He studied his little, at least compared to the Staraban, attacker from the day before while she slept. She looked so small, so relaxed, and so beautiful. He could not understand how such a delicate looking creature could have attacked him with such speed and strength. *Are all humans hiding these types of skills?* He did not think so. The others he had fought had not been so capable and they would have used all of their skills to try to win. Would they not?

After searching the terminal, the day before, based on an assumption that had proven correct, he had decided to monitor all retired terminals within a ten-mile radius for unusual activity. When she had accessed the terminal nearby an hour before, he had rushed over as quickly as possible.

Now, he crouched waiting for his prey to open her eyes. He had so many questions regarding her. Why did she have no heartbeat? Why was she able to not breathe? He would have thought she was dead if he had not witnessed the occasional facial twitch. Was she even human? What had happened yesterday before she fled? When *could* he get her out of her clothes? *Should* he even try to get her out of her clothes? He was sure the answer to the last question was a huge no but he was equally sure he did not care.

He sensed the instant she woke up. Her eyes had not opened and, in fact, nothing seemed different but a part of him, the animalistic part, could tell she was aware. Then she did open her eyes and stared right into his.

Neither said anything for a time and just continued staring.

"Found you, *apura.*"

"Looks like it. What now?"

At that, he had to smile. "You are not happy to see me?"

"No."

While she said she did not want to see him, her gaze said something else. It traveled, with appreciation and banked lust, over his whole body settling back on his eyes.

Well, he was happy to reciprocate. He took in her body head to toe like he had been doing the whole time she had been sleeping.

Like he had been doing in his mind all night. His gaze moved down over her beautiful round breasts, her curvy hips, up to her luscious lips and back to her deep, brown eyes.

"Who are you?" He spoke softly. He hoped it would indicate he was not a threat.

"I am no one. I told you to stay away from me or I would have to hurt you." She spit that back at him and it was obvious his tone of voice had not made a difference at all.

"I am not here to fight but I am sure you are not no one." If quiet and unthreatening was not going to work, he would try something else. "I will not allow you to continue getting into our system. Now tell me what you are searching for?"

"I don't know what you're talking about." Jack tried to look totally innocent. Tried. Sneaky she could do—vampire upgrades and all—but she sucked at subterfuge. "And even if I did, you may be gorgeous, but that doesn't mean I would betray my purpose and therefore my people to you."

Did I really just say that? Get your libido under control Jack! Why this guy? So many human guys and she keeps getting wet for this one. Damn you hormones! Do vampires even have hormones? Stop it. Stay on topic.

His full lips turned up into a sexy grin. Apparently he liked her accidental compliment. Jack needed some distance. And fast. She stood up against the tree. He stood up from his crouching position in response. *Damn!* He was so tall, standing didn't feel any more empowering. He still loomed large and firm and well-formed and those arms could probably dead lift a truck and those giant hands could probably engulf her breasts, and—*What is wrong with me?* Jack's teeth were starting to elongate again and she couldn't afford a repeat of yesterday. Distance. Now.

"Who are you?" she blurted out as firmly as she could, but she feared it came out overly high pitched instead.

"That was my question," he paused and her skin tingled as he gave her another once over, "but I do not mind answering first. I am

36

Tarc." His voice had gone deeper, sexier and it did something very, very yummy to her insides. She was sure, by his sudden inhale, that he could smell her arousal again. Then, realization of what he'd said washed over her like the successful icy shower she had wanted last night.

"Tarc? Did you just say Tarc?" *It can't be.* "Is that a popular name amongst your people?"

"Not a popular name. No." Tarc stared back at her, assessing, pensive, and then his eyes narrowed. "You know who I am." A statement.

Jack's hands nervously picked at the bark. He was the leader of ARC. *Oh shit! Think Jack.* She had the leader *here*. Should she try to reason with him, interrogate him, bring him in as a prisoner? *Mmm…My prisoner.* Jack shook her head to clear that thought. *I could kill him.* She instinctively cringed away from that idea and then avoided thinking about why it bothered her so deeply, murder aside.

May as well start with a Star Trek style intergalactic peace talk. Now if only I can come up with something brilliant to say that will save all of mankind. Yeah. Likely.

She looked up, started to speak, but lost her voice completely because Tarc was no longer ten feet away. He had closed the distance between them. *How had I not sensed him? Distracted or maybe he moved that silently?* She gaped up into his blue, blue eyes and her libido went from zero to one hundred. They studied each other intensely. Tension ticking ever higher with all the suppressed power and attraction they were holding at bay.

Something shifted and her energy level instantly skyrocketed breaking the dam. Tarc pressed her firmly against the tree and she felt his aroused body up against hers as he took ownership of her mouth.

Oh God! I am in so much trouble, was the last thought Jack had as her body went up in flames.

He reveled in how good her body felt in his arms. She was soft and hard and challenging and pliant and it was so confusing, intriguing, alluring. He lifted her and pressed her against the tree, perfectly aligning their bodies. He had not planned for things to head this direction. At least, not yet, but he was not about to stop either. Not when she returned every advance with her own, wrapping her arms and legs around him and owning his mouth in turn.

He leaned his body into hers and her breasts pressed against him through their clothes even as he pressed his erection right where it most wanted to be. His cock could feel the heat of her pussy and grew even harder. His tongue probed her lips begging for entry. After a pregnant moment, she opened for him on a sigh. His hands drifted down to cup her ass. Such a beautiful, tempting handful of ass. He practically growled as he deepened the kiss further. Their tongues moved in an epic duel.

The kiss could have lasted hours or moments. He had no clue. His left hand moved up from her ass, to the curve of her hip, up along her waist, settling in between their bodies on her perfectly rounded breast. Her nipple was hard underneath and he rubbed his thumb back and forth over her shirt, teasing it. His tongue explored every inch of her mouth until it touched on something exceedingly sharp.

Was that a tooth? Yesterday she had drawn blood.

He moved his tongue again in the same way, and once again, encountered her sharp, really sharp, teeth. Two of them.

Slowly, so he did not startle her, he lifted his head and looked down at the amazing bundle in his arms. She looked dazed with lust and before she had a chance to close her mouth, he saw her protruding canines. He studied her while he could and took stock.

She is exceedingly fast, strong, and her teeth can get...sharper?

"You are *not* human. What are you?"

Her mouth closed tight, her legs dropped down, and she started squirming in his arms to get away. *Damn! Really, really strong.*

"What I am or am not, is none of your fucking business. You need to keep your extremely strong hands and enjoyable lips off of me." She pushed him away. Her hands actually started to hurt him, where they touched.

He released her and stepped back with a cocky grin. "So you enjoy my lips? Why should I keep them off of you then? My lips can do a lot more enjoyable things to you than a simple kiss, my little *apura*." He looked over to the terminal. *Stop behaving ridiculous with lust. Focus.* "But business before pleasure, I believe is your human phrase, and before you get to see what else my mouth can do for you, I need to know who and what you are and why I keep finding you accessing our terminals. I ask again, what are you looking for? What do you hope to accomplish? Are there others like you?"

She stared at him. He stared back. He could be patient.

She opened her mouth to reply, but he stopped her.

"Before you answer, know that I do not take well to lies."

"What reason do I have to answer any of your questions? It's none of your business. *I* am none of your business."

"Wrong. You have been caught gathering information from our terminals. That is most definitely my business, and you know it. You obviously recognize my name." His voice dipped much lower. "And you, *apura*, are most definitely my business. I plan to make all of you *my* business."

Jack couldn't breathe. Okay. She didn't need to but it was still a weird sensation when not on purpose. *So screwed!* It was hard to know what to react to first and the mix of her reactions stopped her cold. She most likely should be dealing with fear that he was on to her and had her in his crosshairs. She should probably also be annoyed at his tone of voice suggesting she was a child just being difficult instead of the enemy reasonably staying quiet. Then there was indignation at his claiming some right over her, all of her to be exact. Somehow she found the let's-be-reasonable emotion lurking and decided to give that one a try. She was about to talk and remembered her lack of air situation, she may not need to breathe but vocal cords were demanding she fix the situation. *How long was I without air? Could he tell I wasn't breathing?* She nervously began again.

"Okay. Fine. Seeing as how you told me your name, I suppose

39

it's only fair to share mine. My name is Jack, but that is all you're getting from me." She stared at him belligerently happy to let the annoyance take control at least a little.

"Jack? I thought that was a name given to the males on your planet and I have personal knowledge that you are not male. Are you? Perhaps I am mistaken about humans or whatever species you are?"

"No. I don't identify as male and was also assigned female at birth. The name is a long story and like I said, that's all you'll get from me." She wasn't going to tell him her sob story about how she was named for her abusive mother's favorite whiskey.

"No."

"What do you mean, no?" She attempted to mimic his deep voice with the last word. *Great idea genius. Mock the leader of the alien group you're trying to deal with.*

"No. That is not all I will get from you. Especially since I plan to have all of you." His voice did that seductive thing again. Her knees wanted to either give in and crumple back down to the ground or wrap around his hips again. *Bad knees.*

Her attraction only fueled the fire of her annoyance, so she ratcheted her tone a notch to irritation. "You don't get to decide how little or much of me you get, Tarc."

He smiled at her. He actually smiled, the bastard. "I enjoy how you pronounce my name." She didn't know how, but his voice grew even more deeply sensual. "Your accent *rolls* around it much like I want to roll around with you. I need to hear you scream it while I—"

Jack coughed hard to cut him off. *Am I drooling? Maybe I should check?* Jack subtly ran a hand across her mouth as if in frustration. *I must only be drooling on the inside. Small miracles.* The look on his smug face told her he knew exactly what he was doing when he used that tone of voice and said those things to her. And now irritation gave way to livid, roiling anger. "How dare yo—"

"I dare much and you should remember that. But you are correct, time for that later." That later held every promise any lover had ever made to another. Goosebumps ran up and down Jack's arms. His next words were all business. "For now, my interest in you is information based. Anything that endangers the human relocation or any of my crew is under my jurisdiction. From what I have seen, you could pose a danger and I will not *allow* it to continue. I expect to have my questions answered because you will find there is no other choice."

"There is always a choice. We all want things, but sometimes we don't get what we want. You must have been a difficult child if you never learned that lesson."

"Speaking of children, now you are just being petulant. I have not shown any aggression towards you and yet you resist every attempt I make at negotiation and conversation. Yesterday you attacked with no provocation. Should I just assume you are primitive and unable to be reasoned with or prone to a violent disposition?" Now he was the one sounding irritated and damn if he didn't have a point. He took a few deep breaths and continued in a softer voice, "I understand that you might feel we are a threat. That *I* am a threat."

"I do not." she said in a purposefully petulant voice, because fuck him and his condescension. *She wasn't scared of anything, thank you very much.*

"Well. I am a threat to your continued access to our terminals, but not to you personally. That is true both because we are here to help and because I have a very strong attraction to you. Not just the sexual part, which we both can agree is quite intense, but to what I already know of you. You are beautiful, and strong, and fierce, and loyal, and determined, and if you were able to learn our system language and how to hack it, I believe is the human term, you must also be very smart. I will not harm you, but I must find a way for us to negotiate a path forward that does not leave my people vulnerable."

Why did he have to sound so reasonable and complimentary? Maybe she could try to negotiate that path forward with a partial truth. "I like computers. I thought it would be fun to learn your programming language and play around in your technology. A girl has to have her fun and there are not as many movies or TV shows to watch since your arrival. I'm just filling my day with something exciting." Her mouth tried to get her out of the situation even as her brain kept running his complimentary words around and around. A warmth was spreading inside her and she needed to put a stop to it.

Maybe I can picture him with scales on his body or spikes sticking off of his ripped arms. Maybe then I'll stop thinking he's hot. Oh! Maybe I'll imagine he's got some horrible alien venereal disease or... uh oh, did he say something?

"... leave that topic for now but—" his voice deepened again "—if you need some excitement, I am happy to provide you with something to fill your time, *apura*."

She gulped. His eyes were twin blue flames as he looked at her. Had he noticed that she stopped paying attention? It sure seemed that way and then she smelled the air and yep, he knew she hadn't thought about negotiations just then unless it had to do with negotiating their way horizontally.

He took a few steps towards her, gaze roaming over her body hungrily. If the interactions from the day before, as well as earlier, were any indication, there was no way she could withstand him if he got his hands on her, so she threw her hand up between them and said, "Stop."

He stopped and even took a step back. And then he smirked.

Jack wanted to snarl at that smirk. *Arrogant bastard.*

"Answer me a different question then?"

"Not likely." She raised her chin and attempted to look down her nose at him, but considering his massive height and their relative closeness, she gave up the pose and just glared.

"What are you?" He practically whispered it in his velvety tone.

Oh shit!

"Jack," he said firmly. "No lies. Tell me the truth."

"What are you going to do if I lie, spank me?" She scoffed.

"I like your suggestion. That sounds like a good plan."

"Um...I...I..." She cleared her throat. "I was just kidding about that."

"I am not." No. He really did not look like he was kidding and it sent a shiver up and down her back. She couldn't decide if the idea offended or intrigued her. She shook off the idea of his hand striking her bare backside and got back to the conversation at hand. *He was probably kidding any way. Right? Do not try to test that theory now Jack!*

It was decision time. Just yesterday they discussed trying to convince Tarc that his mission here was unnecessary. Perhaps... well...perhaps it was time to start thinking and working this out verbally instead of reacting to everything he made her feel, as a rebel or as a woman. She deliberated, briefly, and with a slight nod of her head, she decided. "Okay. But this only works if I get to ask questions that you have to answer truthfully as well."

"Done." His lips turned up in a Cheshire smile.

"Since I just gave you my name, it's my turn to ask a question." She chose the most pertinent question. "Why are you here?"

"To find you."

Jack rolled her eyes and frowned at him. "If you aren't going to play by your own rules, we may as well stop now. You know that isn't what I was asking. Tell me why you, the Staraban, are here on Earth trying to relocate us? Do you want our planet? Are you actually exterminating us when we are being relocated?" She couldn't help herself, and so she said the last word in full sarcasm mode with air quotes. She wasn't exactly a negotiator by profession. Hackers were mostly a sarcastic bunch.

Tarc's body tensed and his eyes narrowed. "I will ignore your offensive conclusions. We have been clear and honest about our purpose from the beginning. We were commissioned to save humans and relocate them off of Earth because all of the scientific research said your planet is dying and we were convinced that humans were worth saving. For such a short-lived species, you can be very innovative. Your people invented peet-zza, doughnuts, wine, smart phones, baseball, movies, tacos—"

Jack broke out in a fit of laughter. Her hand covered her eyes and she shook her head. "Are you—Hold on. Hold on." She held her hand up like a stop sign and tried to catch her breath. She looked at him again with crinkled eyes in bemusement. "Are you telling me that all of this is because of pizza, doughnuts, wine, and the rest that you listed? Oh. My. God."

She doubled over hands on her knees. Hysterical, uncontrollable laughter had her in its grip. "I mean. Don't get me wrong. Pizza is the food of the gods and I myself have been known to finish off one, okay two, okay maybe four doughnuts at a time. And sure, wine is a girl's best friend and smart phones really were a revelation, but, but…that's just…it's insane." She was struggling to get her composure back. Her body and mind knew that if she wasn't laughing she very well might have needed to cry over the ridiculous situation. She almost did transition between the humor and the weeping but then she looked over at Tarc and that sobered her up completely.

His body was radiating waves of anger. His arms were crossed over his chest, he was scowling, and glaring. *Okay. He does not like to be laughed at. Note to self.*

His words came out clipped. "Perhaps you find saving a species from extinction a laughing matter, but I suppose considering the wars you wage on each other, you might well be that ruthless. We are not. The point was never the food, electronics, or entertainment. The point was to save an imaginative and productive species. Humans should be grateful that we are willing to help. For all of your inventions, you have been utterly short sighted regarding intergalactic space travel or else you would have been able to make the appeal for relocation yourselves. If we had waited for that, which is our standard protocol, you would all be dead." She thought she could sense some pain, at her earlier reaction, under all his hostility. *And yet he isn't turning violent. Also a note to self.* Then something he said stood out.

"Who?"

"What do you mean who?"

"Who commissioned you? Who convinced you we needed saving?" Jack was wary of pushing too hard too fast, but she needed this answer. She wanted confirmation that the information from the emails was reliable and that Tarc was being truthful. She watched as Tarc took a deep breath. And another. He uncrossed his arms and the waves of anger receded. Jack felt muscles she hadn't known she was tensing, relax. Her energy level, which apparently had been high, receded.

He grinned. Actually grinned. Mood change much? A part of Jack found it hard to follow, but another part really appreciated his ability to control himself and his attempts to stay on a positive path. She remembered thinking him "in-charge" yesterday in the clearing. Clearly, he was a natural born leader. One leader to another, she had a lot of respect for him.

"I would answer you, *apura,* but that is another question and it is no longer your turn. It is mine and you already know what I want to know. What. Are. You?" He raised an eyebrow at her.

Aaannnddd the tables have turned. Energy level back on alert, she said the first true thing she could come up with. "I was born a human." *Take that alien eye candy! That is a true statement.* "My turn, I believe."

"Jack." He said her name, his voice low and full of censure. "You may have been born human, but you are not human. At least, not just human. After the lecture you gave me and the answer you got, I expect a real answer."

Well shit. He has me there. What can I say? She answered him again slowly. Choosing her words carefully. "You're right. I am not *just* human any longer, but my people are a hidden group and I do not know you well enough to trust you with that information." Jack needed a deep tissue massage to deal with the tension building in her shoulders. She forgot to breathe again while waiting to see if he would accept her response.

He just kept looking at her for a while before he spoke. "I will accept your answer, for now." He flashed her his sly grin once more. "We both know I will eventually find out."

Her breath rushed in unnecessarily, because some instincts stay the same, and she was feeling lightheaded from her reactions to him. "Um. Okay. My turn." Jack meant to go back to her earlier question. She meant to. Apparently she was rather sluggish though because her brain forgot to tell her mouth the correct words and before she knew it, she asked, "What does *apura* mean?" *What! The! Hell!* "Um. That is not what I meant to ask as my next question."

He gave a brief laugh and flashed her a wide smile. "Too late, Jack. That is the question you did ask. *Apura* is a term of endearment." His voice did that deepening thing again. "Since I plan to have you as mine..." He left the last part to dangle in the air between them.

Jack's energy level rose for a whole other reason as her anger and lust raged a battle for supremacy. Anger was safer. In an icy tone, she hissed. "I am no one's."

"We shall see."

"No. We won't."

"I know you can feel our attraction. I want you. You want me." He shrugged like the conclusion was obvious. Inevitable. "You will be mine."

She began protesting their connection, but the look he gave her reminded her they promised each other truth.

"Fine. My body responds to you, but that doesn't mean anything." He raised a brow at her and she grew even more annoyed. "*You* are forcing my people off of *our* planet. Tell yourself it's for our own good, but that is a lie and you said you don't like lies. I don't much like lies either. So here is a truth for you. I don't know who convinced you we needed your help but we don't. They fucking lied." Her body was vibrating with her righteousness. She needed a soapbox for this speech. Maybe some protest signs.

"I understand why you would want to stay on this planet. It is a beautiful place. It makes me sad to think it will be gone soon, but, Jack, science does not lie. My people know what it is to live somewhere beautiful and have it become unstable and uninhabitable. The reason my family created ARC and travel around helping to relocate different species off of their planets to new ones is because we went through this ourselves but without sufficient notice. Many of my people perished before we had a chance to relocate everyone. You cling to what you know, I understand, but doing so might be the death of all your people. It is not like we found you a horrible place to move to. Earth Two is beautiful, as well. Admittedly, not as beautiful as this Earth, but it is also extremely stable and with human influence, who knows what you can make of it. My own people moved to a less beautiful planet but we have turned it into paradise." He gave her a genuine and relaxed smile and her heart skipped a beat, well, if it had been beating at all, it would have. "I would love to take you there. Show you my world. I think you will see that different can be beautiful too."

And now, her unbeating heart broke. She could never see his planet. Whatever this was between them, she needed to put a stop to it because he was right. The attraction was intense but there was more, and she couldn't let there be more. Something in her recognized something in him and she was going to have to deny that part of her. They were still on opposite sides of this equation but on top of that, this could only lead to pain, a lot of it, for her. For her people, leaving Earth was a death sentence.

"I need to go. Now. Are we doing this the hard way or the easy way? I'm done playing I'll show you mine if you show me yours with you." He looked so disappointed and she shouldn't care, but she feared she already did.

"You know that I cannot allow you to leave. As I mentioned before, it is my job as the Commander of ARC to learn what danger you pose. It is also my interest, as a male, to keep you at my side since it is what we both want."

The hard way then.

She usually preferred a fair fight, but in this instance, she couldn't afford one. Staring him straight in the eyes, she issued out her power of persuasion and spoke in a deep lyrical voice.

"You've had a long day and feel quite exhausted. Take a little rest against this comfortable tree. Forget the last couple of hours and assume you were sleeping, and you can continue with the rest of your plans for today. Just a little rest first. Go sit under the tree and relax. Close your eyes. All will be well in twenty minutes."

At first it looked like he was resisting her will, so she pushed out more power and eventually, Tarc moved to the tree and did as she had commanded him. She leaned down and kissed him gently on the lips, whispering. "I'm sorry, my beautiful warrior, but this is for the best."

After that, Jack didn't miss a beat. She couldn't be sure how long the compulsion would hold him. She zoomed to the terminal, grabbed her drive, and left as fast as a speeding vampire.

*At least he is susceptible to my glamour. Of course, I'm waaay too suscep-
tible to his eyes and his voice when he goes all deep and seductive. To his honesty
and his control. Maybe he has a form of glamour too. Well, that's my delusional
story and I'm sticking to it. Definitely can't be that I'm hot for teacher with an
alien, an enemy, no... the head of the enemies. But damn he looked good lying
under that tree.*

Forget him Jack. There's really only one path forward here.

If I avoid terminals, I shouldn't run into him again.

That thought should have elated her, but instead it left her
singing the sad vampire blues.

[3]

CLOSE ENCOUNTERS

Adventures of a Supernatural Geek Girl

October 2, 2025
Dear reader,

Have you ever believed something about yourself? Known who you were? What personality traits you understood you had and could live with? We take the good, bad, and the ugly and assume that is who we are. It makes sense to us. Then, something happens or someone happens and you find yourself behaving in inexplicable ways. You look at all that you thought you were and discover a part of yourself that you have never seen before. Never *been* before.

I thought becoming a vampire was challenging, but I adjusted relatively quickly. This, now, I...I don't really know what the fuck I'm doing. Who is this new vampire and where did the original model go? I'm not even sure I know what I'm saying here. Over the years, many people have asked for the story of how I became a vampire. I've always been embarrassed to tell it, but it is a perfect example of me. I'm placing this under Fun Facts because it gives away how a vampire is created.

. . .

Fun Facts:

I like to jog. A lot. Alone. Brilliant...I know. Stay with me.

I was out running early one morning on a relatively deserted trail. A vampire saw me and decided to have an early morning snack. What he hadn't prepared for—I assume—was for my having been a teenage runaway who lived on the streets for a time. When he grabbed me from behind, pulled me off the track and started drinking from me, at first, I admit it, I panicked. Vampires are not supposed to be real, right? That allowed him to big gulp my neck for a while before my brain kicked back in. Even as I was growing weaker, my fight or flight adrenaline along with my street kid fighting skills and instincts kicked in.

I took him by surprise and flung him away. I *wish* that was how he'd gotten impaled on the branches, but nope, that would be a different person with a different, much more awesome, story. Instead, as he came at me again, and I was trying to run away like the good prey I was, I tripped. Yes. You read that right. As I over-corrected, I fell back into him, and we both went flying. I passed out after that. Imagine my surprise at waking up around dusk with something wet all over my face. Something that tasted good. Something that was coming from the form impaled through multiple body parts on multiple branches right above where my head had landed. Something that... Oh, nevermind. Blood. It was blood.

I bet you always thought I was joking about my short version vampire origin story, but I wasn't. My maker didn't make me, I accidentally made myself. With him so thoroughly impaled, he was unable to escape the sun and eventually succumbed to over exposure. All before I woke up to being a new vampire. I had gotten lucky and fallen under the shade of the tree, so I was spared becoming a raisin.

So you see, brilliant and awkward I can handle, but awkward is not the same as out of control and out of my freaking mind. I feel trapped in someone else's reality. Again, I'm not even sure I know what I'm saying. None of it makes any sense. None of *me* is making any sense.

Confused and Shaken,
iByte

Gobble Neighborhood, Mountain View, CA, USA, Earth

October 2, 2025

This is becoming unbearably repetitive. If I tie her up, maybe I will not have to chase after her so much. Tarc had to acknowledge he was enjoying the chase. Especially since he was sure that he would capture her. It was inevitable. He also had to acknowledge that images of her tied to his bed, were exciting him quite uncomfortably.

Their last interaction replayed through his head. Jack had looked into his eyes and told him to go lay down under the tree. The power that had emanated off of her felt like it was pushing him, trying to force compliance, and it was strong. But it had not worked. One more piece of her puzzle. For a moment, he had considered ignoring her command—grabbing her to take her back to his base for interrogation—but he chose to pretend he was no threat, and see where that led him instead.

With that decision, he had gone to the tree, and as instructed, leaned back against it pretending to drift off for a rest. Her kiss and parting words were so unexpected and sweet, he had almost broken from his performance to haul her into his lap. Almost. Instead, he watched from the corner of his slitted eyes, as she blurred towards the terminal, grabbed some sort of external device, and left. When he was sure he was alone, he began his pursuit. Again.

Two times in as many days, he followed her through residential and business areas. Eventually, she slowed down and arrived at the still populated area of section fifty-five. The humans called this area, Mountain View, if he recalled correctly. He took note of the sign reading Gobble Neighborhood and remembered Gobble playing a role in negotiations between the businesses, the local government, and ARC. Interesting.

Is Gobble trying to steal our technology? Are they just information gathering? Are they part of the resistance? Partnership in pursuit of a peaceful relocation, his ass.

Her scent indicated to him where she slowed down. It grew heavier in the air. An aphrodisiac he had to ignore to keep his wits sharp. He carefully made his way forward attempting and mostly failing to hide in the sparse foliage of the Gobble neighborhood. He tracked her to one of the buildings deep in the neighborhood. *Does she live here?* He clicked on his uniform emblem to mark his location.

Shek! He grimaced and put his hand to his neck. It came away with something metallic and glass that dropped from his grasp as his vision dimmed and he fell to the ground. His last thought was of beautiful, troubled brown eyes and soft lips.

"Jack! You need to get to the lower holding cells now." Will's agitated voice came through her communication device loud and, well, loud.

"Did you detain another programmer for surfing Twitbook, Will? I'm kinda busy. I was just about to review my latest downloads."

"That can wait. We've had a breach. Meet me at the cells."

"Okay. Okay. I'm on my way." Will hung up on her. "Hal. Can you please start sorting the data while I check on what has Will's panties in a bunch?"

"Already on it. Do you really think Will wears panties? Are you going to tell them about your most recent alien, ehem, interrogation?"

She groaned. "Of course you were on for that. Do you ever mind your own business? Actually, never mind, just don't ever talk about what you see and hear and we will mostly get along as badly as usual."

"You say the sweetest things, Jack."

"Clearly." She could swear she heard Hal snort in her head. She issued out her senses and knew her path was clear, so she ran down the hall and stairs at full vampire speed. She made it to the holding area swiftly. Upon exiting the stairwell, she noticed a bunch of guards standing in the hallway while Will waited nearby.

"Oh good. You're here. That was fast." He said the last with no small amount of suspicion.

"I wasn't too far when you calle—"

"Yeah. Okay. Come with me."

She inwardly sighed in relief that he believed her explanation. Or was too distracted to care. Or was in denial because he didn't really want to know. "Who has breached us?" She followed him forward even as her nose was trying to tell her something. They entered the first door on the right and against the other wall was the holding cell with a figure slumped onto the floor in front of the bed. Jack stopped walking and stood ramrod still. She knew exactly who had come to HARM HQ and it was impossible. Wasn't it? She'd left him sleeping against a tree. Dammit. *How did he get here? I'm in so much trouble!* His scent swirled around her like a dense fog and she purposefully stopped breathing so it wouldn't affect her.

Will didn't seem to notice her tense new posture. She pretended at breathing when he looked back at her but inside she was freaking the fuck out as Will spoke.

"How did he find us? You think it was dumb luck? Maybe we shouldn't have brought him in and he would have passed us by? He's still sleeping. We could put him back outside and pretend we'd never seen him."

She really liked that last idea but even as Will turned back to the figure of Tarc, she could sense that he was no longer asleep. He was pretending and there was no going back from this. With a resigned sigh, she replied. "No. We can't drop him off back outside. He's completely aware of us and playing at sleeping beauty right now."

Will eyed her with a questioning look. He'd been doing more and more of that as they got to know each other, but he never asked her why she could do things or see things others couldn't. She'd never done anything overt near him and so he was left speculating. She appreciated his willingness to leave her to her secrets. Especially since Will was not a fan of anything science couldn't explain.

Tarc, clearly having heard her reveal his awake state, stood up facing away from them and she had to take a moment to inwardly fan herself off at the sight of his wide, muscular shoulders and firm, perfect ass revealed by the all too clingy alien uniform. Yum. She had clearly done too much running and not enough chasing.

Then he turned and looked her right in the eyes, amused, and her already stopped heart, stopped harder. "Hello, *apura*. I was not as tired as you wished me to be."

Will looked back and forth between them until settling on her. "You know each other?" His voice was low as he looked at her questioningly, almost suspiciously. Well, shit.

"I may have run into him yesterday while gathering information—"

"You what? I asked you, point blank, if you had run into any problems and you assured me that I didn't have to worry nor up the number of guards. Thank logic I hadn't listened. The guards are the ones who caught him snooping around our building and tranqued his ass." Will's tone was like a billboard saying "I'm mad as hell. Proceed with caution."

She replied while anxiously tapping her finger on her thigh. "Yesterday, I didn't think that we had any problems. I knew he didn't follow me yesterday. I knew it for a fact. Unfortunately, I..." Jack felt as though she was standing in front of her elementary school principal again. She cleared her throat. "I may have run into him again today while I was out gathe—"

"What? You have to be fucking kidding me. You ran into the same alien again a second time and when you got back here your first thought wasn't to tell me? 'Hey. Will. We have a big fucking problem. There's an alien that keeps popping up everywhere that I am.' You see how easy that is? What the hell were you thinking?" Will was yelling with his voice and his hands. He looked angry enough to punch a wall. Of course, he'd never actually do that since it was illogical to potentially break your hand on a perfectly good wall, but he probably wanted to.

Tarc's voice was booming yet arctic as he growled, "You need to stop yelling at her and back away. Now." He looked at Will like he might just kill him if he weren't trapped behind the cell bars.

She was chagrined he was coming to her defense and sheepishly responded to Will, "I had reason to believe that he wouldn't follow me today, either. I obviously miscalculated. You know I'd never endanger anyone here."

"We're a team, Jack. You don't get to miscalculate on your own. You should have come to me and told me everything and then we would've made a mutual fucking decision."

"I told you, human…Stop. Yelling. At her."

"You are not in a position to make demands, alien."

She straightened her shoulders and faced her co-leader and friend. "I'm sorry I didn't tell you, but you need to stop and listen. Please." She'd never seen him behave like this. She hated the idea that he may not trust her now, but would have to deal with that another time. "Let me explain it all. Okay?"

"I do not trust this male near you, *apura*. He is not treating you with respect. I do not like him."

"Yeah, well, the feeling is mutual, buddy. And who the fuck do you think you are? You don't trust *me* with her? You're not her partner."

Will looked like he was about to approach the bars so she jumped in front of him, putting her hand on his chest in an effort to stop him. That's when a ferocious growl came from behind her. She turned her head to look at Tarc and his eyes bored into her with jealous intensity. His scent changed and waves of aggression rolled off of him as he continued to growl. She pulled her hand back, which at least stopped the growling, and turned back to Will. "You *really* don't understand who we have here. You need to stop and let me explain before you get us into even deeper water. Please be reasonable, Will." She then turned to Tarc and approached the bars. "You need to quit it."

Tarc glared down at her. "He is your partner? You forgot to mention you had a partner when—"

"Stop right there. Will means that he and I run this place. We work together, though I'm not sure what business it is of yo—never mind. Just stay here and be good. I am taking my work partner somewhere where we can talk. For now, until he and I can figure out what happens next, do you need anything? We will bring you water and food soon."

"I need nothing. For now. I will wait for you to come back. Do not be long. I am not a patient male." With that command, Tarc

57

dismissed them all and went to the bed, reclined with one knee bent, covered his eyes, and seemed to settle in for a nap.

Humph! She turned and grabbed Will by the arm, ignoring the low growl coming from behind her. *Sheesh!* "Oh, be quiet in there. Let's go."

Will grudgingly allowed her to drag him away, though it took some effort. They walked up the stairs one level, down the hall, and into Will's office.

As soon as they entered, he whirled around and used his angry hands to yell at her again. "What the hell is going on, Jack?"

"Please sit dow—" One look at his face and she switched gears. "Okay. Standing then. Yesterday, as I told you, he chased me out of the clearing but I got away. Turns out he is quite smart. That's my bad. I saw all of his Hulk-like muscles and figured he might not be the brightest bulb. You know? Well, this is why to assume makes an ass of u and me because he figured out that I was connecting to the terminal in the clearing and somehow also figured out which terminal I'd hit today." She paused in momentary contemplation, which allowed her to regroup.

"When I think about it, I'd guess he set up an alarm of some sort for when a retired terminal went live. I should have planned for that. I'm not usually so sloppy. I was so excited that we'd found some leads yesterday and couldn't wait to get a more specific search and download going today. Regardless, he caught me napping, which was a total accident. I set up my download and sat under a tree, I was just so tired after a bad night of sleep and—"

"Jack! Take a breath. Did you just say that you fell asleep? While doing something dangerous? While on your own?"

"Well. When you put it that way, it does sound a wee bit irresponsible." Will didn't understand just how capable she was, so, of course it sounded stupid as hell to him.

"We would punish any guards caught napping while on duty. How could you have allowed yourself to become so vulner—You know what? I'm going to move on. What happened after he found you?"

"We talked."

"You talked."

"Yes. We talked. We exchanged questions and answers. It was informative."

"So informative, you didn't bother to come right to my office and tell…you know what, never mind that too. Moving on. What did you learn?"

His condemnation and disappointment settled in her stomach even as she continued, "The alien we have in the cell…his name is Tarc." She let that word hang between them and could tell when Will finally remembered that name and what it meant.

"*The* Tarc? From the emails? Holy shit."

"Exactly."

He walked around his desk and slumped into his chair with a confounded look on his face. "I really don't know what to make of that." He paused looking off into space. Pensive. Concerned. Angry. Unsure. He radiated a lot of feels, his scent muddled. "What else did you learn?"

"He genuinely believes that we need saving. He is convinced of it. Based on what he said, I believe the other alien mentioned in the emails, Qisto, has something to do with his conviction. Also, as I said before, he is a good tracker, better than I had expected or I would have come to you. He's also stubborn, arrogant, seemingly reasonable and of course dangerous. Regardless, I am hopeful that Hal and I will find something in the new batch of information that may help us eventually convince him that his information about us is wrong."

"Did I hear my name? Hi, Will. I'm sorry you have been driven to irritation by our dear Jack. Were you telling him about your interrogation practices?"

She groaned.

"What is he talking about?"

"It's nothing. Hal is just being Hal." She was such a bad liar, though, and Will looked at her with frustration etched on his face. *Dammit.* He was already doubting her. If she didn't tell him the truth, he would know it and she would once again be proving how little he could trust her. "I would really, really rather not say."

"I must know everything if I'm to keep our operation safe. Surely you can appreciate that, Jack." His laser focus was not letting up.

Deep breath in, and out. She looked anywhere but at him. "I, um...I may..." She tried to clear the lump in her throat. "Ahem. I may have accidentally had my lips fall onto his lips both yesterday and today."

"You what?" Will jumped back out of his chair.

"Her lips. Her hands. Her body. Her—"

"That's enough Hal! You weren't supposed to talk about it."

"I am only talking about it, after you are already talking about it, so really, it doesn't count."

Will's look of betrayal and disgust lanced through her. Each word coming out of his mouth damning. "Who are you and what have you done with my partner? More to the point, though, how can you throw out our mission like this? Does he have some kind of mental control over you? Should I be even more worried HARM is compromised? That *you* are compromised?"

She deserved his distrust. Like her mother always told her, the only thing she was good for was being a pain in the ass to everyone around her.

"I promise I'm me and I have no good explanation how or why our lips keep ending up on a collision course. I've been wracking my brain trying to figure out how to stop, but I'm pretty sure that if you put us in a room, we'll be like a negative and positive magnet. You know. Bow chicka bow wow instant magnetism."

"Yeah. Enough. I get it, though I wish I didn't."

"Trust me. I *wish* it wasn't true. I've never had this problem before and I'm not sure what to do about it." She slumped into one of the chairs across from him defeated. "The mission is still the most important thing. I haven't forgotten my goals, our goals, and, in fact, that was the first thing I was going to do when I got back here, look through the new data I collected for something that might prove helpful. I have not betrayed any information about anyone here nor anything we are working on despite my uncontrollable libido around him."

She had to implement some serious self-control not to squirm as he just stared at her for some time. When he took his seat again, her tension uncoiled minutely. "Why does he keep calling you, ap-ur-a?"

"He told me it was an endearment. He is under the mistaken belief that he and I will be a thing. I have tried to dissuade him when I'm not accidentally all over him, but the message isn't getting across. That may have to do with all the, um, accidents, because, let me tell you, they are unbelievably, scorching—" She stopped at the tortured sound coming from across the desk.

"Right. Listen. After talking with him, I truly believe they mean everything the pamphlet advertised. In fact, I've developed some amount of respect for him, them, after hearing about his own people needing to relocate. Long story. So far, I haven't successfully convinced him away from their plan to save us from Earth. Maybe given more time? I don't know, but I also think it's a mistake to hold him here. They'll come looking for the leader of the company, don't you think?"

His face was full of disappointment, in her, and she had to work not to let show how much that hurt. Then he nodded in agreement.

"Does seem likely. I'm not sure we can let him go, though. It will be a challenge to relocate everything we have built here. It's not something that can happen overnight. He knows where we are and can bring others back with him and wipe us out or detain us until relocation."

Shame felt like a leaden stone in her gut and tears burned behind her eyes. She didn't let them go, though. She didn't much like to cry. What was the point? Her mom hadn't cared when she cried. Crying often meant a slap was heading her way. Instead, she closed her eyes counted to three and opened them again. "So we can't keep him and we can't let him go. We're not resorting to murder now, are we?" She didn't know what she would do if Will made that suggestion.

His look of revulsion was answer enough. "Of course not. We are not murderers."

She threw her hands up in utter frustration. "So what do you suggest? Could we ransom him to buy us time to relocate?"

"That's unlikely to yield a happy outcome. We will still come off as the bad guys considering it would mean holding him for a few days."

"Fuck!"

"Pretty much."

"May I suggest something?" Hal queried.

"You've never asked if you can interfere before, I don't see why you are now."

"Fine. Then I'll keep it to myself."

"No. Wait. I'm sorry Hal. I welcome any and all suggestions. The last forty-eight hours are just taking a toll on me."

There was a pause and they were all silent.

"Okay. Apology accepted. If I were you, I would negotiate directly with him. Try to make a deal by which he gives you his scientific data and you help prove one way or another, whether Earth really is in dire jeopardy or if his science is wrong. Ask if you can work together."

Will sat forward in his chair, with renewed interest, and leaned his forearms against his desk. "That just might work. Jack? Do you think you could negotiate with him? I don't think he and I get along too well. I definitely don't plan to accidentally tongue tango with him."

She was abashed. *Oh my god!* "I don't plan on a tongue tango either. It just seems to keep happening. It's hard to explain except to say something about his scent speaks to me." She realized she was verging on discussing something she shouldn't. She looked at Will and sure enough, he was looking at her with speculation again.

"His scent?"

"You know. Like pheromones. Certain people just smell better than others to different people. He happens to smell really good. It's hard to explain. I'm sure you've probably enjoyed a woman's scent before." She was rambling. Time to change the subject. "Regardless, I don't have a problem negotiating with him, but I think it would be better after I have had a chance to review the information I gathered today. It might give us more to negotiate with."

He didn't answer right away but instead continued to assess her.

She sat perfectly still and looked right back at him. All her anxiety buried under a cool façade.

"I think you're right. You should review what you gathered first, but do so quickly. I'm sure we don't have long until Mr. Pheromones has people looking for him."

"Oh good one, Will." Hal sounded like he would have fist bumped Will if he had a fist.

"Who asked you, Hal?" Jack snarled at her own ear which didn't really work and so she just glared into the room as a whole.

"I'll send someone with food and water and to notify our prisoner that you will be down to talk to him as soon as you can."

"Great. I'm off then." Jack swiftly scrambled out of her chair and exited. "I'll let you know how my talk with Tarc goes."

"You better. I won't be kept in the dark again, Jack. Partners don't do that."

"I know. I screwed up. I'm sorry, Will. Truly. I know I let you down. I hope you can eventually trust me again."

"I do trust you, but we are supposed to be a team. No more secrets. Deal?"

"Deal." She turned at the door and tentatively smiled back at Will. "And, thanks."

He flashed her a toned-down version of his million-dollar smile. "Of course."

Heart heavy and unsure, she left to do what she could to help make things right.

Tarc looked up from his prone position at the sound of the door opening. He wanted to see Jack again. He still had a lot of questions for her, but that was not the main reason. He needed to be sure that she was okay. He did not like seeing the male named Will angry at her. When he saw the person entering was said male, he fisted his hands at his sides as he sat up and glared at him. "Where is Jack? Is she okay? She better be okay."

"Huh. Yes. She's fine. She tells me you're the leader of the Alien

Relocation Cooperative. Is that right?" Will appeared less angry and more curious than before.

He thought about ignoring him completely, but decided better of it. He may not like this male and how he had handled *his* female, but he still had questions that needed answers. He sat up and faced the bars. "Yes. That is correct. Who are you?"

"I will ask the questions." Will leaned back casually against the far wall. "She also mentioned that you two keep finding yourselves intimate. I don't remember reading that you can affect females with your scent. Anything you want to tell me about that? I've known Jack since the Staraban arrived and she's not behaving like herself. Are you manipulating her?"

Before he even had the thought, he was at the bars of his cell. In a voice iced over with anger, he responded. "Are you trying to say that I manipulated her into doing something she did not want to do? I have killed males for lesser insults."

Will glared back at him. "I am telling you that I have not seen my partner—" he could tell the other male had thrown that word in with purpose and he could not help the growl that escaped him at the mention of it, "—ever move so quickly into a physical relationship with anyone. But now she's doing so with an enemy. It makes me wonder why. I have to question if someone is influencing her."

Tarc considered what he was saying and calmed. "Your information pleases me. Would it help to know that I am equally affected by her?"

"Really?" Will looked at him like he was studying a scientific experiment and trying to understand the data presented. Quite similar to the look his sister, Caran, got on her face when studying something in the natural world. "I suppose that is mildly better, assuming you are telling me the truth."

"You need to stop questioning my honor. An honor fight will not end well for you, human."

"Anytime, anyplace."

They both glared now, taking the measure of the other male. While he utterly disliked this human, he had to respect his strength of character and the way he was trying to protect his friend. "I have not lied to you."

"Then perhaps there is something in your biology that affects human females that you are unaware of? Interesting as all this is, I am currently not acting as a scientist but as the person in charge of this location. Why did you follow her here?" Tarc stowed that information away. Apparently, Will was a scientist. He was clearly also a fighter, though, and he would store that fact as well.

"I wanted answers and to get close to her again. What is this place? Is Gobble trying to steal our technology? What is Jack involved in?" He watched Will's reactions as he asked each question. He had not reacted to the Gobble question, but to Jack being involved in something. What? "Are you doing something dangerous here?" This time the male tensed. Tarc's eyes narrowed. "Are you a part of the rebellion?" The muscles around the male's mouth drew his lips into a thin line. It was a tiny movement, but Tarc's tracker abilities allowed him to see such small movements in his opponents. Then a possibility occurred to him, that he really hoped was not true. "Is this the Humans Against Relocation Movement?" Tarc inwardly cursed. He could tell from Will's reaction that he had gotten it just right with that last one and—*Shet!*—Jack was one of the leaders. He was going to need to give that more thought before dealing with the implications. "I see. How long do you plan to keep me here?"

"Undecided. Of course, now that I know you've deduced who we are, it complicates things. What do you know about HARM?"

"We know that HARM has sent out information recruiting humans to join a resistance movement. You promote the false idea that humans should not be relocated. You convince others we are spreading lies regarding the health of the planet. You say you are a scientist. How can you deny all of the problems on Earth and still call yourself that?"

"I know the Earth and all of its problems and its instabilities better than an invading alien species who's done a hack job with their scientific research."

"Do you deny our technology is better than yours?"

"No. I deny your willingness to do a full study of the matter."

This conversation was not going anywhere. Will was obviously not the person he needed to talk to. To reason with. "I do not think I am talking to the correct person about this."

Will scoffed. "Jack may be good with technology, but she is no scientist. She is also not very good with people. Of course, you're not a person, but an alien. You're going to get your wish, though, Jack will come back sometime soon and we shall see from there what we do with you." He looked like he might want to say more, but he did not. "For now, I've brought you food and water." The human went to the door, opened it, took a box and a bottle from the guard outside, then handed them over to Tarc through the bars.

Tarc recognized the shape of the box and the smell. *Peet-zza*. At least they were feeding him well.

"I have some work to do but let me be clear." Will looked him directly in the eyes. "You do anything to harm her, and I will make it my mission to end you." He walked out the door and Tarc was left growling at the delicious smelling peet-zza instead of at the human he wanted to get his hands on.

He sat back down, took some deep breaths to calm himself, and began to eat. He could have attacked Will if he had wanted to, but he was not a leader known for behaving in irrational ways. At least that was true until he had met her. He needed to get back to thinking strategically. What should his next course of action be? They clearly underestimated his kind because the cell bars would be all too easy to pull apart. Situation analysis. He was in HARM headquarters. Scenarios played through his head with pros and cons of each decision swiftly filtering through. He did not intend to cause unnecessary harm to the humans. Well, maybe with Will he would enjoy causing some harm, but the others, he would prefer to exit without undo violence. If he stayed, the base would be attacked and Jack and the other humans would likely get hurt. It would be better for them if he left, but he was not going alone. *That* he was decided on. He needed to find Jack.

He could track her scent to find her now, but decided it would be easier to be patient and wait for her to come to him. At least, that was what he thought at first. He was not a patient male, though, and upon further reflection, the faster he was away from their base, the better for everyone involved. He could decide how to handle HARM later. For now, he wanted to get Jack in his power and protection and to get back to his own base.

Jack was still stinging from her conversation with Will when she got back to her room. She had royally fucked up and Will would probably never trust her again. He said he trusted her, but did he really? She threw her body down into her computer chair in frustration. She was not her mom, dammit! She didn't drop everything for any man and yet, because of her ridiculous reaction to Tarc, she'd put her position at HARM in jeopardy. *Stupid! Stupid! Stupid girl! Have you learned nothing from your mother? Nothing from being a woman in tech? Nothing at all?*

She could hear her mom's alcohol slurred voice clearly in her head.

"You think you're going to be better than me? You're just a stupid girl. You'll have nothing, be nothing, just like me. Stop sniveling and clinging. I really should have given you up at birth. You may not like the men I bring home, but they're all I've got, and you will stop all this crying and get back to your room. Let me have my little bit of happiness."

Shaking her head to clear it, her mother's venom still coursing through her veins, she snarled. "Hal! I hope while you were busy being an asshole, you were also busy getting the work done that I had given you."

"Sorry, Jack. I have."

Jack had never heard her PAL sound contrite before. She took a few calming breaths before responding this time. "I'm sorry, Hal. That was a bitchy thing to say. I'm agitated and taking it out on you."

"I didn't mean to upset you so much. I've never heard you like this. Are you okay?"

Was she okay? Not really, but she had a job to do, and she would rather focus on that. "Hal. Tell me wher—"

A knock at her door stopped her words and then it swung open as Rory strode in. "Hola, chica. Everything okay? I heard that you and Will were speaking rather loudly with each other in his office. He's usually so stiff. Other than getting frustrated with the requests the programming pit makes, which I'm pretty sure they now do just to pull his tail, I don't think I've ever heard him raise his voice." Her friend stopped talking, really looked at her, and concern flooded her features.

Jack sighed. "Did you also hear that we captured an alien right outside? That the alien is the same one I told you about from yesterday? That said alien caught me again today and that I practically jumped his bones, again, and when I thought I had gotten away, he followed me back here?" Jack could feel her own tension pouring out into the words.

Rory's eyes grew rounder and rounder with each new revelation. "How did he follow you? You got your groove on with him, again? Where is he now? What did Will have to say? ¡Ay dios mío!"

"I thought I had glamoured him but apparently it didn't take, at least I think that's why he was able to follow me. And, oh yeah. I got my groove on all right and I also accidentally almost drew blood… again. He now knows I'm not exactly human. He is in one of the cells downstairs. Will might never fully trust me again, and who could blame him, since I didn't tell him rather vital information to keep the base safe. And yes. ¡Ay dios mío! And the kicker? The alien and I actually exchanged enough words instead of tongues for me to learn that the alien downstairs is, drumroll please, Tarc. Yes, before you say it, *the* Tarc. The head honcho himself."

"Fuck." Rory leaned against the desk and put her hand on Jack's shoulder, lending comfort Jack wasn't sure she deserved.

A snort escaped at her friend's summation. "Exactly."

"What happens now? And I'm sure Will will trust you again. Give him time. He'll calm down."

Hal cheerily chimed in. "Of course he will. Will is the best after all."

"No one asked you, Hal." Sigh. "Sorry, again, for snapping. Just please. No 'Will is the best, Jack is the worst' talk right now."

"Sure thing, Jack. I'll finish up sorting the files. Almost complete."

"What did the alien, I mean Tarc, say about you being a vampire?"

"I didn't tell him what I am, I just confirmed that I wasn't totally human. I assume he knows that I was trying to use some sort of power on him or that I had used a power on him that didn't last long since I tried putting him to sleep and yet he was awake fast enough to tail me. Maybe they are like you, immune to my power?"

Rory replied matter-of-factly. "Sounds to me like you had reason to believe all was well. Will doesn't know what we know about your powers, so from his point of view, there was no reasonable way for you to be sure Tarc wouldn't follow you. Perhaps it's time to let him in on your secret?"

Shaking her head vehemently she squealed, "No! He may never look at me the same again. He *really* doesn't like the aliens for approaching us before we, humans, were ready and he *really* hates anything unscientific or magical and I can only imagine how he'll react if he finds out that I'm not human. It won't go well." She frowned and pinched her fingers between her brows in agitation. "I don't want to lose his friendship or my position here. I truly believe that I can help save us all from relocation. I'm needed here and have access to the data herd to do everything I need to do. Anyway. Are you planning to share your secret with him?"

Rory grimaced. "¡Diablos, no! I'm not sure he'll react badly, but I, too, don't plan to risk it. Anything I can do?" Rory reached out and took hold of her hand.

Jack placed her other hand over Rory's and shrugged. "Thank you for your support but I think the best thing I can do is get back to work. I just need to stay focused."

"And what about your need to get under, over, and around the alien head honcho downstairs? I really need to see this male perfection you can't keep your fangs off of for myself." She raised her eyebrows up and down lasciviously.

"Perhaps when I go downstairs to negotiate with him, you can come with me." She was finally able to genuinely smile. "You'll totally understand when you see him. So, what are you up to now?"

"I have to go test something I worked on last night. We set up an area in the empty building next door so as not to disturb anyone. Still. If you hear a big sound in the next hour or so, just ignore it." Her face scrunched in disgust. "Sometimes the idiots I work with can't be allowed near the explosives lest they kill themselves, so I'm going to supervise. Just come and get me in about an hour when you're finished and heading down." Rory smiled back over her shoulder as she went for the door. "Oh. And do try to keep all of your clothes on while I'm in the room. Or don't. That might be fun too." She ran out laughing just as the pillow Jack threw hit the door.

She couldn't help laughing, too. Rory was the best thing that ever happened to her. She'd never known what it would feel like to have a family, a real one, but she loved Rory like she assumed you might love a sister. Somehow her friend always found a way to lift her mood.

"Are you ready now, Jack? I have compiled everything and just need to organize it."

"Thank you. Please continue organizing it and then transfer the pertinent folders over to my wrist. I'm famished. I'll check it out either in the food hall or when I get back."

"Will do. Jack?"

"Yes, Hal?"

"You know I love Will, but I think you're right that he might not take it well. I do think he would get over it, though. Consider giving him that chance."

"Okay. I'll think about it. And now I'm taking advice from my own creation. You really have taken on a life of your own." Jack felt lighter as she walked to get herself some food. She thought she heard a mumbled, "More than you know," in her head.

Twenty minutes later, feeling quite satisfied with the chicken risotto the food hall had served for Italian night, but unsatisfied with the risotto she had to eat off of her shirt, she came back to her quarters. She distractedly entered her room while mid-removal of the offending garment that coincidentally read, "Sloppy food, always. Sloppy code, never." Her door closed behind her just as her hands and shirt were above her head and she froze. *No way!*

Tarc had found it very easy to bend the bars and pressure point the guards asleep. They would be out for a while. It was really hard to believe these humans actually believed they were a match for the Staraban warriors at all. The only one who even raised a concern was Jack and he could take her and planned to, over and over again.

He carefully avoided running into anyone in the stairwell and down the hallway while following her scent to where it was the strongest. He opened the door and saw that no one was inside. Stepping in quickly, he closed the door and was enveloped in her essence. His cock went stone hard instantly. *Damn!* He adjusted himself and settled in behind the door. Hopefully no one else will come in to check for her. Erotic daydreams played through his mind and mingled with the memories he had of how her body felt under his hands from the last two days.

He also studied the room. Her room. It was not a very big space and reminded him of many of the living quarters on one of their spaceships. Along the right wall was a desk with a computer screen and a well-loved chair in front of it. He imagined her sitting in it working. Her fingers flying swiftly across the keys. Along the back wall was a rumpled bed he was not sure he could actually fit into. Above the bed there was a picture of a cat with a headset sitting in front of a television and seemingly playing a video game? *Strange!*

To the left of the bed sat a bookshelf which had books lining the three bottom tiers, a couple picture frames on the fourth tier, and some other things he did not recognize on the fifth tier. Along the left wall were two doors. One was partially open and he could see it led to a closet. The other he assumed led to what they called a bathroom.

He had not been waiting long, his perusal brief, when he heard steps coming down the hallway towards the room. He tensed. The door opened and her scent intensified as she walked through the door. He helped it close gently, quietly turned the lock, and was completely transfixed by the image she presented. She had her arms reaching up over her head with her t-shirt pulled up most of the way. Her breasts overflowed the black human breast restraint with the little red bow in the front. They were full and lush and his hands opened and closed needing to feel them. His mouth started watering for a taste as well.

It was obvious the moment she realized he was there. Her body went rigged and her scent, which had already thickened like a blanket around him, changed first to a twinge of fear and then to a heady, spicy lust.

He snaked his right arm around her middle, pulling her back and slamming her firmly against the door. A gasp escaped her. His other hand tangled into her shirt effectively tying her hands together and held them up over her head.

"Tarc." Her breathy voice whispered his name. "What are you doi—"

He did not give her a minute to think, but instead slammed his mouth over hers devouring her as his right hand made its way up from her waist to one of her breasts. She responded instantly. Kissing him with the same intensity he was giving her.

Nothing and no one had ever felt like this female. She was incredible in every way. So smart and so passionate. He growled and leaned his hips into her middle so she could feel his hard length, how hot she made him. He moved his right hand up to take over restraining her so he could free up the left. It made its way down her arm, her head, her throat, at which point he felt her breath hitch.

The hand at her wrists brushed against something metal and he gazed up while still kissing her and saw a hook on the back of her door. *Perfect!* He maneuvered her twisted shirt so he could suspend her wrists on the hook and now that he had both hands free, he grabbed her under her thighs and lifted her legs to straddle at his waist. She hooked her legs around him while he pressed and rubbed against her hot pussy.

She was all sensuality, so completely open in her response, and he was going mad with the need to get inside her. His original plan had been to knock her out and take her with him when he left. His original plan had him getting her back to his base and then having his passionate way with her. The original plan was discarded with one look at her half-dressed body and being overwhelmed with her erotic smell. He became oblivious to his location. His mission. Anything. He could not even bring himself to care when he felt her sharp teeth make an appearance. She was moaning and growling and her little sounds drove him that much more insane with lust.

He reached behind her back and attempted to unclasp the breast cover, but was not used to such a device since the Staraban female did not wear such things. In his urgency and frustration he gave a sharp tug on the front of it and ripped it apart. He caught her gasp in his mouth as he continued his assault on her lips. They were practically breathing for each other.

He pushed the torn material up to join her t-shirt on the hook and finally lifted his mouth from hers so he could skim his way down the column of her throat and over to lick and tease at her left breast.

"Oh my god. Oh. Oh." Her words of pleasure brought about his own pleasure. His desire, to make her feel good, intense.

His hand engulfed her breast enjoying the soft weight of it, the perfect fit of it in his palm. He used his teeth to graze over her right nipple while his fingers tweaked the left one. She moaned. It seemed she enjoyed both the pain and pleasure he was able to give her. Her body was strung so tight she was quivering and panting in his arms.

He switched his mouth and hand locations so he could get a taste of them both. All the while, he kept grinding his hips mimicking exactly what he wanted to do with her. *Would* do with her. He sensed the tension coiling in her body like a spring bringing her ever closer to orgasm. He wanted to rip both their clothes off and forget any and all consequences. Forget where they were, who they were outside of this intimacy.

He rubbed and plundered and pinched until she was reduced to whimpers, her body perched on a precipice. Then, he pushed her over, rubbing himself hard into her hot, needy core. He covered her mouth with his to swallow her scream. Her orgasm as beautiful as she was. She was quaking in his arms and when that subsided, she melted into him.

He only had a moment to enjoy the feel of her relaxed weight, before he became aware of footsteps in the corridor. The footsteps stopped as someone knocked at her door. He moved swiftly to cover Jack's mouth with one hand and pressed the other to her trapped one's to keep them still. He then used the rest of his body to hold hers immobile. Leaning his forehead against hers in frustration, he tried to get his hearts to stop racing.

Another knock sounded. The handle wiggled as whoever was on the other side attempted to come in. "Jack? Are you in there, chica?" A female voice inquired. "I finished early because someone forgot to adjust the radius on the blast zone and testing had to be suspended until it gets fixed. I thought maybe you'd be ready to go torture or negotiate with our prisoner."

Torture?

He heard her mumble. "Since when do you lock the door. Oh." In a louder voice, she said. "I guess you're a little busy with your bad self. Enjoy. I can't wait to see this prisoner of ours who's got you so worked up you're masturbating midday. Damn. Now I need to go find the good doctor again. Come get me when you're, um, finished. I'll make it a quickie." He heard the moment the female stepped away. He lifted his head and looked into Jack's angry eyes. Their interlude was over. *Shek!* His cock was tired of going hot and cold, hard and unused would be a more apt description.

He momentarily closed his eyes to gather his control. When he felt calm settle over him, he moved his hand from hers in a slow caress along her forearm. Some of the angry tension left her as her body reacted to his touch, their continued proximity. He loved her responsiveness. The eyes above the hand still covering her mouth held residual wariness. Smart female. He stroked down her arm, around her shoulder, and then applied pressure to a specific spot that left her unconscious.

Jack slumped into him. He carefully lifted her off the hook and completed removing her shirt and bra. His eyes feasted on the breasts his mouth had feasted on before and his hard response was

74

immediate. *Mine.* The thought was just as immediate and not completely welcome. Still, he would not take her anywhere without proper coverage, so he gently laid her on the bed and found a stack of t-shirts in the closet. Grabbing the top one, he put it over her head noting that it amusingly read, "Hacking is facing a closed door and finding the key or sledgehammer to get through it." Every time he looked at her his dick felt like it could hammer through a door too. He had to adjust himself at that thought.

After a brief search, he located a small backpack in her closet and put a few more clothing items in it. He threw it over one shoulder and picked her up, tossing her over his other shoulder.

It was past time to go.

He had finally caught his prey.

[4]
JACK IN THE BASE

Adventures of a Supernatural Geek Girl

October 3, 2025
Dear reader,

I am actually expecting today to be rather busy, so this post was written last night while eating dinner. I'm sitting here contemplating my risotto. Actually, I'm contemplating my life, but if you saw me, you would think I was finding the answers to the universe in this risotto. Perhaps it will know how I can bring my life back on course. You see, I ran into the alien again. And again, I was possessed by the ghost of a porn star. I've been in charge of my life since I was 15 years old. I was a runaway who created a great existence out of nothing. Taught myself everything I needed to know. I falsified documents to get into college. Basically, I'm good with the details. I'm good at plotting the course of my journey. I am really good at control.

Until now.

I'm shaken. So. I've vowed to myself, as my risotto landed on my shirt, that I was done with the crazy. I'm taking charge of my life again. No one will ever control me. No hormones are going to either. I am not a prisoner to my libido!

I am large and in charge.

Again.

Just not of my risotto.

Flashback Fun Facts:

I know I've discussed glamouring before. For the new readers, yes, we can glamour you. There are pluses and minuses to it. If we do, then you'll never even know we were there. On the other hand, it does ring of violation. For this reason, most vampires adhere to a code of conduct. We only glamour bad people to drink from. It makes the drinking experience distasteful to us, but also ensures we don't violate the innocent. The only other source we have, after all, is volunteers and those are hard to come by when most people don't believe vampires exist. There are some of you out there who are even immune to glamour. That makes for a difficult situation as one of us tries to explain why we're speaking all weird and issuing orders. "Yeah. Um. I just like to imitate lines from vampire movies. Hehe. It's a thing." Awkward all around.

Rededicated to the mission.

Hugs and bites!
iByte

Staraban Headquarters, Portola Valley, CA, USA, Earth

October 3, 2025

Jack woke slowly. She couldn't remember the last time she'd felt so well rested. She was engulfed in warmth and felt as though she was enveloped in a giant hug. Something smelled amazing and she didn't want to get out of bed. She yawned, moving her hand to cover her mouth when she realized she couldn't.

Her eyes flew open as her last memories began filtering in. She found herself staring at a perfect and powerfully built male chest. Deliciously bare male chest. She tilted her head up and stared into Tarc's hypnotic eyes as they studied her warily. How long had she been out? Why was he in her bed? Had she passed out? God he felt good. She recalled the hot moments they'd shared against her door and then—Rory had knocked— She couldn't remember past Rory walking away. *What the hell!*

"What happened? What are you doing in my bed?" She struggled to sit up but his arm around her kept her immobile unless she used her full strength and that would likely hurt him. She wasn't quite there yet. She was also distracted because her left arm still wouldn't budge. As her senses expanded beyond the perfect feel of him, she registered the cold, metallic feel of something like a chain cuffing her to the bed.

His gravelly voice answered her. "We are not in your bed, *apura*. We are in mine."

She looked beyond him and, as he'd said, she was no longer in her own room. The bed they were lying in was quite massive and covered with a soft grey cloth. The large room was furnished with a couch facing a wall TV, a giant chest sat in one corner of the room, and there were a few smooth, handle free doors leading to who knew where. She looked at him again through slitted eyes. "How did I get here?"

"I brought you here."

"How? I..." She looked away. "I only remember Rory coming and knocking on the door and then...nothing." She couldn't stand

CHAPTER 4

the idea of feeling out of her own control. The fact that she couldn't remember anything from that time horrified her. She turned back accusingly. "Did you do something to me?"

He was looking back at her with amusement, which made her ire rise. "Of course I did. I was escaping and taking you as my prisoner. I think it is all quite self-explanatory."

"Your prisoner? If that were the case, I would understand the restraint, but not why I'm in bed with you. How dare you?"

He cupped her face with his hand and softly said. "I dare much. Especially with you. Remember? You are both a prisoner and the female I want in my bed, I accomplished both with this configuration. I could not bring myself to treat you as a normal prisoner. You know why—"

She scoffed. "You have to be kidding me. As if I would allow you to touch me while being your prisoner." She snorted in derision.

Before she knew what was happening, she found herself on her back with Tarc lying on top of her. He wasn't crushing her, though. He was cradling her face while supporting some of his weight with his other arm. The bulge of his impressive erection lay against her core. "We both know that is a lie I can disprove easily."

He leaned down, gently nipping and licking at her lips, asking permission to delve inside. Jack didn't want to respond—shouldn't respond—but she did. She couldn't contain her need in in the wake of all that damn nipping mixed with the heady scent of him as it enveloped her. Not to mention her body's delight at the feel of his weight. Lust struck her hard and fast. *Fuck!* A moan escaped as her lips begged his lips for more.

Instead of more, she found herself flipped once again on her stomach and heard as well as felt the smack he delivered to her backside. "Ouch! What the hell?"

"I warned you not to lie to me. I see you need a reminder. I think a punishment for your transgression is in order and a spanking was the suggestion you made yesterday. I find I like your suggestion." Another hard smack hit her backside at that pronouncement.

She ignored how much she enjoyed the bite of pain and focused instead of her irritation. "You fucking asshole. I'm going to kill you for this."

She heard him sniffing the air behind her. Obviously checking her scent so she did the same and…shit. She was totally giving off more arousal pheromones not "you're a bastard" ones.

Thwack. Thwack.

Arousal be damned. She was not one to lay here and take anything. Fucker would pay! She yanked at the bound hand, broke the chain, and whirled around at Tarc. The look of shock on his face would have been comical if she wasn't in such a rage. She flung herself at him knocking him back off the bed. They wrestled on the floor, rolling and pushing for dominance.

Tarc was rethinking his decision to sneak her onto the base so he would not have to put her in a prisoner cell. If she killed him now, he might well deserve it for stupidity. Still, even as he fought with her for dominance, a part of him respected her will and her strength. Respected it and wanted to dominate it. He wanted all that fire writhing under him sooner than later. The last couple of days had left him masturbating or in pain and sleeping next to her, holding her all night had done nothing but make his aching worse.

He had to admit that while he knew she was strong, he had no clue she was strong enough to break his cuffs. He would have to get stronger ones made for her. That thought made him smile in the middle of their wrestling match and she growled at him in response. He couldn't help but smile even bigger.

While he was enjoying the fight, he needed to get back to the main topics. He pinned her under him. "You are amazingly strong, *shela*, but I am stronger. Stop this."

"You spanked me, you asshole."

"I did. You lied. Do not lie and I will make sure it is a pleasurable spanking next time." He licked his lips and grinned in anticipation.

"Don't flash that sexy grin at me. There won't be a—"

CHAPTER 4

"Watch it. You are about to get another unpleasant spanking."
"Fine. I'm going to ignore that topic completely. Let me go."
"No."
"No? Just 'no'? What do you mean no?"
"You keep asking me that like you do not understand what that word means. In this case, I mean, I am not letting you go. Putting aside what is between us, you are also my prisoner as I was yours. I need to know what you have been doing with our terminals and what are HARM's plans."
She stilled completely and her face went blank. "You should already know I won't betray my people."
"Are you so willing for there to be bloodshed?"
"You don't get that there are those of us willing to fight to stay on Earth. Maybe you should ask yourself why, instead of trying to stop the resistance." His mouth thinned and he was about to say something when she rushed on. "Regardless. Yes. I am willing to have bloodshed for what I believe in, though it is a last recourse."
He leaned back surprised by the vehemence behind her words. Could they be wrong or are humans that confused about their own planet? He did not like mysteries, and he had to figure this one out before things spiraled out of his control.
Pain erupted in his balls, before he even registered her moving beneath him. "*Fash!*" He laid his full weight on her again and held her wrists even more tightly. "All you have proven so far is that you are a very violent species. When I escaped your facility I attacked no one." He swiftly moved his hand down and pressed on the same spot as the night before. Her body went limp beneath him as she fell back asleep.
Thirty minutes later Tarc was ready to kill his brother.
"This is the female that keeps attacking you?" Bren laughed at him.
They were standing outside of the most fortified holding cell they had on base. It was built with human amenities to hold any Earth fighters they came across. He gritted his teeth as he stared at an immobile Jack. She was on the bed he had moved into the room because he could not stand the idea of laying her down on the hard

82

cot that used to be there. He only wished he had been able to place her there without his brother finding out.

"I would love to see you try to battle with her. She is deceptively small and weak-looking. Before you know what hit you, she——"

"Taps you on the shoulder?" Bren was nearly in tears he was laughing so hard. And then the ass slapped him on the shoulder. "Oh. I am sorry. Did I hurt you big brother?"

Tarc growled back. "Say one more thing and I will put you in that cell with her. She may well rip your *fashing* head off."

"Please do put me in there. I will have that beautiful creature purring for me like an Earth cat."

He had Bren up against the wall, hand wrapped around his throat before he even recognized what he was doing. It was instinctive. Necessary. "You put one hand on her and I will cut it off."

"*Fash.* Is there something you would like to tell me brother?" His eyes were inquisitively looking back at Tarc, but Bren had left his hands at his sides, non-threatening.

He moved back and let Bren go. "*Shek.* I am sorry. There has been more than just fighting between Jack and me. She..." He shook his head in confusion. "I do not know how to describe what she is to me. All I know, brother, is she is mine. No one touches her." He looked his younger brother in the eyes, conveying the seriousness of his position.

"I have never seen you like this about a female. Not even, Stala. Are you sure she has not done something to you? There is much we do not know about these humans." Bren was now looking at him with concern etched on his features. "Maybe it would be better if you let me interrogate her? You said she was a leader of HARM?"

"No. I will interrogate her myself and yes, she is one of their leaders. I will be okay. I know how important it is to avoid bloodshed. Speaking of that. Bren, I have something I want you to look into. Ask Caran to help you. Jack has been questioning the validity of the reports we were given regarding Earth. The way she spoke... They are willing to die over this issue. They honestly do not believe they need to be relocated. I know we did a first run review of all that Qisto gave us, but... Jack raises questions. I would like Caran to do an independent analysis while you investigate the Vrolan for any reasons they would have for deceit."

Bren just looked at him for a time. He was clearly studying his features the way they were always able to read each other. Then, he nodded. "I still have my concerns that you are not in a position to be unbiased about this female but there is no harm in doing the checks and tests you have requested. If it all comes back as we expect, we can reveal the results of the testing to the governments and media of Earth so they can see for themselves another basis of information for their move. As you know, our sister is quite thorough." Then he grinned. "And she does not like these Earth males. She finds their dick pics quite offensive. We've been trying to figure out how they find a way to text or mail her, but as soon as we close an avenue, they pop up elsewhere and the pics keep coming. She would be overjoyed to have us be wrong and leave this place."

"Thank you brother." He put his hand on Bren's shoulder and squeezed.

Jack, once again, woke slowly. She took stock of her body and turned on her side to relieve the dull ache of her butt. It reminded her of exactly what caused the ache and she jumped out of bed into a fighting pose in an instant. She couldn't sense anyone around so she relaxed and took stock of her location.

Well, Jack, you asked him why you weren't in a holding cell if you were a prisoner. Way to go. The bed she had been sleeping in was plenty comfortable, but, otherwise, on three sides of her were blank metal walls. The fourth wall had a section of bars between metal walls. Exceedingly thick metal bars. There was a toilet and a shower in one corner with a drape for privacy and a small sink next to it. She walked over to the metal bars and attempted to bend or break them but they didn't budge. Apparently, they put her somewhere quite fortified. She sighed and turned back towards the bed.

On the floor near the bed there was a bottle of water and something wrapped in paper. Taking one last inventory to make sure she was truly alone, Jack settled onto the bed and grabbed the object off the ground and unwrapped it. Tarc had provided her with an egg, bacon, and cheese sandwich. She wasn't sure what time it was nor when she'd had her last meal, but she was starving. The problem was, she was starving for food and blood both. Considering she had eaten blood only a couple of days ago, it was surprising.

A vampire's intake of blood was directly correlated to their power. The more they used—sun exposure and healing being the main draws on it—the more often they needed to feed. Usually, she could go a week without feeling the need for blood. She must have used up her power somehow because she was downright ravenous. If she didn't make her way out of here and find someone to eat, she was going to end up eating someone at random. She'd prefer to avoid that scenario. Except a vision of eating Tarc passed through her mind and she had to work hard to dislodge it.

She tapped at her ear. "Hal? Are you still there?"

"I'm here Jack. I made sure not to talk while around the aliens so that they wouldn't know you had me. I have transmitted your location to Will. I'm sure he'll find a way to come save you."

Her internal feminist and her fang side chafed at the idea she needed saving, but considering where she found herself, maybe just this once. "Thanks, Hal. I'm glad you're here. Um...I have a problem. I haven't fed on anyone since the guy in the alley a couple of days ago. I can feel the need to feed rising. I don't have a lot of time before I will become feral."

"May I suggest you go feral on your alien boy toy?"

"Har, har. Very funny. Will you let me know if you hear anything from Will regarding the timing of the rescue mission? I'll work on figuring out if I can escape from here myself until then."

A sound came from the hallway outside her cell. Jack jumped to her feet and shushed Hal back to quiet. A beautiful male alien appeared at her cell, but not the one she expected. It wasn't Tarc. He did have some resemblance to him, though, and seemed familiar. It hit her that this was one of the aliens she had observed in the clearing with Tarc the other day. He was studying her just as intensely and with as much suspicion as she assumed showed on her own face as she studied him.

"You are awake. Now tell me what you have done to my brother."

"Your broth—do you mean Tarc?" Then taking in the rest of his statement, her jaw dropped in disbelief. "What I have done? Are you fucking kidding me?"

"Yes, I mean Tarc and I am very serious."

"I have done nothing to him. He on the other hand, is an asshole who won't leave me alone."

The alien started laughing. "He can definitely be, as you say, an asshole."

Well damn, these aliens are hot. He had looked so forbidding, with the scar across his face and his hulking build, bigger than even Tarc, but when he started laughing it transformed him. He had similar facial features to her alien irritant, though, now she could see his eyes were more accustomed to laughter than glowers. His hair was also wavy and black, and while still tousled, was cropped closer to his head. The thing most notably shared was the blueness of his eyes. He was scrumptious and yet she felt nothing. *Why do I go crazy around his brother?*

He leaned into the bars and looked at her leeringly. "Perhaps I need to investigate you a little closer to see what you've done to my brother."

Oh wait. Asshole apparently runs in the family. Jack was off the bed and had her arm around his throat through the bars before he had a chance to react. She ignored the need that came upon her to feed and instead warned him in a hiss. "You lay one finger on me and I will kill you." He wasn't laughing or leering any longer.

He looked back at her in shock, which was very satisfying and then wrenched himself out of her hold and backed out of arms reach. "Tarc was not kidding. You *are* fast and strong. Are you human?"

"Tarc hasn't told you?" That surprised her. She pushed away the thought that Tarc may be trustworthy. She wasn't going to be that stupid. She knew she had genetically bad instincts about men. "What's your name grumpy?"

"Grumpy?" He began laughing again. "Bren."

Bren apparently had emotions that shifted like the tide. The only other person Jack knew who had similarly chaotic emotions was Rory. That girl could go from laughing to ripping your head off from moment to moment. It also meant she never stayed mad for long. The idea was to always stay on her good side or get her back there. Perhaps, if she kept Bren laughing, she could convince him to let her go.

"Well, Bren, it seems your brother needs to work on his wooing skills because I don't think holding someone you are interested in, in a cell, is the way to go about winning her. Perhaps he's rusty?" At his look of confusion at the last word, she continued. "You know, forgot how to treat someone so they choose to stay around. Or maybe courting is done differently within your species?"

He smirked. "You realize when big brother finds out you have questioned his ability to court a female, he might feel the need to punish you, again."

Now, *she* gaped in shock. Her indignation colored every word as she shrieked, "He told you? That rat-fink-mother-fucking-ass-wipe-alien-scumbag! You better not be laughing at me, you—"

"Stop. Stop." He was practically bent over in his humor. "I am not sure what some of what you said even means, but you have quite the vocabulary. Maybe you can give me lessons?" After collecting himself he continued. "And yes, he told me. Tarc and I are very, very close. We have other siblings but there is something that connects us as the two closest in age. Will it make you feel better if I tell you that he promised to cut my hands off if I touched you?"

"He did?" Undesired warmth spread through her.

"He did. So you can see why we started this conversation the way we did. My brother is never possessive of females. I was concerned and am not completely dissuaded from the idea that you may have some sort of power over him. I do not trust him to inter-rogate you properly and between you being one of the leaders of

HARM and having unusual skills for a human, as his second, I need to make sure we get answers."

Jack shrugged. "You can ask me all you want. I won't be answering any questions about HARM or myself. Do your worst, Grumpy." She decided that made a fitting, hopefully annoying, nickname. She moved back to the bed and sat down, taking the time to organize her argument. "Bren, there is something I need you to know. You can't keep me here much longer. I can't explain, but I will become dangerous. I don't want that and neither will you. Convince your brother to let me go before this all goes to shit."

"Is that a threat?"

"No. Just fact."

He studied her with aggravation clearly visible on his face. "Tell us what we want to know and we might be able to let you go. What are HARM's plans? Why have you been accessing our terminals? What do you hope to accomplish? Are there others like you? What are your abilities we need to be aware of?"

She looked back at him and willed her irritation towards him so he could truly hear her. "Like I said. I will not answer any of your questions, but, if you don't let me go soon, we might all regret it. If you won't help me, then go fuck with someone else." She was about to turn away when she smelled him.

Tarc walked down to the containment area. He was uncomfortable keeping Jack in a cell despite making it as comfortable as possible. Seeing her behind the bars earlier left him conflicted. The sooner he convinced her to cooperate with them, the better. He entered the hallway and two things registered simultaneously.

His brother had ignored his direct order not to visit the prisoner and after hearing Jack tell him to fuck someone else, he was going to have to kill him. He roared as he launched himself at Bren and punched him in the face.

"*Fash!* What are you doing?" Bren queried as he used his right hand to feel his jaw while the left hand was up in front of him as a shield.

He replied menacingly. "I told you to stay away from her and I definitely warned you to keep your *fashing* hands off of her." He approached his brother for another swing when Jack's voice penetrated the haze of rage that had descended upon him.

"*Tarc!* What the hell is wrong with you? Stop it, you oversized ogre." Jack had her arms through the bars reaching to grab and pull him back. "Are you always so violent towards your brother?"

He growled at her. "I am never violent. I heard you clearly say he should fuck someone else. I warned him not to touch you. Are we that interchangeable for you?"

She flinched as though he had hit her and her gaze slid away in what looked like...pain? "That kind of belittling is uncalled for. What keeps happening between us is unexplainable and a mistake but it only happens with you, you ass. And with the way you're behaving, it won't be happening again. For your information, the word fuck has many meanings. I didn't mean it in the sexual way but in the annoying-me way. I wanted him to go annoy someone else with his questions."

"*Shek. Apura*, I am like this with no one else either. I, too, cannot explain what controls me around you. I am sorry if I hurt you." Any and all anger drained away leaving remorse in its wake. He could not be sure, but he got the impression that something he had said had hurt her deeply.

"Hurt her? I am the one you punched. She is right. You are an asshole." Bren said indignantly.

"Maybe you will follow orders next time. Now, leave."

Bren spoke through gritted teeth. "I do not think it wise to leave you alone with our prisoner, brother. You practically just admitted you do not think clearly around her. Also, what is she? She is not a normal human. I had a demonstration of what you told me earlier. She is dangerous, Tarc."

"I am fine. She will not harm me even if she is tempted to try. I am not asking you, Bren. I command you to leave."

Bren looked at him with concern then turned to Jack. "I do not make a habit of hurting women, but know that if you hurt my brother, you will answer to me." He stiffly turned and walked away.

Tarc waited for the door to the elevator at the end of the hall to close before turning back to Jack. "I do not like seeing you here, but you must know I cannot ignore the danger you pose. Please, just answer my questions so I can release you." He did not know why it was so imperative, but he needed her to trust him even beyond the question of HARM.

"I can't. No. I won't. I won't risk all my friends, my family, or betray my cause. It's not a reasonable thing to ask of me. But Tarc, you have to release me. I tried to explain to your brother but maybe you will actually hear me. You know I am not completely human. I..." She paused looking concerned. Scared. "My kind. We eat food, but we also eat something else and if you don't release me soon, I'm afraid I will do something that we will both regret. Please. Please let me go. It's getting harder every minute that passes."

He drew his brows together in concern. "You are in pain?"

"Yes. It is becoming painful and will continue to grow worse."

"I will provide you with whatever you need. Tell me."

She shook her head. "No. I don't want to tell you. I just want to go. Please."

"Jack. I cannot let you go but I would not have you in pain. Tell me. Trust me. I will not harm you." He quickly swiped his hand, entered the cell, and closed the bars behind him.

Now she looked utterly panicked. "No! What are you doing? Get out of here. Please Tarc. You don't know what you're doing." She backed up from him until her back was against the farthest wall. "Don't get any closer!"

Tarc paused at her rising panic, but it was obvious she did not intend to harm him. She was worried that she might and did not want to. He softly whispered to her. "Trust me. Tell me, *shela*. Let me help you."

"Oh God. I...I...I can't. I'm sorry Tarc." He saw a flash of her elongated teeth pop out of her mouth and then she was behind him, her mouth at his neck. At first, all he felt was pain, but then, nothing but pleasure. Her fangs had spiked into his skin and she was...

drinking his blood? He remembered some of the mythical creatures from the movies and video games that Qisto had given them as part of the sales pitch to save the humans. Of course, the Vrolan had promised they did not exist.

He tried to keep his mind working but the pleasure spreading from the point of her mouth through his whole body, was intense, overwhelming. "Jack. Oh goddess. I need you." He felt her mouth lift off of his neck and that was the end of his control. He spun around, grabbed her, and threw her on the bed, covering her body with his. His mouth found hers and he poured the lust coursing through him into her. She met him passion for passion. "Jack. I cannot slow down. Next time will be slow. I need you now." He kneeled up between her legs and tore her shirt in half, throwing it to the side even as she started struggling with her pants. He took over and made quick work of them and her underwear. She was gorgeously naked below him. "You are so *fashing* perfect, Jack. Absolutely beautiful." He growled.

Jack had tried so hard to control the hunger gnawing at her. It had been building and building until it was clawing at her insides turning her into her most base animalistic self. When he had come into her cell, she hadn't stood a chance. She may have needed blood, but she *wanted, craved* his blood.

It. Was. Ambrosia. No one had ever tasted like him. His blood was everything in those first few moments. The beast in her took over completely. She needed and so she took while aware of very little else except making sure to release the essence that would turn the pain into nothing but pleasure for him. Sated, the blood lust subsided, but she wanted more. More of his blood. More of his taste. More of his everything. She had heard that sometimes the vampire's bite could become sexual, but she had never felt it herself before today. Now, with Tarc's blood coursing through her, her energy shifted to an all-consuming desire.

Once again, their mutual arousal blended and engulfed them.

His words were tinder to the flames inside her, growing into a full-blown inferno. When she stopped feeding, shocked he didn't hate her now, she thought about apologizing or explaining but she didn't have a chance for either. He'd moved too fast and she found herself tossed onto the bed with his body pressing her into the mattress. Their kiss ramped her up even higher and the way he attacked her clothes even more so. She was momentarily frustrated when his uniform confounded her fingers until she decided, fuck it, and ripped it as badly as he had torn her clothes, leaving the halves dangling off his thighs. They never even stopped to remove his boots.

His long, thick and very hard erection had popped out of that uniform and it was a beautiful and formidable sight just like the man who wielded it. She had her hand on him before she even realized that was the plan and it felt so damn good. So hard and soft all at once.

"Your hand feels amazing, but Jack, I cannot wait. I need more than your hand. Tell me you want this. You want me."

She did. She really, really did. She'd never felt like this with anyone. She couldn't even claim it was some weird thing that aliens did to human females since she hadn't felt it in his brother's presence. Tarc called to her on some deeper level that she didn't understand and maybe didn't want to. She knew all too well that the overthinking things road often led to truths better left unknown.

With the taste of his blood still in her mouth, and his cock at her mercy, she wanted another taste of him. A different one. Instead of answering his question, she leaned forward and licked her tongue against the weeping slit of his penis.

He moaned and moved one of his hands to grip her hair at the back of her head. "Yes. Suck me Jack. I want to feel your mouth on me."

She was about to do just that when she felt a tug on her hair which lit her scalp with sensation and also had her looking up into his now stern looking face. "No biting. Can you do this without injuring me?"

She had to smile and flash him her fangs. Poor guy. "You'll have to risk it to find out. You want me to continue?" She flicked her tongue out and once again caught the tip of his penis hovering nearby.

He groaned deeply his eyes flashing hot with his passion. "Yes. Take me in your mouth. I need to feel you."

He pulled gently on her hair maneuvering her mouth forward. She swirled her tongue around the end, loving the silky feel and musky taste of him. He tasted just as good here as he had with her teeth in him. Then she put her lips around his cock and tried to take another inch with each pass in and out. She got to a point where she thought she had taken as much of him as she could, but his hand firmed at the back of her head and he took charge gently fucking her mouth. She breathed through her nose, the familiar sensation helping to relax her muscles and jaw.

Their eyes stayed locked to each other as he continued moving in and out. His blazed a fiery sapphire blue. "Goddess you are so sexy. I love seeing my cock in you finally and I find I am impatient to fuck you wild. You have been driving me mad for days." He said that last as he pumped his cock deep enough she felt him at the back of her throat. "That feels so *fashing* good. One day soon I will have you swallowing me, but today, I want to be buried deep inside your sex."

He yanked backwards on her hair as he pulled out of her mouth. Then he pushed her down onto her back and once again kissed her passionately. While his left arm supported some of his weight, his right hand played with her breast, rubbing his thumb over the hard bud and then squeezing it between two fingers. She arched her back wanting more. Needing more. She was burning too hot. She needed relief. He left her mouth and kissed his way down her jaw, her neck, and down further until his mouth clamped around her left breast. "Tarc. Yes! Oh god. Please. I need you."

She was so lost in her passion, she couldn't tell which of them growled, but she was pretty sure it was him as he moved back up her body. "Next time. Slow." He reached down with his right hand and pushed a big, long finger into her, finding out for himself just how wet she had gotten. "Mmmm. So ready for me yet so tight."

He pushed yet another big, long finger into her and she couldn't contain a low moan from escaping. "Tarc!" Her hips were pressing into his hand. She needed more.

"Look at me." She hadn't realized she'd closed her eyes. She opened them at his command. He pulled his fingers from her eliciting a whine of protest and brought his fingers up and into his mouth. "You taste so sweet. So good."

He leaned down and she tasted herself on his mouth as he kissed her again. It drove her energy even higher, her body to become even wetter, and her need skyrocketing. "Please. Please!" She begged him and then felt the head of his cock at her entrance. "Yes. Please."

Inch by inch, he entered her, stretched her. He lifted his head and groaned. The strain of entering her gently was written across his features. She felt his muscles strain for control and then he was completely inside and she greedily wanted more. She wanted him to move his fucking hips.

"You are so tight. You feel so very good." Then he moved and it was glorious. The speed of his thrusts ramped up fast as she moved her hips to meet his. "You are mine, *shela*. Mine."

Jack was incoherent with need. All she registered was the desire in his eyes, the energy level in her at a strength she had never felt before, and the precipice she was quickly nearing and wanted to jump off of. Some instinct she had never felt before claimed her and she bit him again.

He grunted and then moaned and his pace grew even faster, his pounding hard and frenzied. He reached down and flicked his thumb over her clit and she went soaring, releasing his neck with a scream as a burst of energy escaped her. Tarc was right behind her as he gave one last hard pump with his hips and his own yell. Her name. "Jack." He collapsed on top of her, cradling her as he rolled over them so she was on top. She had a moment of pure bliss.

Sanity crashed into Jack like a freight train. What had she done? *Oh god!* She must've tensed, because his hands stilled their rubbing up and down her back.

"What is wrong? Are you okay? Did I hurt you?" He sounded more and more concerned with each new question.

"Did you hurt me? Are you kidding me? I hurt you. I'm so sorry, Tarc. I…I never lose control like that. I don't know what's happening to me. Clearly you aren't safe around me."

She felt his chest moving under her cheek even before she heard his chuckle. "*Apura*, I am fine. You did not really hurt me."

"How can you say that? I bit you. Did you miss that part? Not once. Twice!" There was a note of hysteria creeping into her voice and she didn't care. "Now you can see why you have to stay away from me. Please just let me go."

"No."

"You don't understand."

"I think I do. You are a—the word I think is vampire."

She lifted her head to look him in the eyes. They lacked the condemnation she was convinced would be there. Instead, he just stared back at her. Could she trust him with the truth? Should she? He seemed to be handling what happened with more calm than she was. And he kind of already knew, so it wouldn't really be a betrayal of her people to confirm it. Would it? As he patiently waited, she thought about all of their interactions so far, and couldn't find a time where he hadn't been truthful or fair with her. Potentially making a huge mistake, she chose to trust him. "Yes."

"I assume humans do not know you exist?"

"Most don't," she said warily.

"Some of the material we were shown about humans included monsters," she flinched at that and he must have noticed because he amended, "or humanoids that were not human any longer, and we were told they were all imaginary." He raised an eyebrow in query. "Not so imaginary, then?"

"Many of the depictions of vampires are imagined, but I suspect the reason someone imagined us was because at some point in the past, they saw something they shouldn't have. Not all vampires, since the beginning of my species, have been discreet. Still. Many of the things you see aren't accurate."

"I have seen you in the sunlight."

"Yes. Like that. I can't be in the sunlight indefinitely, because I can be overexposed and bad things happen then, including potentially dying, but I can be in it in small doses."

He suddenly went pale and through gritted teeth said, "I could have killed you."

"What?"

"When I took you from your base. It was sunny and I would not have known how much was too much. I could have killed you. Oh, Goddess."

Jack put her hand to his cheek. "It wouldn't have been your fault. You didn't know what I was or what my limitations were, though that does explain my very urgent need to feed."

"You think I care if it was or was not my fault?" He was growing agitated. His jaw rigid. Angry.

"Oh."

"Oh?"

She bit her bottom lip. She couldn't fathom why he would care about her one way or another. No one ever did. Well... except Rory. "I guess I just figured I would have been one less irritant. One less resistance member."

Tarc exploded off the bed, pulling up the sides of his jumpsuit as he did. She clutched the sheet to her as she sat up.

"What? How low your opinion of me is to imagine that is all I would think about. Especially now. How can you believe that?" Every word felt like a blow. *Could this be a boomerang of the pain she might have caused with her words?*

He paced savagely back and forth across the small room. When she didn't answer him right away, he continued in a nasty tone waving his hand at the bed. "I thought you said you never do this kind of thing, but if you would do this with someone who you think would not care if you lived or died, I find that hard to believe." He walked towards the bars. "I have a job to do. It is time I focused and finished saving your species per the contract, and leave you all to your own demise so I can get back to saving a kind, peaceful, and grateful species. I will not bother you again. I will send someone with clothes."

Where there had been a sweet scent of lust and hunger and fulfillment moments before, there was a horrid scent of anger and betrayal that was rolling off of him while choking her. He was truly furious. She had to make this right, but what could she say? She could clearly hear her mother telling her, *"All you do is cause problems and men don't like problems. You'll never be worth anything... to no one."* Could still feel the years of training at her mother's side to be as silent as possible during her tirades.

She was not that girl anymore. Still struggling for words, she looked up to make him understand, but he was gone, locking her in before she could get them out. She sat, shell-shocked, and just stared at the wall across from her. Her mother's words mingled with Tarc's angry face.

Worthless. Slut. Troublemaker. Alone.

[5]
JACK BE SWIFT

Adventures of a Supernatural Geek Girl

October 3, 2025

MIA – I'm sorry but iByte can't come to the blog right now. Please leave your comments and she will hopefully be back to her regularly scheduled postings after a short rescue.

– Her PAL

Staraban Headquarters, Portola Valley, CA, USA, Earth

October 3, 2025

She couldn't be sure how long she had sat there. There was a sound from the hallway, but the steps were too light for it to be Tarc. The tall female alien from the clearing stood in front of her cell looking at her with an analytical, assessing gaze. Jack returned her gaze analysis for analysis. She had long flowing black hair, a slim muscular build, but what really gave her away were her eyes. She would bet everything that the alien was related in some way to Tarc and Bren.

Jack took her first impression in like a list of facts and nothing more. She felt hollow. She hadn't been ready to deal with what happened from the moment she started feeding on Tarc until they came together like fireworks, but the aftermath so soon on its heel and it was just too much. So she just kept staring. Waiting to see what happened next. Emotionally shut down, just like when she was a little girl. It was safer to shut down sometimes. She knew that well.

"Don't you dare answer me like that, girl. I'll slap you until you learn to shut your mouth. You hear me? You're just lucky I'm willing to put up with you, but I won't if you keep irritating me."

She was startled from her thoughts, as the female swiped her hand to the side of the bars entered and swiped again closing them in together. She walked over toward the bed, toward Jack, and put a container on one side while sitting on the other, clutching what looked like an array of clothes in front of her. Jack turned her head to keep looking at her while neither spoke. The female reached her hand up towards Jack's face very slowly. She didn't flinch. If she attacked, Jack would defend herself, but anything else and she couldn't care at the moment.

The alien ran her hand on one side of Jack's face and then the other. She only then realized the female was wiping away tears she hadn't known were slowly streaming from her eyes. The gesture was surprising. Now that they were closer, they stared again, eye to eye for a time. She had no words, so she stayed silent. Finally, the alien spoke.

"My brother asked me to bring you clothes and food. He was quite angry at the time and would not explain his obvious distress. I came down expecting to want to shove you out an airlock, but I see there must have been some mistake for you are also in distress. I must deduce that he misunderstood something or you did? Clearly by the look and scent of this room, you two were intimate." She sighed then ordered. "Put on the clothes I have brought you, and perhaps we can figure out what mess you two have created."

Jack was surprised by her clear deduction and kindness. "Thank you. Do you mind giving me some privacy to clean up before I change into the clothes you brought?"

The alien showed her the clothes. "I do not mind. These clothes are ones Tarc brought from your base."

Jack gratefully took the clothes and went behind the curtain. She swiftly cleaned herself from a sink with the small hand towel. She pulled on the jeans and then slipped the shirt over her head and peered down curious which shirt he had grabbed. It read, "You are here" and had a red arrow pointing down. She couldn't help but laugh. Otherwise she might end up back at crying.

"Something wrong with the clothes?"

Jack stepped out from behind the curtain. "No but of all the shirts for Tarc to grab for me—You have to see the irony." The female read her shirt and laughed.

"Very much accurate. Do all of your shirts have silly phrases on them?"

"I haven't met a time in my life that couldn't be made better with the right shirt slogan." She shrugged. "We haven't actually been formally introduced yet. You know I'm Jack and I know you are Tarc's relative. A sister perhaps?"

"Yes. His sister. I am Caran."

"So Caran, you're the lucky woman who has Tarc and Bren as siblings." Jack gave her a sympathetic look.

Caran snorted. "Yes. They are sometimes a lot to deal with. Also, we have another brother who is the youngest. I assume you saw him as well in the clearing when you spied on us." Jack fidgeted at that. "I am the only daughter. Do you have siblings?"

"No. My mother never wanted kids and especially not me. I was quite lucky to be born."

Caran looked horrified. "Why would she not want you? And how do you know she did not?"

"Let's just say that she was quite vocal about her objections. I was quite clear on where I stood. If I had been a boy, it might have gone better for me, but maybe not. Who knows?" Jack shrugged.

"That sounds terrible. I cannot imagine a mother not wanting her children. What kind of species are you humans? The things you do to each other sicken me."

"At least we don't try to move anyone forcibly away from their home." Jack heard the familiar voice and saw Will standing at the bars. He moved his hand like she had seen Tarc and Caran do, and the bars slid open. He walked in like an avenging angel with gun drawn and pointing directly at Caran. He was still tall, dark, muscular with beautifully set eyes but this was the first time Jack looked at him and felt nothing. A strikingly gorgeous man, but the only male she seemed to want anymore was the one who hated her right now. It figured.

"Who are you, human—" Caran practically spat the last word out. "—and how did you get a cell pass?" She demanded jumping up to her feet, hand starting to reach to her belt.

"Uh, uh, uh, sweetheart. No grabbing for your weapon. Slowly. Very slowly, give it to Jack."

"I am not your sweetheart." Caran hissed back. She also didn't comply right away, but ultimately did as Will requested. Tension was rolling off her filling the room and Jack with the scent. She had to move. She walked to stand between Will and Caran.

"Will. What are you doing here? No wait. Obviously trying to rescue me, but how did you get in?"

"We can discuss it later. For now, we have to go. Have they harmed you? It's clear to me you've been crying."

Caran answered him. "Of course we have not harmed her. *We* are not the barbarians."

"No. They haven't harmed me. We can talk about that later, too." *Or never. Never was good for her.*

Will looked around the room and stared at the bed for a time. "I'm going to kill that bastard." He looked at Caran. "You call us barbarian? What did your leader do? She is obviously upset and looking at that bed, I can guess why. And who. Maybe your species doesn't think rape counts as harming—"

"I wasn't raped, Will. Stop this!" She was burning with embarrassment now. "I'll explain later. We have to go. You can't get caught here."

He stared at her with frustration and then turned to Caran. "We may need a hostage to get out of here."

"You touch me and I will make you regret it." Caran narrowed her eyes at him. "Regardless, it is illogical to want a hostage. You will move faster without my attempts to escape nor my dead weight. Even without me I doubt you make it off this base." She smirked back. "You may have found a way here, but you will not find a way out, *sharta*."

"I truly can't stand your species." He bit out.

"Feeling is mutual, human." She snarled.

"Stop it! Both of you. I can't decide if I should send you to your rooms or tell you to get a room. Caran. I think it's best if I leave. I don't think there is anything to work out. Everything was just a momentary lapse in judgment. Please tell Tarc...Tell him...I'm sorry if I offended him." She had to blink back the tears that were lacing her confused emotions. "You have been kind to me..." She looked back and forth between her and Will, "I'm really sorry but I will need to tie you up so we have a chance to get away. Please. I really don't want to fight with you but I do have to get away."

Caran looked between her and Will and the gun he held and then back to Jack. "I will do as you ask, but I think you are making a mistake." She looked at Jack with such concern, that she had to look away.

"You're wrong. The mistake was already made. Now I'm just leaving before it gets worse."

Tarc could not remember the last time he had been this angry. He never got angry. He was the cool headed one. The one in control. He never said or did things he did not mean or intend and yet, when he left Jack he had been anything but in control.

Taking the time to change into a new uniform had not calmed him. He had to get himself together before seeing her again. He needed his answers, and he needed her, despite what he had said. There was no way he was going to be able to stay away from her. Even now his body urged him to go back to her, to claim her until she had no doubt that her death was completely unacceptable to him.

He would not do that. Not until he was in control. Stala, his past *braif*, had taught him all too well to never fully trust himself with a female. He had grown up with her and believed himself in love. He had never thought to control his feelings for Stala but that had turned out to be his mistake. She had left him the day before their commitment ceremony and he learned an important lesson.

"I am sorry, Tarc, but I never really loved you. Our families have wanted our commitment since we were young. You are attractive and strong, you are my friend so I agreed to this. I knew what you wanted to hear, that I loved you. In a way, I do, so I said it, but I have never been in love with you.

I am sorry this hurts you, but I have found someone I truly love. I cannot go through with our ceremony. I must follow my hearts in this."

He had been planning their lives together, imagining the children they would have. She had been cheating for months with a mutual friend. No. He would never play the fool for his feelings and he never tolerated lies. He never again wanted to hear a falsehood from someone because it was what they thought he wanted to hear. He respected truth in all things.

Had Jack been truthful about not feeling drawn to anyone else like she was to him? He did not know, but with a mildly cooler head, he did not think she had been lying. He had seen her confusion and then pain at his words. It was not even about the sharing of their bodies. She could have done that many times and he would not care. It was their connection that made him crazed with jealousy. He owed her an apology. It was cruel to have said what he had. To have treated her so badly. He had been insulted by her assumption he would not care if she lived or died, but that was no excuse for his behavior.

He was staring out the window at the beautiful open space preserve just beyond their chosen base location when he heard his door slide open. "Leave."

"I see you are in just as bad a mood as our sister relayed to me. Something happen that I should know about?" Bren moved to stand right next to him but was staring at Tarc instead of the view.

"I told you to leave. I meant it." He said sternly. His brother should know when to leave him to his own thoughts by now.

Bren said nothing for some time and Tarc knew that he was trying to read his face. *Fash* their ability to literally read each other. There were times he found it useful and then there were times like now. He tried very hard to smooth out his features.

"You may not want to talk, but I believe you need to. What is happening?"

He sighed in resignation. His brother seemed like the easy going one or the scary one depending on what mood he was in when you saw him, but what most did not realize is that he was also the stubborn one. When he got like this, he would not stop until he got what he wanted.

"Tarc, you are my leader but more importantly, you are my brother. You need to figure something out. That is what I am here for." He paused and then lifted one side of his mouth into a crooked smile. "And if that is insufficient, we can kick the *shek* out of each other and that will make you feel better too. I still owe you for your punch earlier."

He smirked. "That last one has merit." Bren was probably right, though. "I do not know if I can explain it. From the moment I first caught her scent, I have wanted her. I want to know everything about her. I want to know she is safe. I want to claim her. It is completely insane. Irrational. My control slips around her and I do not like it, but I also cannot stay away. Things happened between us

I will not go into detail about and after, she said something I did not care for and I said things. Things I did not mean. I was…unkind. *Fash*. No. I was cruel. I hurt her. I do not thoughtlessly react to things. I act. But with her, I find myself reacting mindlessly." He shook his head. "I know the right thing to do and I do not care. I want to claim her anyway."

Bren had been silent. He allowed Tarc the space he needed to get everything out in the open. Now he tensely waited for Bren's response and then it came. "What the *fash* are you doing up here? I do not claim to understand the way you are feeling, but I did see how you reacted when you thought I had touched her. There is obviously something between the two of you. If she is yours, then you need to go and do as you say. Claim her and perhaps then we can get the answers we nee—"

Alarm bells sounded and one of his warrior's voice came through the internal speaker system. "We have had a breach! I was knocked out and my ID as well as my cell badge are missing."

"*Fash!*" Tarc was already running for the door with Bren right behind him.

He ran down the corridors yelling for others to move out of his way. He went down the stairs taking them two and three at a time to the lower cell level. He made it through the door and to the cell where Jack was being held. Where Jack had been held. He found Caran tied up and sitting on the bed, instead. He let out a growl.

"Caran are you okay?" Bren asked as Tarc moved to undo her ties. First the one gagging her and then her hands.

"Yes. I am fine. A human male named Will came for Jack. He was very unpleasant but neither of them hurt me. He did seem like he wanted to kill you, brother, after he saw the state of the bed. Is he her lover?" Once released, Caran stood looking closely at him. Probably looking for his reaction.

"He is not her lover." He growled. "Where did they go? How long ago?"

"I think our brother is not in the mood for an analysis, dear sister. I suggest you answer him quickly."

"Yes. I see that. It was not long ago. Maybe five minutes. They should still be making their way out. They went to the right. Probably thinking to make it out of the supplies loading area would be the logical conclusion."

"Are you sure you are okay?"

"Yes. Go find her, Tarc, but when you do, you should know... I found her here in an emotional state. She had been crying. Whatever happened between you, she did not mean to hurt you. She even left me a message saying she was sorry if she offended you. I do not think she will be stopped from leaving easily."

"Thank you for that information. She may not think to stay right now, but she will not have a choice. She *is* staying and we will talk then. Bren. Perhaps you should stay—"

"No. He should go with you. I am fine."

"I am right behind you, brother."

They were out the door in a flash, heading down to the supplies bay. When they got to the main loading zone, Tarc stood still, closed his eyes and breathed deeply. He would always be able to pick up on her scent. It took him a moment and the trace was faint, but they were at the far corner of the room.

He looked at his brother and once again, their ability to communicate silently was back to being a good thing. Through mostly gesture, Tarc indicated that if the two got separated, he would go after Jack while Bren should get Will. They both nodded and silently worked their way from two sides of the room. Cornering his escapee and the human thorn in his side.

Jack's tension escalated when the alarms began to go off. They were running out of time. She vehemently whispered behind her. "Shit. Will, you should never have come to get me without a better escape plan."

"This was a good escape plan, dammit. I couldn't leave you to the mercy of these aliens. Who knows what really goes on here? The female alien we left in your cell for instance. She might be beautiful on the outside, but who knows what evil lurks underneath.

She was even dressed as a scientist. Maybe she had come in to run experiments on you after he raped you."

Jack rolled her eyes. "Stop saying that. I keep telling you, he didn't rape me. Nothing like that happened. Well. Something happened but—Sheesh!—Can we just focus on what's important here? Oh...And by the way, everything else you are speculating about...Seriously? Are you going mental on me? Alien experimentation? Come on. Tarc's sister was perfectly friendly the whole time. I kinda like her."

Will's jaw appeared to unhinge it dropped so far. "That was his sister? Shit!"

"Why does that matter? You know what? Never mind. Like I said, we need to stay focused. You said that there will be a way to get out of this area. Will that still be true with the alarms blaring?" Jack didn't see any way to safely cross to the door on the other side.

"I don't know. I hadn't expected us to still be here by the time the alarms went off. Shit. I must have miscalculated the amount of sedative I gave the guard. I have to assume he's the reason alarms are now blaring at us. I'm sorry Jack, but I'll get us out of here. Originally I had someone on the inside helping us, but I don't see them and have to assume that they aren't able to come here while security is high. We may just have to make a run for it. I'll have your back." He pointed at the closest opening to the outside. "On three. One. Two. Th—"

The hair on the back of her nape stood at attention and she felt eyes on her when Will started counting and then she could smell him. *Bren!* "Now. Go now. Run!" She took off, but was hampered since she couldn't actually use her vampire speed with so many able to observe her. She also didn't want to leave Will behind. As they rounded a set of containers, Jack was slammed to the ground. She had been so busy running away from Bren and worrying about Will, that she hadn't sensed the danger ahead of her. "Will! Keep going. I'll find a way out another time. Run!" Then she was looking up into Tarc's angry hot eyes. "Miss me already?"

He glared at her. "I did not give you permission to leave."

She glared right back at him at that. "I thought you said you wouldn't bother me anymore. That seemed pretty dismissive to me."

He flinched. Her comment had, apparently, hit its target. He closed his eyes, took one of those deep calming breaths she was growing to recognize as him taking control of his emotions, and then looked at her again. His eyes that had been blazing a short while before were now fathomless, cool pools. A part of her preferred them filled with passion.

"I spoke in haste. I was angry and said something I did not mean." He spoke in a calm and controlled tone of voice.

"Tarc." The sadness she was still feeling from earlier, seeped into her again. "Just let me go. You know I won't give you what you want."

"I cannot. I will not. There is much I want from you and with you, Jack. I think you want them with me, if you give us a chance."

She was so tired of arguing with him and going in circles. The fight left her and her limbs felt leaden. She would need to conserve her energy for another chance at escape, anyway. She looked to the door to see if Will had made it and saw him and Bren were battling near the exit. It looked as though Bren was about to get the upper hand when someone entered from the door and Bren turned to look at who was coming in. Will, no slouch when it came to fighting and tactics, took the advantage. He punched Bren and then wrapped his arm around his neck, gun pointing at his head. Other Staraban warriors were flooding into the room from the other side.

"Will! Run! Go! Get out of here!" He was going to get captured soon if he didn't make his escape. He backed through the door with Bren as his prisoner.

"No!" Tarc was yelling from above her. "Let him go! If you harm him, nothing will save you from me."

Will spit back. "As though anything will save you from me, you bastard. I saw her cell. I saw her tears. I don't know what you did to her, but I will be back, I will make sure you pay." Will continued out the door with Bren held at gunpoint. Tarc gestured for his warriors to follow.

Jack could only hope Will would get away without harming

Tarc's brother. She didn't want things to escalate and Grumpy had kind of grown on her. She didn't want to see him harmed.

Tarc stood and pulled her to her feet, one hand wrapped around her arm as he pulled her back towards the main building. "He better not harm him." A note of frustration, anger, but also pain laced his statement.

"If Bren doesn't give him any reason to, he won't. Will isn't like that." She protested.

He looked her in the eye and he must have found the reassurance he needed, because he gave a curt nod and continued walking. She thought he would bring her back to the cell she had been held in, but instead, he moved towards another section she hadn't seen before.

A few stairs and a few hallways later, he slammed through a door, locked it, and Jack found herself right back where she started. His bedroom. She couldn't help the sigh that escaped her nor the thrill that ran up her spine when she spotted his bed. Why this guy?

He must have sensed her body's betrayal, because he pulled her towards the bed. "Tarc! This is a bad idea. Just take me back to the cell."

"Clearly, I need to keep my eye on you at all times. You cannot be trusted to stay where I put you."

"Of course I won't stay where you put me. I'm your fucking prisoner. That is how it works. You didn't stay where I put you either."

He grinned at her, "True."

That grin melted something inside her. "Listen. We can't keep going around and around like this. Maybe we need to sit down and try to work out some sort of a deal where we live and let live. What if I promise to stop hacking into your system and you leave us alone?"

He scowled at her. His grin had been so short lived. She got the impression, he didn't smile or laugh nearly enough and she sure had a habit of making his good mood disappear. She really was just trouble. Why couldn't he see that?

"Will and Caran both mentioned you had been crying." She

hadn't expected such a sudden change of subject. Apparently he was just going to ignore her suggestion.

"I was just wanting to get back home. That's all."

"Jack. You are lying. Shall I remind you what happens when you lie to me?"

A part of her kind of thrilled at the idea, but she put up her hands to ward him off instead. "No! No. Okay. What you said hurt. It's no big deal. I hadn't meant to hurt you but apparently I did and you hurt me back. It's fine." She shrugged nonchalantly. She could play it cool. She *would* play it cool.

"It is not fine. I did not mean to hurt you either. I do not believe what I said. It was cruel. I lashed out and that is not like me. I will not do it again." He looked so contrite. So sincere.

"Don't worry about it. I often bring out the worst in people." She looked away from him. She didn't want him to see the pain she carried around with her. The knowledge that she only brought trouble, anger, sadness, or hardship to those she cared about hurt deeply.

He put a finger under her chin and lifted her eyes back to his. "Jack, that is not—" She put a finger over his mouth to stop him from saying anything else.

"Please, Tarc. Just kiss me." She needed him. She may not want to need him and she may well regret this later, but right now, she was still raw from their earlier intimacy, their fight, the failed escape, and she didn't want to discuss her failures. She just wanted to feel what she had felt earlier in his arms. A different escape than she planned, but an escape none-the-less.

[6]
SERENITY MY ASS

Adventures of a Supernatural Geek Girl

October 3, 2025
Dear Reader,

Have you ever had a day where it just didn't pay to get out of bed? Me too. As many of you noticed I was unavailable earlier. Thank you for all of your concerned comments. I am fine and my PAL overstepped himself in posting for me. I apologize. He may be in for a reprogramming soon. That said, I have definitely had a crazy few days and I am not sure it was in my best interest to have woken up today. So much crazy and the day isn't over. So, I don't really have anything I can share right now, but know that I am doing okay. I'm just a little tied up at the moment.

Flashback Fun Facts:
Some movies and shows like to portray vampires as lacking morality. They talk about how we no longer have our humanity or that we have some internal switch to cut off our humanity. It's total

BS. We are still ourselves after the change. If we were bad before, we are bad now. If we were good before, we are still good. We hurt, we care, we get sad, we laugh, and we love. If you run into one of us, treat us as you would anyone else. Most of the vampires I know are quite caring and loyal and we make excellent friends with our super skills.

Hugs and bites!
iByte

Staraban Headquarters, Portola Valley, CA, USA, Earth

October 3, 2025

Bang. Bang. Bang.

Tarc had been about to do as Jack requested because he did not want to go one more minute without kissing her, but the knocking was insistent. "What?" He growled at the door while still locking gazes with her. Frustration washed over her features. He did not like the disruption either.

"Commander. We followed the human male and Chief Bren out of the building, but the human had a hidden transport and was able to get away with your brother."

"*Fash!*" His face contorted as a predatory snarl escaped. "I will be there shortly. The armorer is working on something for me. Please retrieve it and bring it here." He heard the footsteps recede before continuing. "Like I said, *apura,* he better not harm my brother or I will kill him painfully."

She paled. "He wouldn't do that. You have to see that all of this is going to end poorly for everyone. Exchange me for Bren and let's be done with it. Someone is going to get hurt if you don't put a stop to this."

He growled and turned away from her. She had a point, but he could not let her leave. He may not allow his feelings to be engaged but he also recognized how much he wanted this female. She fired his blood like no one ever had. Reason said he would eventually tire of her, but for now, he was unwilling to let her go. Some part of him worried that if he did, she would never be his. He did not want bloodshed if he could avoid it. The right call, the safe call, would be a prisoner exchange.

There was another banging on the door. "Commander! I have what you ordered." He walked to the door, opened it and grabbed what the warrior offered him. "You will stay here, posted right outside my door. If the prisoner tries to escape, you will stop her, but do not harm her. Also, do not underestimate her. She is unusually strong and fast for a human."

He closed the door and headed back to Jack. He braced himself for the fight he was sure was about to commence. "Do you need to use the bathroom, as some humans call it?"

"No. Why?" She was looking at him warily now, all her previous need dissolved from her eyes as her predator instincts came to the fore. He could relate. He wished he did not have to do what he was about to do, but it was necessary. It was obvious she had not taken note of what he had in his hand yet.

"Climb up on the bed, Jack. Now."

"No!" She yelled back defiantly.

"Do you really want me to have to put you to sleep again. We both know that I can."

She grumbled to herself something about assholes, murder, and dismemberment but then climbed on the bed and leaned against the headboard. "Now what? I thought you were leaving."

"I am." Moving swiftly so she would not have a chance to react, he placed a newly reinforced cuff around her wrist. It was attached to a strong, unbreakable chain. He attached the other side to the heavy headboard. She bared her sharp teeth at him. "Flashing your teeth at me is not going to do what you want it to, *shela*. I still remember how amazing those teeth felt biting into my skin. All you are doing is making me want to stay and claim you, again."

"Fuck off!"

"I assume you do not mean you want me to fuck you now, though I wish I could do just that, so it must mean something not very nice. I will not let your anger affect me, though. I told you I will not react the way I had earlier, and I plan to keep that promise." He leaned in and pressed his lips to hers. She was stiff at first, but he felt the moment she melted into him and he groaned in satisfaction. The kiss was about to turn incendiary, but he broke it off first. "Later."

She looked dazed but it did not last. She narrowed her eyes and frowned. "I doubt it."

He looked back at the beauty chained to his bed, and if it was not for his brother, he would not be leaving her now. The thought that he would never leave her was one he refused to acknowledge.

114

A few minutes later, in his command room, Tarc checked in with his security team. "What information do you have for me, Nial?"

Nial had pulled up the map of the base as well as the surrounding land on the holo-display. "You can see he had a hidden jeep behind these hills back here along Alpine Road. We were unable to get close since we were worried about him shooting the chief and we did not have any of our transports with us to follow. We were able to track his progress with the cameras. He did not seem concerned with them, which is surprising. The cameras were down near Gobble, which is where I believe he headed."

"He is not concerned because I already know where he took Bren. I was their prisoner for a few hours, until I escaped, yesterd—"

"*Shet!* And you did not think to let us know? I assume the human female that he was trying to break out plays a part in all this? You want to tell me about her or do you expect me to secure this location without any knowledge of the dangers that we might encounter?" Nial glared daggers at him. He was convinced if there were no observers, his friend would break protocol and try to beat him. Deserved or not, it was good he kept his control.

"I told Bren. I also underestimated the human's ability to organize. I was certain it would take more time for him to notice her missing, work to locate our base, and figure out a plan of action. Apparently, I was mistaken. I acknowledge my mistake. The only thing to focus on now is how to get my brother back."

"Obviously we offer to exchange the human female for him."

"No." He replied with vehemence until he realized how he sounded. A breath. "I will only consider that as a last resort."

"Clear the room." Nial was a good, levelheaded warrior, but right now, he was red-faced and his hands kept clenching and unclenching into fists. The other warriors looked between the two of them and, knowing he was not going to escape hearing what Nial wanted to say, he waved them out.

As soon as they were alone and the door was sealed he turned to his third. "What? Speak your mind."

"Who is this female? Why did you not reveal her before and why the *fash* will you not exchange her for your brother?"

"First, I owe no explanations, Nial, but I will excuse your tone because I, too, am upset with Bren being taken. In answer to your question, her name is Jack. I have been tracking her for a few days. I did not reveal her because, while she is my prisoner, she and I are also more. It is the same reason I will not be letting her go unless I absolutely have to. If there is no other way to avoid violence or Bren getting hurt, then I will do what I must." He hoped that his friend would accept the very broad information without attempting to dig into more details. He did not want to dig into those details himself, like why she was so important to him.

"That is it? That is all you can tell me?" He still sounded exasperated, but his body no longer seemed as coiled with anger and he no longer resembled an Earth tomato.

"No. You should also know that the female, along with the male who has Bren, are the leaders of HARM."

Nial was back to full redness and looked as though he would break something. And so he did. He picked up the little statue of an Earth creature, called a cat, that Bren had brought in to decorate the table and threw it at the wall. He threw it so hard, the indentation of whiskers, a small nose, and pointy ears was left in the wall. "They are the leaders of the biggest rebellion movement we have ever had to deal with and you did not think it was important to warn me? Wait..." Nial turned to him in inquiry. "You said you escaped from their headquarters? When I showed you the map, you knew where he was heading. You know where their base is. We should organize a team to attack them and extract Bren."

"Like I said before, I want to avoid bloodshed. While I was their prisoner, brief as it was, I observed mostly non-violent, non-warrior people there. I believe they are called programmers. Also maybe some scientists. Their security was not very challenging to escape from but I am sure now they are going to be more alert. They treated me well, even giving me peet-zah to eat. I do not want to hurt anyone if at all possible. It is not part of our purpose for being here. We do not kill the locals who are peacefully protesting."

"Since you have all the information and answers, what do you suggest? We will not leave him there." Nial appeared to deflate after all of his ranting.

"Jack has assured me that Will, the human male that captured Bren, will not harm him. I have no reason to doubt what she said. We will proceed with devising a few different extraction plans and choose the one with the least casualties. We will not rush in."

Nial did not respond right away but examined him. "You feel something for this human female?"

"You know that I feel nothing for females, besides my mother and sister, after Stala, but I do want her."

"Okay. Okay. I will go work up some scenarios."

"Yes. That will be appreciate—"

"Commander. Third." The voice of his head of communications came over the intercom. "We have an incoming call from the human connection line. He claims to be the man who took Bren."

They looked at each other in surprise. Nial ordered, "Pass it through."

A beep indicated the call was connected to the room.

"Will. You better not have harmed my brother."

"Your brother? Fuck! How many siblings do you have? Nepotism much?"

In the background, Tarc heard his brother's voice. "Get this woman to stop torturing me." Then they heard a female voice. "¡Cabrón! I will cut off your balls! Do you even have cojones? Tarc, what have you done con mi hermana? If you've hurt her in any way, I will come and play slice and dice with all of your cocks. Believe me when I say, I can do it."

Tarc gritted words through his teeth. "Are you allowing my brother to get tortured?"

"Only if you call a tongue lashing from Rory torture."

"Yes! Torture." Bren yelled.

"You blue-eyed diablo. I will do more than just lash you with my tongue if you don't convince your asshole brother to return my friend. Oh look. There *is* something to cut off." The female called Rory sounded quite serious.

"Get your hand off of those! Tarc! She has me by the balls here. You know, if you are that interested in getting your hand on those, release me and I will show you how you're supposed to handle them."

"As if you would know what to do with those with a woman like me. I am way too much woman for you."

"I would have you eating your words and begging for my balls in five minutes flat."

"Rory! Stop groping the alien. It's hard to bargain for Jack's release while you're fondling the enemy." Will sounded about as annoyed as Tarc felt.

"Enough!" In his coldest and most authoritative voice he tried to take control of the situation. "Tell the female named Rory to get her hands off of my brother. Then... release him. I believe we would all like to avoid bloodshed. You realize I could order an invasion of your base, but that would be bad for everyone."

"You don't get to issue orders around here asshole and your brother gets released as soon as Jack does."

He attempted again, using the voice that always sent his warriors scurrying. "Will. This is not a game. My warriors could kill everyone there if I order it."

"But not before we kill your brother. Are you willing to go down that road?"

Tarc hissed under his breath. *"Shet!"*

Over the speaker he heard. "You are the most infuriating female. Stop threatening my balls. I am not the one holding your friend. Go threaten someone else's balls."

"¡Te castraré!"

"You know our technology allows us to understand all of your Earth languages. You will not castrate my brother. Will. Get that crazed female away from my brother. Now!"

"Rory! Seriously. I can't even stand hearing all your threats without cringing. Let up. It's not working." He heard Will's sigh over the speaker. "I promise. I will make sure we get Jack back."

Tarc considered the situation. Perhaps there was another way forward. "Will, I am working to resolve some things and I need Jack to be a part of that. Can you promise not to harm my brother while he is in your custody? Promise to treat him the same as you treated me when I was a prisoner?"

"We're not the barbarians that you are, despite what Rory is saying at this moment. We wouldn't actually do anything gruesome to your brother while there is a chance of getting Jack back. But, she must also be unharmed and considering what I saw earlier, I'm not sure you could claim such a thing. I will accept her assurance that it was consensual, but it was clear she'd been crying from whatever happened before I arrived."

He flinched like he had been struck at hearing that. The human male was right. It was not the sex that was the problem, it was how he handled himself after that hurt her. Hiding his shame from Nial's gaze, he replied with as much sincerity in his voice as possible. "She will not be harmed. What happened earlier was mutual. Afterwards, we shared some angry words. That is all. It will not happen again." He resolved to make sure that would be so. "May I speak to my brother?"

"As long as you speak in English and in brief. Rory. Stop tormenting the alien and bring him over here so he doesn't have to yell."

There was some shuffling and sounds of movement from over the line. "Hey! Jefe. Did I hear you correctly and you and Jack slept together?"

Tarc groaned. "You are not Bren."

"No. I'm not. But, you need to go through me to get to him." Her voice changed then. It stopped sounding like it could skin you alive and instead took on a concerned note. "Please. Be gentle with her feelings." The woman paused, but then continued hesitantly, like she was not sure she should say what she was saying. "She is not skilled with men. Her behavior with you, it is not something she is used to. If you won't give her back, then please, don't mess with her heart. Oh, and, um…There are certain things she needs that— ¡Mierda!—How do I say this?"

119

"Rory. I think I know what you are trying to say and I already know it all and it will all be taken care of."

"What is he talking about?" He heard Will inquire.

"I'm afraid it's private female things. You don't really want to know about our private things, right?"

"It is for Jack to tell you. Leave it be, Will. Also, Rory, I appreciate the concern you have for your friend. I will not harm her. Not intentionally. You have my word. Now please put my brother on the communicator and leave him intact."

"I make no promises if he doesn't learn to stop eye-fucking me."
More shuffling.

"Hey, brother. You cannot leave me with the hot, crazy female."

"You haven't even seen hot and crazy yet." Rory's offended voice hissed at his brother.

"Bren. You can handle one human female. I need some more time and having been their prisoner before, I can tell you it is not bad. You may actually get peet-zah out of it."

"What is it about you aliens and pizza?" Will grumbled loudly in the background.

"Tarc. Are you really leaving me here?" He sounded confused.

"Not for long. Like I said. I need more time. I will figure out something. Trust in me, brother."

"Yes. Okay." He could hear the deep breath Bren took, just like he had taught him.

"Are we done here for the day, then?" Will asked.

"Yes. We are. Shall we plan on daily conversations until we come to an agreement regarding prisoners?"

"I think that's wise. It occurs to me that while you have had the chance to talk to Bren, I have not talked to Jack. How do I know she is okay? I want to hear her and know she is well."

"Tomorrow. You can speak with her tomorrow. For now, she is resting from your attempted escape."

"I don't like it—"

"I promise you that she is well."

"She better be. And, she better be there tomorrow."

"We shall talk then. She will be here."

As he closed the communication, something else hit the wall of his meeting room and when he looked over, there was a similar indentation of a second cat statue imprinted on the wall. He looked at Nial. "Bren will be angry if you destroy his statues. He has fallen quite in love with the Earth creature known as cat."

The other warrior reminded him of the deadly *rapan*, from their home world. All teeth showing and muscles tensed for attack.

"What happened to me coming up with different scenarios? Now you just plan to leave him there with that dangerous female? The human female you have here cannot be worth more than your brother and his male parts."

Tarc had known Nial all his life, in fact, he was like another brother. In this, though, he was his subordinate and while he did not mind having opinions when it came to running his company, he did not stand for being challenged. "If you have a problem with my leadership or with my decisions, I will make sure to send you back to our planet where you can find alternate employment. I will tolerate a lot from you, Nial, but I will not tolerate complete insubordination."

Nial stiffened. Tarc could feel him leashing his anger one moment to the next. The warrior then tilted his head in acknowledgment. "As you say, Commander. What are your orders?" His tone was distant and aloof.

Fash! "I still want extraction scenarios just as I had asked. Eventually, we will need them." He was saddened by having his friend retreat so completely behind formality, but he would not let anyone question him when it came to Jack. "You are dismissed."

Nial turned and strode out of the room. Tarc's mood was grim until he thought of the beautiful, infuriating prisoner tied to his bed and not only did his mood rise, but so did his cock. He stopped to grab some food on the way back to his room. They would both need sustenance after today and in preparation for the night he hoped they would have. He picked the two statues off the floor where they had landed and placed them on the table. *Time to learn more about my...vampire.*

Jack looked around the room, back at the manacle on her wrist, and sighed in resignation. After her initial attempts, she'd given up trying to break the new and improved cuff. She needed to keep busy, though. She didn't want to let herself think too deeply about what might happen when Tarc returned. *Get it together, Jack. Thinking about him will just make you anxious the whole time he's gone.*

She used her free hand to tap at her ear. "Hal. Are you there? You've been awfully quiet through all this."

"I didn't see where I could be of help and didn't want to give away that I was here, but yes, I'm here with you, Jack. How can I be of service?"

"I need something to do. Since I missed my normal blogging time, I thought maybe we could work on a blog post together to reassure everyone I'm still here."

"Since you were unavailable earlier, I took it upon myself to post something in your stead."

She bristled at that. She loved her blog. What had Hal done? "Are you fucking kidding me? What did you say?" He filled her in about being MIA and needing rescue and she cringed. "I can't believe you did that. What are the comments like?"

Ten minutes later, Jack was moved to post for some damage control. On the one hand she tried to be as open as possible with her readers, but on the other, she didn't want anyone to know about the fact that she was a prisoner. Tarc's prisoner. Her vampire followers were readying to mobilize on her behalf. Things could get really bad, really quick.

She dictated her post to Hal and when she was finished, she remembered they had unfinished business. "Hal, did you end up finishing the sorting of the emails we had downloaded?"

"I sure did. I have a folder I believe you will be very interested in."

She heard the footsteps outside the door and some voices talking. She whispered, "Hal. Later." She tapped her ear and steeled herself for whatever was about to happen between her and Tarc. It seemed that they were destined to fuck or fight and she didn't feel equipped to deal with the first and didn't want to keep pursuing the second.

The door opened, and there stood her yummy tormentor. He closed the door behind him and locked it. He looked so fucking beautiful, so sexy, and once again, she felt her libido slipping out of her control while he radiated control like a second skin. She couldn't go down that path, so she went on the attack instead. "Is locking a woman to your bed, the only way you keep one here?"

A sharp inhale of breath told her that her aim had been true. He hated it when his honor was questioned, and there was no pretty way to color the words she'd hurled his way.

"I see leaving you here did not improve your mood. It was unavoidable. You may be interested to know that while I was away, Will contacted us and tried to request a prisoner exchange. I refused. He has promised to leave Bren unharmed as long as I do not harm you. For now, we are leaving everyone where they are. Based on your word, I am trusting that he will not hurt or allow any others to hurt my brother. Please. Assure me again, that I can trust you in this."

She saw the concern clearly on his face. The easier thing would be to lie and say he had to agree to the prisoner exchange or else something bad would befall Bren, but she couldn't do that to him or risk him attacking the base.

"Will keeps his word. If he said that nothing bad would happen to your brother, then you can trust him. Why, Tarc? Why are you keeping me? You must know by now that I will not give you information about the resistance. I can tell you love your brother. Why wouldn't you ensure his return with a prisoner exchange? I don't understand you." She knew the last came out as a sad plea. She *really* didn't understand him. A beautiful alien like him, someone who wields the kind of power he wields, has to have his choice of alien females. In fact, there were probably many women on Earth who would be happy to be with him who would be infinitely less trouble.

"I told you already, Jack. I will not let you go. What we share…"

He looked pensive. Perhaps trying to find the right words? Then he shook his head. "I do not know what to say, except I want you. I want you more than any female. I am not ready to ignore my desire for you. I can tell you want me, too. I touch you and you burn so hot for me. Even now, I can smell your arousal in the air. I am sure if I touched you between those amazing legs, I would find the evidence of it as well."

She gasped at his words as she felt more wetness pool right where he described. He'd been right that she'd been wet. True from the moment he'd entered the room but his words made her arousal notch up even more. Fuck. She wanted him. Now. Dangerous. He was so freaking dangerous. She had to try to control the situation. Had to.

"It doesn't mean anything. Yes. You're hot and I'm attracted to you. It changes nothing. You're the leader of the aliens trying to move my people off of our planet and I'm the leader of the group opposing you. Nothing good can come of this. You have to see that." With her eyes and her power, she implored him to understand.

"All I know for sure, Jack, is that I want to be inside you again. Now."

Just like that, she was on fire. Lust rushing through her as the scent of his desire started to flood her system again. "Dammit." He was across the room, sitting on the bed next to her hip, and invading her personal space and mind as she breathily said his name. "Tarc. Sex is definitely not the answer."

"Perhaps it is."

"No. I'm pretty sure it's not."

"Hmm."

"Hmm?"

"It is hard to negotiate when all I can think about is your taste. How it feels to be inside you. If you wish to negotiate, then it would make sense to me, to have as much sex as possible to stay focused."

"That's what you're going with?"

"Yes."

"Damn. It's a good point."

With that, his lips were on hers, cutting her off before she could say another word and her brain shut down completely. His hand caressed the side of her abdomen right under her breast and she wanted to beg him to grasp it. She couldn't. His mouth was plundering hers. His tongue teasing in and out of her mouth. Stroking. She wanted to do some of her own stroking. She couldn't.

She attempted to move her right hand and couldn't, reminding her that she was still locked to his bed. That both disturbed and excited her. More heat cascaded through her body. She matched his kisses with her own instead. Feeding him back the heat and passion he ignited in her.

A gasp escaped her as he grabbed her hips, pulling her to lay down on the bed and positioning himself along the length of her. She could feel all of his taught, hard muscles matched by his long hard cock pressed to her hip. Once again, a sexy breathless voice she barely recognized as hers spoke. "Tarc. Oh god. I burn. Please."

"I do too, *shela*. You can see why I cannot let you go. I need you. I need to be inside you." His voice was no better than hers coming out all deep and guttural. He growled as he took possession of her mouth again. This time his hand did cup her breast and she arched into the feel of his hard fingers.

"Yes!"

"Your breast fits my hand perfectly and your body amazes me. So delicate and yet so very strong." His hand moved again as he pushed her shirt up to reveal her tits. Since he hadn't brought her a bra with her clothes, his hand closed on a bared breast and she once again gasped as pleasure painted every inch he touched. He continued to push her shirt up over her head twisting it and securing it, effectively trapping her left arm to her right. Her skin felt scorched everywhere his eyes looked as he took her in. "These are so beautiful. All I can think about is getting my mouth on them and sucking and playing until you are moaning under me." He put action to words and sure enough, as he sucked and played and let his teeth run over her nipple, she began to moan.

"Oh. You feel so good. Too good." He switched between each breast like he was worried they might get jealous of each other. All the while, the intensity of her passion continued rising along with her power. "Yes! Tarc! I want more. I need more. Please."

His hand trailed down her abdomen, unclasping her jean's button, and yanking down her zipper. He trailed delicate fingers right above the area that had been revealed and she nearly flew apart just from his teasing. "Tarc. I can't. I need you. I need to feel you. More."

"We went so fast last time, *apura*, this time, we will be going slow so I can savor every inch of you." She heard his deep groan as he pulled her pants off and threw them away. Her frustration made the few minutes he took to take off his boots feel like hours. When he returned she sighed in relief as he kissed his way down the same path his fingers had taken earlier. Did he mean to do what she thought he meant to do, because, hell yeah, she was down for that. He took her thighs in his hands, positioning her legs over his shoulders and... Yep. He totally did mean to do exactly that.

His fingers found her folds and spread her open. He blew at her hot core eliciting a squirm as her body wordlessly begged him for contact. His eyes met hers over her mound and the experience was like staring into a blue flame. She melted even more under the intense heat. Then he dipped his head and licked at her clit and her mind short-circuited. Her energy level kept rising with each stroke of his tongue. Her body grew taught as a bowstring prepared to fire. "Tarc."

He moved his tongue into her pussy licking at her like a cat with a vat of cream and then moved back up to suck on her clit as he pressed two fingers into her. He moved his fingers and tongue with more and more insistence until she couldn't take it anymore. Her body shook as she screamed. Her power burst out of her, shaking items throughout the room and wrapping around and through her lover. "*Fash!*"

Tarc had never before felt anything like Jack's release of power. He was momentarily transported beyond his body. The power did not just surround him, it flowed into him, it infused him. He was normally very strong and virile, but her power boosted him. Made him feel invincible. He was overcome.

He licked at her pussy one more time to capture more of her sweet cream on his tongue. Then he spread her legs even wider as he moved back up her body. His cock was in agony, trapped as it was in his uniform, and it was going to rip its way out if he did not release it soon. He leaned over her satiated, relaxed body and took her mouth with his. He wanted her to taste herself and when she did, she moaned. Her eyes looked up into his, swirling with desire, and a shy smile played around her lips.

In a guttural voice, he barely recognized, he told her, "You are amazing. I loved having you come all over my mouth. I loved feeling your hungry pussy squeezing my fingers. And…I think that burst of energy would have dropped me if I was not already laying down." He looked at the magical female in his arms with awe and wonder.

She moved her hips against his erection as though in agreement with its wishes. "I want to feel you. Please. Tarc. Release my hands." He debated between the enjoyment of having her trapped for his delight and giving her what she wanted. Considering the state he was in, the torturing-with-pleasure part of their mating was finished for now, making way for the feel-her-hands-on-him part. He pushed his thumb into the side of the cuff and released her. In a languid yet curious voice she said, "Huh. Fingerprinted handcuffs. Neat."

He brought her shirt off of her arms and then massaged her wrist. "You are not harmed?"

"No."

"Good. Now touch me, Jack. I want your hands on me, too."

She brought her hands down to his shoulders, fisting them in his lapels, and nudged him back into a kneeling position. He had a moment of disappointment thinking that she had used the opportunity to get free and they were about to go back to fighting. Instead, she tore his uniform in half. Again. "You will leave me with no uniforms if you continue like this."

She flashed him a mischievous smile and it became clear her sharpest teeth had extended. "You should make them easier to get

127

off if you don't want me to rip them. Perhaps it's time for a wardrobe change for you and your crew. I recommend everyone wear red shirts." She laughed briefly to herself, which left him baffled. He didn't like the feeling.

He busied himself removing the remains of his uniform as he asked, "Why red?"

"Never mind. Earth joke. Right now, I have something else red that I'm much more interested in." A hungry, predatory heat flared in her eyes and he braced. It proved unnecessary. Apparently, she had more control this time, because instead of attacking his throat, she gripped his shoulders and pulled him back down to lick and nibble lightly all along his neck, sensitizing the area. "Tarc. I want to bite you so badly, it hurts. I usually only bite people who deserve it. Otherwise, only with permission. Please. I need to hear that you want me to bite you. I need your consent."

He heard the pleading note in her voice and remembered just how connected it had felt the last time she had bitten him. He wanted it. He wanted it bad. "Bite me, Jack. I want you to." She struck. The pain was brief, but then the pleasure started and the pain moved south to his erection. Her hands were all over his chest and arms. They tested and teased his muscles. His nipples. Driving him senseless. He reached between their bodies and fisted his cock. Pumped it.

He only got a few pumps off before one of her hands pushed his out of the way. Now she was working her hand up and down his shaft. "Goddess. You feel so good. So damn good. I need to be in you, *shela*."

He pushed her hand away, and as Jack kept slowly, almost lazily drinking from his neck, he positioned himself at her drenched opening. With one hard thrust forward, similar to the way Jack struck with her teeth, he drove in to the hilt. He felt the vibration of her moan on his neck, but like the vicious *rapan*, once latched on she refused to give up her treat. He had meant to go slower this time, and considering the speed of their last joining, they had. Now. Now he was driven mad by her bite and everything else they had shared and he wanted—no—needed to finish. But not before she came for him one more time.

He moved in rough, deep strokes in and out angling his hip to thrust towards the front wall of her vagina. At the same time, she finally let go of his neck and the freaky possessive part of him enjoyed seeing the trickle of his blood on her lips. He thrust his thumb into her hot mouth. She sucked at it, though not for long, because he withdrew and used his newly wet finger to rub vigorously at her clit. He sensed when her energy started to rise to unmanageable levels. She was going to hit him with her power again, and he was looking forward to feeling it as he came.

"Give it to me. Come on my cock. Do not hold back from me." One more rub and a fast few hard thrusts later, and she came again. Shudders running through her. And as he released inside her, her power released into him. He shouted. He could not help it. "Jack! Yes! Goddess, yes!"

She responded with her own yell of his name, which gave him great satisfaction. After the sensations began to abate he collapsed to the side of her, spent. She went completely limp underneath him.

Eventually, her hand came up to wipe at her mouth. She tensed in his arms. Again. *Shet!* He tensed too. How was he to keep her from getting upset every time they mated? They were equally excited both times. Just as desiring. As needy. He reminded himself how many times she had begged for more because he was growing a complex around this aftermath. "Jack. What is wrong this time?"

"I left you bleeding. Shit. Let me lick you." He felt the relief pour through him even as he groaned, because that statement conjured up some really fantastic images. She punched him in the arm. "Oh, stop that."

"No. A second time is looking very promising."

"Oh my god. That was just round one? You're going to kill me and vampires are hard to kill."

ALL WORK AND NO PLAY MAKES JACK A DULL GIRL

Adventures of a Supernatural Geek Girl

October 4, 2025
Dear Reader,

You know how I asked you about days you never want to get out of bed? How about nights where you don't go to sleep, get out of bed, or come up for air? You know what I mean without my spelling it out for you, right? I mean, holy shit, a vampire has to rest at some point. At least I thought so until last night. One particular alien has utterly blown my mind. I don't know what to say. He's rendered me incoherent but what the hell am I doing sleeping with the enemy? How does that even make sense?

I don't know either. Perhaps, at this rate, I can excise him from my system and get back to the business of excising them from our planet. Yep. Okay. New game plan. Go hog wild so I can get over whatever insanity is ruling my libido, learn all I can in the meantime, and finally make them go away. Get back to normal. (Confession time… There's a small part of me that doesn't want to go back to normal. That doesn't want to work this alien out of my system.

It's a small part. Itty bitty. Almost non-existent. I WILL stay true to the cause.)

Personally Newly Learned Fun Facts:
I can't believe no other vampire has written about this before. Yeah. I'm looking at you and you know who you are. I was NOT prepared. Didn't expect what happened, that's for sure. Am I the only one to ever experience this? Why? It's never happened before. So here's the deal... while getting my mind blown, my energy climbed (that was normal) and seemed to hit a breaking point at the same time as I, ehem. The best description I have for it is that it unleashed in all directions. It's quite unbelievable and potentially mildly destructive if I had been near anything delicate. Do not try this at home kids. (Okay... if you get the chance, totally try this at home. It's like a jolt soda and red bull had a baby!)

Hugs and bites (amongst other things <wink>)!
iByte

Staraban Headquarters, Portola Valley, CA, USA, Earth

October 4, 2025

Jack slowly came to consciousness. It took her some time to remember where she was, but soon enough, the scent of the sheets reminded her of all that they had done the night before. She couldn't help the smile that curved her lips. Wow. That was…just wow.

She took stock of her immediate environment and it saddened her to find she was alone in the bed. Where had he gone? She opened her eyes, lifted her head, and looked around. The room was in disorder compared to yesterday. Everything was just a little askew or out of place. Her power had apparently done that. She made a mental note to do a specific search to see if there were any surging power references out there.

She flopped her head back down on the pillow. Still stuck at, wow.

She touched her ear. "Hal?"

An acerbic voice responded. "Oh look. She lives."

"You are such a pain. You know that?"

"At least I am your pain. I live for these moments."

She groaned in frustration and wished Hal had a body she could throw a pillow at. Impatiently, she dictated her next blog post, skimmed through the comments to her last one, replying as necessary and was finally mentally acute enough to get back to work. "Hit me with the folder you organized."

"Look folks, she takes a break from the horizontal tango to do some actual work."

Jack screamed through her teeth.

"Okay. Okay. A person would think that after last night, you would be in a better mood. First email that matched your parameters was an email between Tarc and Bren. Bren wrote him saying, 'The Vrolan are being insistent. I do not think we can keep putting off this meeting without offending them. When should I schedule a

133

conference? Their representative Qisto wants to meet as soon as possible.'"

"Interesting. The Vrolan must be the aliens that paid for the contract discussed in the last batch of emails. So they are the ones that want us moved. But why?" Before she could move on to the next email, Jack heard sounds from the hallway. "We'll continue this later." She tapped her ear.

Tarc came into the room carrying a tray. Based on the smells emanating from it, both sweet and savory, he had brought food. Her stomach jumped for joy at the idea of eating something other than just the sex god walking towards her. She sat up clutching the sheet to her chest. He smiled a knowing, sensual smile and Jack's body considered abandoning her stomach in the interest of other pursuits. His voice came out all husky too, "You are awake."

She inwardly tried to shake the impact of him off while he set the tray on a nearby table. "That does seem to be the case. What've you brought me?" She smiled back, because it was getting increasingly hard to remember he was the enemy. No. The leader of the enemy. *Dammit!*

"I thought you might enjoy some of your delicious Earth food. I have wafff-les and bacon as well as coff-eee. I have heard that human's like coff-eee though I find it quite vile. I have some hot choc-o-late, if you prefer it. I understand the appeal of *that.*"

"I do love hot chocolate when it's cold outside, but in the morning, I need coffee. You may well have saved lives by making sure I got some." she joked.

Are you flirting with him? What are you thinking, Jack? Seriously. She sobered, subduing her light mood and flirtations.

"Tarc. What are we doing? This makes no sense considering our opposing views of the situation and all that. This. Between us. I'm not going to pretend it's not there anymore, but, that doesn't make it possible. I sound like a broken record, but you have to see that." A part of her wished she'd kept her mouth shut for at least a little bit longer and just enjoyed the morning with him, but another part acknowledged that down that path lay pain or betrayal, of them or her movement, and she didn't care for either outcome. The food seemed less appealing now.

"I understand your concern and agree, the facts seem to be against us enjoying each other. But, perhaps there is another way to look at it *shela*. Already, I have asked my sister to double check the science that was used to determine your planet was imminently going to be uninhabitable. I also requested that Bren look into our communications and contracts with the alien company that brought you to our attention. Of course..." He flashed a half-annoyed and half-amused grin. "He cannot do that research while being a prisoner that is being threatened by your friend, Rory, of getting castrated. She is lying about that, correct?"

"She didn't!"

"I believe she grabbed him in that location while talking about cutting his male parts," he replied unamused.

She blanched and then rolled around on the bed laughing, gasping out her words. "She...Oh my g...She is so fucking funny... He's in so much troub...Best friend ever."

Once she was able to control her humor, she looked over at Tarc and found him scowling down at her. "Assure me she will not actually cut his balls off."

She reached out and touched his arm. "I'm sorry if that scared you. No. She won't. She likes to threaten men who piss her off with ball cutting. Funny thing is, if you meet her, she is normally the sweetest, most amusing woman, but if you get on her shit list...Oh buddy. You better run. Apparently, Bren made it on her shit list rather fast. I guess she's pissed you refuse to give me back."

He stopped scowling and his shoulders appeared to relax as he righted a chair and sat next to the table where he'd placed the tray. He began uncovering the food. Her appetite returned with a vengeance. She looked around and couldn't spot any of her clothes. "Um. Tarc? Where are my clothes? A robe? Something to wear while we eat?"

His gaze moved back to hers and then drifted down the length of her body. She could swear that he was peeling away the sheet, she had gripped to her chest, with his eyes. "You do not need clothes right now. It is just the two of us and I will enjoy seeing your beautiful, lush body while we eat.

"Not a chance. You're fully dressed and I need my clothes. Actually, I need a shower and then my clothes. The wipe down you gave me last night isn't going to be enough today." He didn't look like he had any intention of telling her, so she started to gather the sheet around her to go investigate for herself.

The next moment, he was right beside her. She paused in her movements, waiting to see what his intentions were. Climb in with her, maybe? She pictured tearing another of his uniforms and getting...

He caught her by surprise while she daydreamed uniform carnage, which made him able to grab the sheet and fling it out of her grasp. She stared dumbstruck. He reached down, and with an arm around her back and one under her legs, he lifted her, went back to the chair, and sat her in his lap. She growled at him. "You arrogant jerk."

Instead of arguing with her, he placed his left hand just under her breast. She felt the warmth from his palm sink into her skin.

"Calm yourself."

"Easy for you to say. You're dressed," she hissed.

He eased his palm up to cup the underside of her breast and she gasped. She wished in protest, but knew it wasn't. Heat pooled in her belly instantly. "Tarc. You keep this up and I'll make a mess of your uniform."

"It would be worth it. I have already put in an order for many more." He chuckled and then squeezed her firmly running his thumb over her increasingly erect nipple.

"Oh god." Her eyes closed as she melted against him. "I thought we were going to eat breakfast."

"We are." His hand moved and she had to bite back a protest. She smelled bacon near her face, opened her eyes and found him holding a piece for her to eat.

"You think you're going to feed me?"

"I know, not think, I am feeding you."

"I can feed myself, you know. I've been doing it since I could grab things with my hands." Indignation raced through her. *I don't need anyone to fucking feed me or take care of me.*

He shrugged. "I am confident that you can. I want to." He took a bite of the bacon himself and then put the rest in front of her mouth again.

It smelled really good and well, bacon. She gave in to her hunger and, though she would never admit it, to him. For now. Just for a little bit. She would allow herself to enjoy a moment in time when she felt special. Treasured. Taken care of. A momentary balm to all those childhood days where she felt none of those things.

They sat eating for a time without talking. He conveniently dripped maple syrup on her breast while feeding her the waffle and licked it off. That had her moaning. It became a little dance of eating and moaning, eating and moaning, and once her appetite for food had been taken care of, her other appetite had been fully awakened.

"Tarc. Fuck me."

"Yes, *apura*. As you wish."

The morning's sexual escapade was more sensual than explosive. They explored each other with light touches, sensuous kisses, licks, and rubs. Sensations built and rolled through her. She had no need to bite him so she just nipped a little here and there along his collar bone.

Their climax was soft and sweet and full of tenderness.

This was a whole new side to their intimacy and if she hadn't been ready for the wild passion, she was especially not ready for tenderness. She only allowed herself a few minutes to enjoy the afterglow before she sat up out of his arms needing to disconnect. "I really do need that shower and my clothes."

He considered her for a moment. "I see. For now, I will let you run, but not for long, *apura*. Not for long."

A shiver ran down her back at his words. To lighten the mood, she changed topics. "Perhaps you let me choose lunch? I can introduce you to some pretty amazing Earth food. I'm quite the foodie."

"Foodie?"

"A ridiculous sounding word describing a person who likes

food." She grinned, "I know all the best food in the area. Well. From what's still open." She moved on quickly before her mood could darken from that thought. "Have you ever tried a burger from Come 'n Go? It's a California tradition. For now, though, shower. Clothes."

"We do not have a shower like you use. Follow me." He got out of bed completely unaffected by his nudity and strode into an adjoining room. She almost took the sheet with her, but realized how ridiculous that would be, and followed him in her birthday suit.

The alien version of a bathroom was all smooth walls that seemed to glow from within. He took her to one part of the room and pressed his finger into a slot. A few panels opened and some long cylindrical objects popped out. "Close your eyes. When your skin stops tingling, you will know it is finished."

She hesitantly closed her eyes and felt the tingles begin right away. "What?"

"It is okay. Relax."

She tried. She did. Then she actually enjoyed. The tingles awakened all of her. She was aware of every inch of her skin. Even her teeth tingled. No need for toothbrushes? Neat. When the tingles receded, she opened her eyes, and saw Tarc still standing right next to her looking refreshed. She felt utterly awake now. Completely aware and ready to take on anything. "Wow. That was...amazing. How do I get one of these installed in my bathroom?"

He chuckled. "I am glad you enjoyed it. We were very happy when our scientists developed this technology. The system releases undetectable nanobots that remove all dirt on the molecular level. They also remove toxins and help to awaken your body. We have sold many of these throughout the galaxy. I am sorry to disappoint you, but I do not believe Earth is ready for this technology."

She sighed. "A girl can dream. Anyway, moving on, now that I am so completely awake, where are my clothes?" She punched him on the shoulder.

He used her punch as an opportunity to grab her arm and pull her into him. He placed a light kiss on her lips, "Follow me."

"You keep saying that." She grumbled. "Don't expect it to last, though." *I follow no one.*

He led her out of the bathroom-like place which was back to just glowing smooth walls and into a corner of the main bedroom. He once again pressed his thumb and giant panels resembling an armoire popped open revealing shelves full of clothes. One shelf was full of uniform after uniform. She couldn't help teasing him. "Look at all those victims just sitting there unaware."

He looked over to where she was staring and let out a bellow of laughter. It came out deep and wonderful and continued for a time. She loved his laugh. It felt good to have gotten this serious control freak to let loose even for a moment.

She also spotted a pile of her jeans and t-shirts. "I assume I have no underwear or bras?"

"Such useless clothing. I do not understand why you choose to wear such things. I did not bring any. If you insist, I can acquire some for you."

"I guess it depends on what happens next. How long I will be away from my base." That statement wiped all the laughter from him and he was he was scowling at her again. She hurried on. "We can discuss that later. Let's just get dressed and deal with one thing at a time."

He nodded and grabbed one of his uniforms. When he looked at her he gave out a brief laugh again. Not as wonderful as the one before, but still a laugh. "*Shela,* your shirts are an endless amusement."

She looked down and saw she was wearing the one that read, "Will code for food. Will food to live. Will live to code." The words written in a circle of life emblem. "Yeah…totally me." She grinned. "A girl's got to have priorities."

She grew tense when she recalled something he said earlier that she hadn't taken note of at the time, distracted by all the things. "Tarc. Did you say earlier that you have set your sister the task of retesting the data provided to you about our planet? Also, that Bren was supposed to investigate communications before he got himself kidnapped?"

Tarc had to wonder where her questioning would lead. "Yes. I did." Everything in him braced for what might come next. She looked uncomfortable and anxiety rolled off of her leaving an unpleasant scent in the air between them. "Why?"

She took a moment before replying. "I. We." She sighed. "Let me try that again. If you are willing to bend enough to listen, to double check, to either realize that what you are doing is wrong…"

He started to protest, but she held up a hand to hold him off, so he kept his mouth shut. He would hear her out.

"…or prove to us, humans, that we really are in danger, then perhaps our groups could call a truce for a time and work together to get to the bottom of all of this."

His shoulders relaxed and he nodded. "I had hoped for exactly such an outcome. Jack, it is not the way of my people to force other species to do something bad for them. We are in the business of saving lives, communities, societies. I need you to trust me."

She studied him. He was not sure what she was looking for, though if he had to guess, she was gauging his sincerity. He waited as she finished her evaluation. It chafed at him to have his honor questioned, but he tried to remind himself that her version of events was very different than his, and if he believed as she did, he would not trust his species either.

Finally, she gave him a curt nod back. "Okay. I will try to trust you, but if you betray me, us, the movement, my people, I will not care if everyone finds out I'm a vampire. I will not care what is between us. If you betray me, I'll make sure you regret it."

He found her irresistible even as she was issuing her threats. So much strength and passion. So much love and loyalty. She was simply everything he could want in a female. "It seems we have reached an agreement."

She looked like she was debating something, so he waited. Gave her space. "Who is Qisto? Who are the Vrolan?"

"I see your investigation at our terminals has been successful." She shrugged her shoulder waiting for him to answer. He indicated the chairs where they had eaten breakfast. They both sat down and he continued. "Qisto is a representative of the alien species called the Vrolan. They are the ones who approached us and contracted our help to move your people from this planet. They provided us with evidence of your ingenuity as a reason to find you another planet to live on and to make first contact. Usually, a species must have achieved interstellar space travel. They come to us themselves with the request and with payment. If they cannot pay, we have systems in place for them to provide payment by other means. We have never turned a needy species away."

"I understand what you do, but I don't understand why you took this contract if it's completely outside of your modus operandi?" The last phrase left him confused and it must have showed since she continued with an explanation. "Meaning, you have a normal system of operations, and this was outside of that system."

"As I said, their evidence both showing your immediate need and showing your species' worthiness for saving, was compelling."

She looked at him with frustration. "You never thought to check whether their evaluation of our planet was accurate? You trust them so much?"

He was growing very tired of having her question everything. He was too used to being the one making the decisions, but in the interest of their new and precarious truce, he let it go. Mostly. Irritation still laced his words. "Of course we double checked their claims. Your weather patterns are violently changing. Your ice caps are melting. Every claim they brought before us has been validated."

Her tone grew heated as she argued. "Then what is your sister doing now that was different than what you did before? And why is she doing anything if you're so sure that everything here is leading to destruction?" She gnawed on her lip, and it took everything in him to ignore his desire to pull her back into his lap and gnaw on her lip too, but their discussion was too important.

"I have asked her to investigate deeper. To scan the planet core, to double check the severity of the changes. She is to verify not only *their* evidence but create our own. My sister is one of the great scientists of the Staraban. She is still young, but her research

141

into planetary science has been hailed as thorough and even revolutionary, at times. She plays a key role in the company; making sure that any planet we move a species to, matches their needs exactly, as well as making sure it will be a stable environment for a long time."

"Did you ever ask yourselves what interest the Vrolan might have in moving us? We, humans that is, often believe that when there's a crime, you check on who benefits from it, and nine times out of ten, you'll find your culprit. Follow the money trail."

"I understand that theory, but *you* need to understand, we have not seen any of this as a crime. Until now, perhaps. I am happy to double check everything, but I am not convinced this is a crime yet." He leaned forward and grabbed her hand, that she had started tapping on the table. "I am not saying it is not. I am saying that without proof, I am not convinced we are dealing with a crime. I promised you that we will look into it, and we will."

She finally softened a bit. Her hand held on to his just as her gaze held on to his gaze. "Thank you. You'll see. There is something very fishy about all of this and I'm convinced the Vrolan are the culprits. Question is…Why? What do they want?"

He snorted. "Fishy? Your language is so amusing sometimes." More seriously, he added. "Jack. Can I trust that you will not try to escape until we have worked all of this out?"

She nodded. "Yes. You have my word."

"Then we should go to my meeting room and talk to Caran. We can see if she has found anything." He pulled on her hand and lifted her up into his embrace, claiming her mouth for a swift kiss. She was stiff at first, but then molded her body to his and so he deepened the kiss. She kissed him back with equal fervor.

It took a lot of will to lift his mouth away, but if he stayed kissing her, they were going to end up in bed again. "Come." He pulled her behind him as they exited his room. "You will not convince me to take you again just yet." He knew that would get her hackles up and sure enough female indignation emanated from behind him and she began stammering profanity as he led her down the hall to his meeting room. It was a good thing she could not see the smile on his face. She might try to hit him again, and he knew where that would lead.

"How is your evidence so far inconclusive?" Jack was growing more frustrated with each passing revelation. "What is it that you aren't sure about? Dammit! How can I prove to you that our planet is not on death's door?"

Caran tapped a finger against her chin. "The problem is that I am using other people's data points. To truly find out the state of your planet, I need to be able to run my own tests. I need to get my hands on some soil and water samples from somewhere deep in the Earth. I have looked for a possible nearby location and I have found one but…"

"Then what's the problem? Get the samples and run your tests." Jack knew her impatience was showing but she wanted to get to the bottom of this and get the Staraban to leave. A part of her hurt at the idea of Tarc leaving but she needed to stay focused on her mission. He probably had a female to fuck on every planet and she was just the female he was focused on now. They were never going to last no matter what the outcome was. She needed to keep her head in the game and her focus on the end goal.

Tarc's sister looked at her in annoyance. "I was going to say, before you interrupted, that the location that is closest and best suited to yield what I need is called the Pinnacles but…"

This time, Tarc interrupted her. "Absolutely not. I forbid it."

"Stop interrupting me if you want your answers, both of you."

"What's wrong with the Pinnacles?" Jack had nothing but fond memories of the caves she'd explored when she'd first moved to the area. The extinct remnant of the ancient volcanic region was beautiful.

"No. Find another location."

Both she and his sister glared at Tarc.

"Have you heard of the group MAD?"

"You mean Make Aliens Die? Of course." She grimaced in

disgust. "Obviously we don't associate with the militia-run nutso resistance movement even if both groups refuse to be relocated."

"That is good. MAD has taken over the Pinnacles National Park. They are using it as their base of operations. It is easy to defend from above and easy to hide in the cave system, which is why I absolutely will not allow this. There has to be a safer location."

Caran threw the device she'd been reading from onto the table and snapped back, "Not as close to here. No. The previous volcanic activity as well as the reservoir and the deep cave system will allow for us to sample some of what I will need to review. At least it will be a good start for answers. I thought that was what you wanted. Answers. Fast. I know I do since it seems you will not bring our brother back without them." Caran's anger at Tarc over his handling of Bren briefly showed in her face before she schooled her features.

Jack couldn't fault her though. Caran had to be wondering why Tarc would make such a choice since Jack kept wondering about it herself. The sex was great but not worth a beloved sibling. Hopefully, it was a sign he trusted her too. Hopefully, their mutual trust wouldn't be misplaced.

She interrupted the tense silence that followed. "Okay. I'll go and get the samples. Just tell me what you nee—"

"No." Tarc's voice rang with finality. Shocked, she looked over at him to find his eyes had gone a scorching blue with suppressed anger. He kept clenching and unclenching his fists as though he was just barely restraining himself from throttling her.

"Be reasonable, caveman, I'm human. I'll get in and out of there very quickly and easily. You know that I can."

His tone was that of the leader he was. "I will not allow it. I will not risk you like this. These militia groups are violent and insane. They will kill you or worse."

Unfortunately for him, he was not her leader. "I'm not asking your permission. I've been on my own for a long time, and I've dealt with plenty of dangerous situations. I'm also one of the leaders of another rebellion movement, which you seem to have forgotten. I can handle myself."

"I will lock you up again." His voice was hard as steel and she knew he meant that threat.

"You could try." She taunted and belligerently lifted her chin.

He stepped into her personal space trying to intimidate her with his greater height. "I think we both know that I would succeed, *apura.*" He was an imposing figure, but she was not going to back down. She was made of sterner stuff than that.

Before she could respond, Caran interjected. "Fascinating as it is to watch someone stand up to you, big brother, this argument is pointless. I have to side with Jack. You said you wanted to get the information as quickly as possible. This is the place to get it."

"Not by risking Jack's life. The information is not *that* important. More than likely it will just prove what we know. Earth is dying and we need to move the humans from here."

She expelled all the air from her lungs as though someone had hit her in the solar plexus. She hurt but she'd be damned before she crumpled under the pain. "This truce is a total fucking farce to you. You don't want to prove that the Earth is okay. You're just playing along so I won't cause trouble and you can keep me in your bed. Well, forget that." She turned and stormed away. Her energy level escalated, crackling just below her skin in fury, at his betrayal.

Her senses on high alert, she felt his movement as he grabbed for her and maneuvered out of the way of his grasp. She crouched down and kicked out, attempting to take his legs out from under him. She caught his feet, but he used the momentum to knock his body into hers and pinned her to the ground.

She was *not* doing this again with him. She was leaving. Jack bucked with all her vampiric power and flipped their positions rolling away as she did. Then she was off, a blur of movement towards the door and out. Unfortunately, she slammed right into a very hard, muscular back which sent them both tumbling to the ground.

Tarc was on her before she had a chance to catch her breath. He restrained her hands above her head and used his shins to pin her thighs to the ground. "Stop! Now! You promised you would not try to escape."

She snarled up at him. "You promised that you would try to prove whether the Earth is really dying. I guess now we both lied."

That was when Jack finally registered all the eyes that were warily watching her. Caran stood in the doorway face full of curiosity. The man she had barreled into was sitting nearby with suspicion etched on his features and behind him, all the aliens in the room looked at her with either fear or disgust. It was hard to tell.

She looked back up into Tarc's angry face and realized what she'd done. "Oh god." Caran had witnessed her move with inhuman speed, they'd all seen her knock a warrior down with her strength, and now her sharp canines were protruding from her mouth. "Oh...Oh god. What have I done?" Tarc's face turned from anger to concern as he took in her growing panic.

"Everyone. What you have seen here today is classified. If I find out anyone has spoken about this, you will answer to me. Understood?" He lifted his eyes from hers and made a sweep of the room to ensure he took in every person's face that was there at the moment. "Am I understood?" He gritted out menacingly.

A resounding, "Yes, Commander." came from all around.

"Caran. Nial. In the room. Now." The man staring at her warily, got up off the ground and stepped into the room behind Caran. "Jack. Come back inside so we can talk about this."

She was still feeling skittish and distraught. It was all becoming too much and she fought back her tears. In a quiet raspy voice low enough so only he could hear, she responded. "I don't trust you. You told me you detest lies and yet you lied to me. Talking will not help since I don't believe a word you say."

He winced at her indictment. Then he closed his eyes and took a deep breath. There he was centering himself again. She was going to have to start calling that "The Tarc." When he looked down at her again, he was almost remorseful. "I am sorry I made you feel this way. It is not my intention to break my word with you. Please come back inside and let us figure some way forward."

Sincerity tinged every word he spoke and scented the air between them. Should she trust him? She wasn't sure, but she also wasn't ready to throw away the truce without first hearing him out.

"Okay. Let's go back in. I won't run…for now, as long as you don't betray me."

He studied her for an extra moment before getting to his feet and helping her up. She looked nervously around the room where everyone pretended to be busy all of a sudden. Still feeling raw and a little wild with her magical version of adrenaline, she couldn't help the small giggle that escaped her at the sight. "What diligent workers you suddenly have."

Tarc looked around as well and smirked. "Yes. So it seems." He then led her back into the meeting room.

[8]

JACK AND JILL

Adventures of a Supernatural Geek Girl

October 5, 2025
Dear Reader,

Today I am going…dun, dun, dun…spelunking. You heard that right. Deep planet dive. I've done this once and I remember it being beautiful. Breathtaking. Today, though, this vampire is on a mission. I can't go into too many details, but I hope that we find what we need to prove our relocation is unnecessary. This is a perilous mission so stay close tomorrow. I'll either come back in triumph or be one deleted byte. Knowing me, I have quite the knack for landing in hot water, and then finding my way right back out. So…Let the adventure begin! Wish me luck. Also, have you ever been spelunking? Let me know in the comments.

Fun Facts:
A few days ago I mentioned that we are environmentalists. I'll let a little more out of the bag about this one. We actually need

planet Earth. Our essence, the thing that made us vampires was derived from the Earth. There are no vampires excited to relocate because we need to reconnect with it on a regular basis to replenish ourselves. And you thought it was all about the blood. Okay. It's that too. But without Earth, we would all die. (I bet my human anti-vampire enthusiasts are ready to board the first spaceship off planet right about now. That's okay. See you later haters!)

Hugs and bites!
iByte

Pinnacles National Park, Paicines, CA, USA, Earth

October 5, 2025

Jack knelt in front of Tarc, arms tied behind her back. Her energy was on high alert. She bowed her head forward anticipating what would come next. She whispered to him. "Whose idea was this?" She lifted her eyes to meet his, a short distance away.

His accusatory stare burned a hole through her. "I am going to spank that ass of yours so hard, you will not sit for a week if we get out of this." He, too, was kneeling with his arms tied behind his back. The ground was covered in dead leaves and dry grass as well as rocks, which were biting into her knees. If Tarc hadn't been with her, she would've already gotten away. She let her own accusations shine back at him and then looked back down.

She caught sight of her clothing choice for the day and cringed. She was going to need to start thinking of her t-shirts as the magic eight ball they had become. Today, she'd chosen to wear her tight faded jeans and a gray shirt that read, "Trapped on the Information Superhighway." *My life, irony be thy name.*

Around them, three MAD militia members were pointing guns in their direction, waiting for someone to come join their little group. "No talking!" One of the militia members with a long, brown beard yelled at them. "There's nothin' I hate more than fuckin' aliens, except alien sympathizers." Brown Beard spit on the ground near her knees. She flinched away in disgust. "Don't you fuckin' move."

Note to self. Spit on Brown Beard's corpse after killing him.

"Bulldog said he would be here in the next few minutes. He wants these two questioned." That guy had a buzz cut and wild, angry eyes. "I hope they don't talk too soon. I'm looking forward to torturing the information out of them." He tapped the long knife at his waist.

Another note to self. Don't piss off Crazy Eyes until I can kill him. Then piss him off all I want.

"Both of you just shut the fuck up until Bulldog gets here." The third member was a woman. She had a long dark braid down her back and spiked leather cuffs. "You two talk more than most school-girls." This one was all business. She was cold and calm.

Yet another note to self. Spikey might be the really tough one to kill. Watch your back with her. Girls can be mean. I do like her cuffs, though.

Honestly, she still couldn't believe the militia members had caught them. Between her senses and Tarc's tracking ability, she would have put a wager stating they would be fine to sneak in and out, but that was not how things went down. Instead, they wandered right into an area set up for an ambush. Bulldog had obviously trained his followers well.

Everyone turned towards the sound of gravel crunching under swift footsteps. She'd been hearing that sound growing closer for a while, before the others in the group took note. It was probably Bull-dog. She didn't have to wait long to find out. A tall, burly man with greying brown hair and beard wandered into the clearing where they were being held.

"What'd you capture for me?" He looked between Tarc and Jack assessing them. "I have to wonder what a Staraban is doin' out here in the Pinnacles with a human woman? Doesn't seem right. Will one of you please save us all time and just tell me?"

"If I do, will you let us go?" She didn't mind sharing their reasons if it meant being released. Still, she couldn't ignore the bad feeling she had, cramping her stomach, telling her that this wasn't how things were going to go down.

Bulldog laughed along with Brown Beard and Crazy Eyes. Spikey just kept being, well, Spikey. "Let's not play dumb. Neither of you leaves here alive. I can make your time here short and pain-less or long and agonizing. Which would you prefer?"

"Um. Are those my only options?" She couldn't help herself.

"Jack! To quote the female over there, shut the fuck up." Tarc looked absolutely livid. "That mouth of yours is going to make things worse."

"How do things get worse from here, exactly?" She wasn't about to let anyone shut her up.

Crazy Eyes answered her. "I could cut that tongue out for you."

"Shutting up now." Jack's shoulders slouched. "But...for the record, I was being asked a question, so if I don't answer it, that does seem rather counterproductive. Back to shutting up now."

"I have a feelin' you'd be rather entertainin' if you weren't in need of killin'. I'm not happy with being out here in the open like this for long. They may have friends comin'." Bulldog looked around. "Bring 'em up to the main hall. I'll meet you there. I'm gonna check on things at the cabins before the torture and fun begins." With that, he trudged back the way he came.

"You heard him." Brown Beard had his evil minion smile perfected. "Stand up. Slowly. No sudden moves or my trigger-happy friends will trigger right into your head. Time to entertain the boss."

"This is ridiculous. If you think I'm going to willingly walk myself into your main hall to entertain you with my torture, you're all idiots." She really, *really* couldn't help herself.

Next to her Tarc growled while getting to his feet.

She fumed at him. "Just because you don't speak much doesn't mean that I plan on going quietly. Even on a good day, I'm not exactly inclined to do as told and here we're talking about compliance ending with torture and death. I don't think so."

Tarc laughed sardonically. "Not exactly inclined?" He snorted. "Never, as far as I have known you. If you had listened to me, we would not be in this situation now."

"If you had listened to *me, you* wouldn't be in this situation at all."

"And let you come alone?" He was walking up into her space again. Why did he have to always do that?

"Well. Yes. I don't understand you. I'm a fucking rebel! Why would you care whether I lived or died?"

"You are the most infuriating female. What does it take to get you to understand that your life matters to me?"

"Re-bel!" She emphasized both syllables of the word trying to get it through his thick skull.

"Are you saying my life means nothing to you, then, because I am a fucking alien? Look you have me using that word 'fuck' as much as you now."

Her voice dipped lower, softer. "Of course not. This wasn't your mission, though. It was mine and your life shouldn't be in danger right now. You should've let me come alone."

She'd completely forgotten the people with the guns until Brown Beard interrupted their discussion sounding quite put out. "What is wrong with you two? We have guns trained on you and your discussing your fuckin' relationship? You disgust me." He spit at Jack's feet again. "We need to move."

"Wait." A single word, but delivered with so much cool authority, they all stopped. Spikey decided to join in the conversation, apparently. "Did you just say that you're a rebel and you're on a mission. Explain yourself. You obviously aren't one of us. What type of rebel? What mission?"

Jack finally started to feel her self-preservation kick in. Should she tell the truth or hedge or straight out lie? What to do? They may not work together but HARM and MAD didn't actively dislike each other. Perhaps she should take a chance. "HARM. I'm a part of HARM."

All three of the MAD members sucked in some air in surprise at her revelation.

Spikey continued with her questioning. "What is a HARM member doing with one of the enemy? And, unless I am reading you both wrong, which I'm not, in a relationship."

Jack would've blushed if she could, but she still felt herself tingle with embarrassment. "It's a bit hard to explain."

"Actually, that part is easy. We cannot deny our attraction and cannot stop fucking each other. Wow. That word, once used, really just keeps coming."

"Tarc! Now? Now you found your voice and feel like answering questions? There is such a thing as TMI you know."

"TMI?"

"Too much information, caveman. Just stop talking and let me figure this out."

He began growling at her again. Oh well.

"Ignoring what he just said, the mission is something that you'd be able to appreciate, actually, if you didn't appreciate the torture and killing so much." She tried smiling at Spikey to see if she'd find the sarcasm amusing, and instead found her stone cold. Tough crowd. "I'm working with the Staraban to prove that Earth is not as close to death's door as they believe so that they will leave us here."

For the first time she saw some interest in Spikey's eyes before she turned to look at Tarc. "Is that true? If you had proof we're okay here, would you just leave?"

"Yes."

Crazy Eyes glared at them. "Your attempt misses the point. We don't wanna relocate but we also do want to make sure these fuckers don't ever come back and the only way to ensure that is to kill as many of them as we can. This is a waste of time. Any longer and Bulldog'll have our hides. Let's g—"

Two shots rang out and Jack panicked. Had they shot Tarc? Oh shit! Power coursed through her and she broke the rope binding her arms behind her and jumped in front of Tarc. She yelled at him over her shoulder. "Are you okay? What the hell happened?" Even as she asked, she saw Brown Beard and Crazy Eyes fall to the ground.

She turned in time to see Spikey spin towards her after shooting her cohorts. The killer looked at her now free hands with confusion and pointed her gun at Jack instead. Meanwhile, Tarc tried to shoulder her out of the way, but then they all froze.

The sound of someone rushing at them caused them all to turn. Something or someone flew at Spikey, crashing into her. A man sat on top of her and pinned her to the ground. There was a lot of that going around. He looked up at them. "Are you okay? I heard the gun fire and thought I was too late."

"Nial? What the fuck are you doing here?" Tarc asked and then turned to Jack. "And how do I stop saying that fucking word? Fuck. Never mind." He wanted to kill, spank, and fuck Jack, just not in that order. "Set me free." He turned and held out his arms to her since she obviously had the strength to break the binds. She complied and ripped through them with both hands. "I will deal with you later, *shela*. You will never step in front of me again when there is danger." He spun to the two figures on the ground that were glaring daggers at each other. "Nial. What are you doing here?"

Nial looked back up at him. "I could not let you go into danger without someone guarding your back. I have been following you."

"You disregarded my orders, is what you mean to say."

"That is one way to look at it, yes."

"Also, later." He looked down upon the female that had killed the other two MAD members. "Female. What is the meaning of what you have done?" He waved a hand in the direction of the two dead men.

She did not take her eyes off of Nial but spoke through gritted teeth. "Tell your guard here to get the fuck off of me."

"Nial. I think it is fine, my friend. Let her stand."

He watched as Nial let the female's arms go. His friend stood up and the female did as well. Then she used her right hand to punch his warrior straight in the face. Nial's head actually swung to the right from the impact, and a string of Staraban curses escaped from him. The female stood shaking her right hand as a grimace of pain crossed her face. "Worth it." He could not help the short bark of laughter that escaped at her words.

"What is your name, female?"

"I've been thinking of her as Spikey." Jack shared.

Now the female glared at Jack. "Spikey? What kind of fucked up name is Spikey? And how the hell are you able to break through our ropes?"

"Ignore Jack for now, I am the one asking the questions. Answer me."

She did not answer right away but instead seemed to be assessing her situation. He waited patiently for her to start talking. Her demeanor shifted back to her earlier cool and calm façade.

"I'm Jill and I'm choosing to defect from MAD. I grew up in this militia, but while I can't say I like you, aliens that is, I'm also not into the kind of torture and killing that MAD enjoys. Since Jack, I think you keep calling her, strange name, is in HARM, I thought it was a good time to make my move and return with her to the saner resistance movement. At least, I thought that until she broke her binding and yours." Now she looked at Jack with wariness. "What are you? Some sort of robotically enhanced government experiment?"

Jack crossed her arms over her chest defensively. He wondered what she would tell the other female, but of course, his Jack went with sarcasm. "W-o-w. Somebody has been drinking the conspiracy theory Kool-Aid for waaaayyy too long. I'm just really, really strong." He chuckled at her claim of normalcy, but did not understand what she meant about cool aide.

Jill scoffed and crossed her arms over her chest as well. "Yeah. And I just come from a slightly dysfunctional childhood. That makes two lies between us, so how about you give me the truth."

Nial was rubbing at his chin where Jill's fist made contact. She must be quite strong, as well. Tarc inwardly laughed. His friend's eyes burned with an interesting mixture of offense, anger, and he thought he spotted interest. She was a striking figure, not classically beautiful with her strong chin and extremely muscular build, but he could see what his friend might see in her. This will be interesting.

"Again, Jill, I am the one asking the questions right now. Jack is none of your concern. I am sure she would be happy to facilitate your defection to HARM when the time comes."

Jack mumbled quietly. "Fat chance." He whipped his head around to her and gave her a quelling stare. She put her hands up in front of her in a placating fashion. "Okay. Okay. I guess she did kill Brown Beard and Crazy Eyes for us. Oh yeah. Speaking of which." He watched as his female walked over to the bearded dead man and spit next to his corpse. She then walked over to the other man and called him all sorts of derogatory names before coming to stand by him again. "Long story. Personal vow. Had to be done." She shrugged. He must really be into the crazy ones now, because her crazy was turning him on. So unpredictable.

He turned and saw the crazy had affected Nial and Jill as well. They wore matching looks of confusion and concern on their faces. He stifled his laughter, but just, and wondered at this newfound ability to find humor in so many places. He clearly had Jack to thank for that one as well.

"We have to move on so we can collect what we came for. Your leader will start looking for us soon since we will not show up as expected. Nial, take Jill and wait for us to join you where we left our transports hidden. I assume you left yours near ours?"

"Yes, but No."

"No way."

Nial and Jill answered in unison. Nial continued, "I will not leave you unguarded. You can punish me for insubordination after we make it back to base. I will follow you whether you allow it or not. May as well make me a part of the plan. I can be a lookout while you are in the caves, for instance. Jill can make her way out of the Pinnacles and we can meet up with her later, assuming she is still around."

"Speak for yourself, Cujo. I know this area and our patrols and can help you achieve your samples. As you can see…" She indicated the dead men. "I'm also a really good shot. I can help to guard the cave entrances as well from above while brute force, over here, stands around looking pretty as bait."

At first it seemed like his warrior might get mad at Jill's commentary, but instead he turned one of his well-known female luring grins on her. "So you think I am pretty?"

She just glared back at his friend. "Get over yourself." He shook his head at her next comment. "How's the chin?" Now, she was playing with fire. Nial loved a challenge and he loved a strong female. She might not like the Staraban, but it seemed that one Staraban warrior might try to challenge that belief, and soon.

Amusing as it was, he needed to get them back on track. "Fine. There is no time for arguments. Jill, we need to get to one of the deepest caves and we need to get to the reservoir for soil and water samples according to our scientist. Think you can get us there without running into any patrols?"

"Yes. Easy… until they raise the alarm."

"Looks like we have our team for our quest. Our ranger." Jack pointed to Jill. "Our warrior." She pointed to Nial. "Our other warrior, because you can never have enough tanks." She pointed to Tarc.

Jill cut her off. "And what are you? Our resident jackass, I mean bard?" Jack looked ten kinds of offended but Jill just kept talking. "It really saddens me that I actually know what the hell you're talking about. Geek." She said the last with a new tone in her voice and a glint of amusement in her eyes.

Apparently, Jack saw it too, because instead of staying upset, she was back to her normal sarcastic self. "This from the Goth militia chick? Choose a subculture, lady." There had to be some female code in there he did not understand because both of them smiled and Jack continued. "I have a feeling I'm going to like you. That is, if I don't kill you first."

"Same to you."

Maybe all human females were just a bit crazy and considering Nial's gazes at Jill and his own feelings for Jack, Staraban warriors might just like the Earth women version of crazy. He thought back to the one that had threatened to cut off his brother's balls and wondered how Bren was faring with her.

Jack stayed in the shade as much as she could as Jill led them through the rocky wooded terrain. Since they were trying to avoid detection, the route they took was anything but straight forward. She had them walking through dried-up river rock, over high ridges to avoid the snipers, and hiding behind giant boulders during patrols. It was difficult and quite frankly, considering the two big strong aliens and with her being a vampire, she hadn't thought Jill could possibly keep up with them. She had been wrong. The woman had obviously spent a lot of time in the area and knew what she was doing.

After a few more tunnels and some high trail walks, they made it to an entrance into the cave system. Tarc turned to Nial and Jill and whispered. "I want you two to stay out here and guard." Nial took up residence in a hidden alcove of rocks, instantly. Jill, on the other hand, stiffened her spine. Jack could guess that she didn't take orders well. They had that in common too. *I really am going to have to like this one. Damn. Thought it was a fluke earlier.* Jill gave a slight nod of her head and disappeared into the higher rock terrain to take up her sniper position.

Tarc grabbed her hand and proceeded to haul her into the cool, dark, dank caves. It felt good to get out of the sun for a time. She was lucky she was full up on blood, which allowed her extra sun exposure. Her power was drained a bit but she was still good.

They wandered carefully through some very tight areas, occasionally using the flashlight she had brought along. Finally, she saw some wet dirt. "Here." She pointed. He nodded at her and stood protectively while she pulled out one of the special containers she'd gotten from Caran.

She scooped up some of the dirt, labeled it, and put the full container back into her backpack. They continued on silently further down into the cave system. At a very low point, they spotted a puddle of water seeping from the rocks. Once again, she pulled out a container, collected the water, labeled it, and put it away.

This continued throughout the caves. She had successfully gathered many different samples for Tarc's sister to run her tests. She was amazed that they hadn't run into anyone else down here. She kept listening intently, because the alarm had to have been raised by then, but nothing beyond their own sounds registered.

She spotted some light up ahead. Following it, with Tarc at her back, they made their way out of the cave. Jill had given them a rundown of what to expect at this point. Now they just needed to climb the stairs carved into the side of the mountain and at the top, they would find the deep reservoir. They made it there without incident and gathered a few more samples from various locations. When she came back near Tarc, she spoke to him in a low, sad, quiet voice. "It's so beautiful here. It's unfortunate that MAD has taken over this park."

"It is beautiful. I wish we could have come under different circumstances to sit and enjoy the view. Back home, I have a place near my home that has a similar look and feel. I spend a lot of time there."

On the one hand, she was excited to learn more about him and his life. On the other, if his people had never come to Earth, this park would still be open to the public. It was their fault that MAD came into existence and took control of the location. Her lips thinned and she answered him tightly. "It must be nice to go to your favorite spot whenever you want." She knew that wasn't totally fair, but her frustration got the better of her.

"Jack." Resignation ran through that one word. "If you insist on continuing to paint us as the bad guys, I am not sure what I can do or say. I am here, at your request. I am diverting time and resources to this endeavor. I wish things were not as they are between us, but I cannot change what has already happened." He grabbed her hand in his. Heat flashed through his eyes. "I am not sure I would want to anyway."

"I don't know what to think, Tarc. I need some time to reconcile everything."

He nodded. "We need to go."

"Yes."

They solemnly made their way back down the stairs to return to the caves.

Distracted with her thoughts, they were about halfway down when Jack heard the sound of a gun. Instinct had her blurring into action and moving to put herself in front of Tarc. She jerked as a sharp stinging sensation erupted in her upper right shoulder. She looked into his horror-filled eyes before she lost her footing on the narrow stairs and fell backward off the ledge. Above her she heard him yell, but she was lost to all the pain of her body hitting tree limbs and boulders on her way to the awaiting creek bed below. She hurt everywhere and then, she didn't hurt at all. Blackness swam in her vision and ultimately engulfed her.

Tarc heard the gun fire and turned to protect Jack but he was not fast enough. With her speed, she had moved to stand in front of him instead. He saw her body jerk, their eyes met, and then before he could register all that had gone wrong, she toppled backwards over the side just as he reached to engulf her in his arms and missed. "Jack!" He watched as her body hit from one object to the next until she landed a crumpled mess in the creek below. Worse than a nightmare. "No!"

Another gunshot splintered the rock just above his head. There were only two options open to him right then, devastation or fury. There would be time for devastation later. For now, he had a gunman to kill. He let the fury infuse his whole body and ran back up the stairs with his hunter's speed and agility.

Part way up, he saw a trail of fallen rocks that he could jump over to get to the other side where the shooter resided. He used all of his strength and skill, ignoring the pain of a bullet grazing his upper left arm and then another grazing his forehead. Nothing was going to stop him from killing the man who killed Jack. Nothing.

The man tried to run, probably because he had an avenging Staraban warrior barreling down on him. Tarc took a flying leap at the man when he was close enough and knocked him to the jagged ground, blood flew from the wounds created on impact. He wanted to rip this man apart with his bare hands, but he also wanted to get back to Jack as swiftly as possible. With a violent lift and twist of the man's head, there was no doubt that the shooter was dead. He wiped his hands on the back of the shooters shirt, got back up, and raced almost reluctantly back the way he had come.

He raced down the stairs to where Jack lay, but became immobilized at the sight. *You have to get to her. You have to keep going.* He told himself what he needed to do, but everything in him rebelled and wanted to ignore the thoughts. If he did not approach, if he did not verify, then maybe she could still be alive.

He lifted one foot in front of the other and made his way to her body. He could not remember ever feeling this desolate emptiness before. Feeling. *Shet!* He was feeling things for a female again just when it was too late. Why did he keep losing the women he loved? Loved? *Shet!* He fell to his knees next to her and tentatively reached out his hand. He paused and just let his eyes take in her mangled form. *Oh goddess!*

Tarc reached out further to touch her, but he noticed something he had never seen before and did not know what it was. The ground around Jack began to move. It snaked up onto her skin creating dark lines, like veins, all around her. For a moment, he panicked. Was the ground trying to take her from him? He had never heard of anything like this in all of the studies they had run about humans.

Of course, she was not human.

Then he felt it. Some kind of energy surrounded her.

Even as he looked on, he noticed small cuts healing, broken bones mending, disjointed limbs getting realigned, and her complexion turned a little less pale. The whole process was probably just a few minutes but to him, it felt like he was suspended in time watching Jack heal with his hearts skipping beats.

The ground began to recede, he held his breath waiting but he was not exactly sure for what. Then she opened her eyes. Relief poured through him, but it was short lived.

Pain erupted on his neck. Jack had moved with her vampiric speed and was latched to the front of his body, biting deeply into his neck. This was not like the times before. She drank fast and hard and there was no pleasure, just lots and lots of pain. He resisted his instinctual reaction to fling his attacker off of him and instead enveloped her in his arms, willing to take any pain necessary to ensure she lived. He could feel himself growing weaker by the moment as he fell to his knees. She might well kill him, but if she could survive, he was going to be okay with that. He was not sure how this infuriating female had gotten so completely under his skin within a few short days, but she was there.

Just as fast as she had latched on to him, she flung herself backwards off of him. She was crouched a short distance away with a look of horror on her face. Such a beautiful face. She really was lovely. He tried to speak and tell her, but he was feeling unusually tired, and forming the words would take too long.

So lovely.

So fucking beautiful.

That word.

Not that word again.

What word?

Lovely.

His first coherent thought was that someone was trying to kill him. There was a disgusting, metallic tasting liquid being poured into his throat. It was an understatement to say, he was not overly fond of it. He opened his eyes and there she was. He was so happy she was okay. What was he drinking though? He had never tasted anything like it. He looked down and that was when he noticed that Jack's wrist hovered above his lips, blood pouring from it into his mouth. He pushed her wrist away. "What are you doing?"

"Considering I almost killed you, it seemed only fitting that I also save you." She sounded defensive but her eyes were filled with remorse, shame. "I'm so, so sorry. So very, very sorry." Tears swam in her eyes, and though she looked as though she was trying to fight them back, she failed and they began to stream down her face.

He reached his hand to her cheek, wiping away the wetness. "Jack. Stop. I am happy that you drank from me. When I saw you fall, saw your broken body, I..." He had to pause to take a calming breath. "I thought you were dead. I would have done anything to bring you back. I still do not understand why you were feeding me your blood?"

"Something else to know about vampires, our blood can help you heal. Well. It can help humans heal and I had hoped it would help you too. Apparently, it does." She stopped crying, but sadness still lingered all around her like a cape.

He felt at the areas that had been grazed by bullets only a short time earlier, and they were completely healed. No sign of broken skin anywhere. "That is amazing."

"Wait." Jack's sadness fell away as she looked at him quizzically. "I can still hear your hearts beating. You aren't a vampire. How is that possible?"

He looked back at her confused. "What do you mean? Of course I am not a vampire. I am the alien. You are the vampire. Are you feeling okay?"

She glared at him. "I feel fine. *But.* When someone is drained of blood and a vampire brings them back with their own blood, that person becomes a vampire. That's how I became one. Unfortunately, for my maker, he ended up feeding me while staked and left to the sun, but I digress."

"Staked?"

She ignored him and continued. "I guess you must be as immune to vampirism as you are to our glamour. Fascinating. I wonder why? Thoughts for another time. I know you don't hear them yet, but the earlier gun shots haven't gone unnoticed, we need to get out of here. There are multiple people heading in this direction and they will be here in a few minutes."

"I want to know what happened with the ground? It seemed to crawl up to you and heal you. Goddess. I thought you were dead until I saw it moving around you. Felt the power coming off of you."

"Can I tell you later? We really do have to go and with both of us having near death experiences, neither of us is at our best to fight."

"You are correct. Of course. Let's hurry to Nial and Jill and get out of here. Later, you *will* tell me." He stood and held out his hand to help her up as well. She took his offered hand and as she stood, he pulled her into his arms for a swift, passionate kiss. Necessary. He needed to feel she was alive. "I needed that. And let me make myself clear… I am not okay with you dying. I was far from okay. Do you understand me?"

Her eyes were liquid pools. "I was not okay either when I thought you were dead."

One more swift kiss, and they were ready to move.

A little breathless, she followed him back in.

[9]

AFTERNOON OF THE LIVING DEAD

Adventures of a Supernatural Geek Girl

October 5, 2025
Dear Reader,

Thank you for all of your responses to my question. I'm impressed with all of your adventures. Spelunking did not go particularly well for me. I may have come close to, you know, dying. The tl;dr version is that I tripped over my feet and plummeted to my death. If I'd been human, there is no doubt that I'd be dead. Instead, I was near death. Kind of one step behind and to the right of death. I don't recommend it. Luckily, your favorite blogger bounced back and lived (kinda) to tell the tale.

My current status surprises even me. I'm working *with* the enemy to help our resistance succeed. No one-way ticket to some random planet thank you very much. I'm reminded of why we're so committed every time I take in another inspiring and lovely place on Earth, like the one I almost died at earlier today. Not to mention that there really is no choice for someone like me, as you know if you're one of my regular readers.

. . .

Fun Facts:

Decapitation really is a thing. I was lucky my fall hadn't resulted in such a messy situation. I have invented a short poem about the subject, just for you.

Keep your wits, Keep your head,
When you don't, You wind up dead.

I didn't say it was a good poem. I'm a programmer, not a poet. Don't wind up dead. Who would read my blog?

Hugs and bites!
iByte

Pinnacles National Park, Paicines, CA, USA, Earth

October 5, 2025

Tarc led Jack back through the caves, towards the entrance. He worked to suppress all of the echoing feelings still rebounding through his body in response to the last fifteen minutes. Had it really all happened that fast? They were not out of danger yet and he needed a clear head to get them safely away. When they emerged, they were greeted by two dead bodies. Nial was busy putting away one of his wicked, custom-made blades. He had obviously used it with the male closest to them. The other body had a perfectly executed, gunshot wound to the head.

"We need to go."

Nial nodded his agreement. "We could hear the gun shots from out here, but these bastards showed up and we did not have a chance to come find you. I am glad to see you are both okay."

Jill joined them, dropping silently out of the trees. "We have to go now or I am shooting every single one of you and saying you took me as your hostage earlier." She was glaring at them all.

His friend turned to her and growled. "You just try it, female."

"Listen beastmaster, Bulldog may be my dad, but he won't give a shit if he learns I tried to defect. He will kill me. If..."

Jack interrupted. "Did you just say that Bulldog was your dad? Holy shit. No wonder you're a crazy bitch. Damn."

Jill rolled her eyes. "I hate you."

"Same." Both women smiled at each other. Nial sported a confused look that probably matched the one he had.

"Can we get going now that you have had your—whatever that was?" Both women stared daggers at him. "Jill, which way gives us the fastest route to our waiting transports?"

After he described the area where they had left them, Jill headed out. With her leading the way, they hiked back as quickly and silently as possible. Jack warned them when she started to hear someone approaching. They passed the meeting hall on the way, but it was empty. Everyone was out looking for them. It took some time, but eventually, they found the two hidden transports. Tarc took Jack into his and Nial, despite a lot of grumbling, took Jill in his. They closed the doors, lifted off to hover a few feet above the ground, and made their way to the Staraban Base.

He should be relieved, but instead he grew more and more apprehensive the closer they got to Caran. What was he going to do if the samples proved that they were sent to Earth under false pretenses? That would be problem enough, but even more troubling was what would happen if Earth really was dying. How would Jack take the news? Would they be able to calm most of the resistance with their findings? He had a bad feeling forming a tight knot in his gut that the way he watched Jack connect to the ground earlier had something to do with why she was so resistant to leaving and, what if they were right and she could not leave?

He looked over at the object of his obsession. Or was that affection? Both? It was obvious to him that she was once again trying to distance herself. He was not going to allow that.

Leaning over towards her chair, he undid her restraint system, and pulled her into his arms. She squealed, which he enjoyed, but she did not protest. "*Shela*, I need to feel you. To know you are okay." He craved her on a whole other level from anyone else before her. She was vital. His arms encircled her tightly and his mouth claimed hers. There were still a few minutes until they arrived back and he was going to put that time to very good use.

Jack felt as the transport slowed in its approach. She wiggled off of Tarc's lap and stared out the window. His lips had made her forget, well, everything while she was in his arms, but now that she regained her distance, she couldn't let go of the image of him falling to the ground because she'd taken too much blood from him.

She had nearly killed him and it terrified her. Even when she'd been a brand-new vampire, she'd never gotten that close to killing someone and now…now it wasn't just anyone she had been seconds away from killing. It was him and once again, she proved her mother right. She was trouble. She was no good. She couldn't be trusted. She had to find a way to leave so he could be safe.

Until then, she had another more immediate problem.

"Tarc?"

"Yes, *apura*?" He turned his head away from the landing site to look at her, clearly distracted.

"I need your help. Do you have a large blanket in here somewhere?" She knew her voice sounded tense, but she couldn't help it. As soon as she left his lap, and returned to her senses, she could tell she was in trouble.

He turned fully to face her. Concern etched his features. "No. What's wrong?"

"Do you remember me telling you that I have a limit to my sun exposure?"

It took him less than a moment to grasp her meaning. "Fuck! How bad? What can I do?"

"I need to get covered up. As long as I can hide myself under something and stay away from sunlight for a time, I will be okay. I just need something to help me get inside and away from any windows."

He looked around frantically as though he could make something materialize if he just thought about it hard enough.

"Tarc!"

He stopped. "Yes?" He sounded angry, almost, but she could see it was fear driving him. "*Shet!* I think it is unreasonable for me to have to deal with your potentially dying twice in one day. *You* are not going to die. Understand?"

He sounded quite insane. "It's not like I want to die. I didn't purposefully throw myself off the stairs, I got sho…"

"Do not think that I have forgotten that you fell because you took a bullet meant for me!" He was bellowing at her now. "I. Protect. You. Got it?"

"No. You. Don't. Dammit."

He began growling at her and it sent shivers down her back. Shivers! Why are none of her responses to him making sense? She needed to leave him. Soon. She needed the safety of her normal life.

Her normal friends. Her normal behaviors. Her normal non-homi-cidal track record.

He reached down and she noticed that he was tugging his shirt up, up, and over his shoulders and head and then, it was off. "What the hell are you doing? We can't just end every argument with sex. I know it seems I can't control my response to you, but you can't control me using my body against me."

He raised an eyebrow at her and answered through painfully gritted teeth. "I would not do that to you. While I appreciate your immediate reaction to me, and trust me, my body does the same thing to me with you, I am not attempting to end this argument with sex. I am attempting to save your life by giving you my shirt as a cover for your upper body. We are lucky I dressed in human clothes today." Then he started grumbling in the Staraban language under his breath.

She caught some words she had earmarked as "would be fun to learn" while she studied his language. She reached out and accepted the shirt. "I'm sorry. It's been a really trying day and it's only half over. I think we both need a cool-off period. Right now, I literally need to hide." She lifted the shirt indicating it with a tilt of her head. "Thank you for protecting me." Jack deftly made a knot in the neck and arm hole areas and effectively made a basket for her upper body. "I'll need your help getting out of here and into the base."

"Of course. Cover up before something else bad happens."

She took her new sun shield and put it over herself. It was made of a super soft cotton and smelled divinely, overwhelmingly of Tarc. She caught hints of everything off of his shirt. His desire. His anger. His fear. His excitement. His...What was that smell? His despera-tion mingled with...desolation.

She gasped. Was that how he'd felt when she'd appeared dead? It was still hard to reconcile that he could feel so strongly for her.

But.

The evidence was tickling her nose. How long was she going to deny he cared? Every time she did, he would get all mad and growly. She sighed. But so what? Really. If it was true, it would just be more proof that she needed to get away from him for his own safety. She was dangerous to him. A vampire out of control was always dangerous. Control was the last thing she had when he was around. Profound sadness settled into her.

A cool breeze swept into the transport which could only mean he'd opened the hatch. His arms reached under and around her and then she was up against his chest, cradled protectively. She was momentarily jostled as he jumped down off the transport and began to run. She heard him yell. "I'll speak with you inside." She wondered at who he'd yelled that to—wait—Caran. She could smell the scientist's scent lingering in the air where they passed. She could see the daylight filtering through his shirt and then it got darker. They must have made it inside.

She considered throwing off the shirt and started to move to do just that, but Tarc stopped her, command in his voice. "Not yet. There are still windows. I will tell you when it is safe."

Amid the background sounds, she heard Jill's voice sounding irate intermingled with Nial's voice sounding frustrated. *Guess those two are still going at it. Sheesh.*

Finally, he put her down in a cushioned chair. With a swift motion, he pulled the shirt over her head and she caught her first lungful of air not completely infused with his scent. She blinked a few times to adjust her eyes. Around her stood Tarc, concern so palatable, she could taste it on the air, Caran looking confused, and Nial and Jill appearing ready to go from verbal sparring into a physical altercation.

Sounding scientifically intrigued, and speaking up over the still bickering duo, Caran asked, "What was that about, brother? And who is this other human? We seem to be acquiring new ones rather frequently right now."

His gaze questioned her about sharing her situation with the people in the room. The day before, when she went vampire in front of so many of Tarc's people, he'd suppressed all questions and refused to give anyone any details. She believed Tarc could keep Caran and Nial in check. She looked to Jill, trying to decide if she could trust this potential new ally. Of course, she knew things about Jill that were dangerous if revealed. Mutually assured destruction should keep them both quiet. She turned her head back to him and nodded her agreement.

"Quiet or get out!" He yelled at Nial and Jill. Both fell silent to the command in his voice though the rebel looked rather put out about it. "What you hear now is confidential. Jill, I know my sister and Nial will heed me and my command, I have no such confidence in you. If you do not think you can keep everything you hear to yourself, leave now."

"Listen here, motherfucker... I know how to keep secrets. The whole fucking militia way of life is one giant secret. Hell, not one person there even knew I wanted to leave. That was a hard secret to keep, so give me a break. The real question is, do I want to know your damn secrets and the truth is, I'm too curious not to."

Jack couldn't help herself. She really couldn't. "Nosy bitch."

"Better than a freaky bitch."

They both smiled.

"Is there something wrong with both of you? Nevermind. Forget I asked. Jill, you can stay, but know that if I hear of you sharing any of this, I will kill you myself. Have I made myself clear?"

"Crystal." Jill replied insolently and crossed her arms over her chest.

He looked at her in confusion.

Jack interpreted for him. "Crystal is very see-through, it's clear. She means that yes, you have been clear with your words and she understands completely."

His only response was a grunt of acknowledgment. "Caran, Jill was a part of MAD, but she defected and helped us on our mission. Now we can move on." He took a deep breath and plunged ahead. "Jack is not exactly human."

She braced for their response.

"Obviously." This came from Nial.

"What? Really?" From a very sarcastic Jill.

"What is she then?" From Caran.

"I'm a vampire." She responded quietly.

All heads turned her way.

"Bullshit!" Jill's tone and face left no doubt that she was unconvinced.

Her "freaky" inner bitch got the better of her for a moment and she flashed her elongated teeth at the woman. Jill's reaction was quite satisfying.

"Holy shit! No fuckin' way. I have *not* gotten in bed with a group of aliens and a fucking vampire. You're not supposed to be real. This is like some Twilight Zone shit or perhaps straight up Twilight shit, come to think of it." She was definitely shaken, which made Jack's smile even broader. The cool cucumber was not so cold anymore. "Oh sure. Smile. I still hate you."

Jack laughed. "I hate you too, Spikey. Don't worry, this changes nothing."

They stared at each other and finally the other woman was back to smiling. Jack really was going to have to be friends with her. Damn.

She scanned to see what Nial and Caran's expressions held. Revulsion maybe? But, no. Nial looked at her warily, much like the day before, and said, "What exactly is a vampire?" Caran's inquisitive gaze seemed to second that question.

She hadn't even gotten around to really explaining to Tarc how she had become a vampire. Now was as good a time as any.

"I was human once. I won't go into the whole story of how vampires came about, I will just tell you that vampires feed on blood, amongst other things. When a human is drained of their blood nearly to death but is then refilled by the vampire's blood, they transform instead of die. I was changed into a vampire about five years ago."

"But...You've been out in daylight with us all morning." Jill looked completely confused and distrustful now.

"Yes. It's a myth that we only walk the night, though you can imagine the fear that gripped me the first time I truly tested that theory." Jack chuckled at the memory and then continued. "I can walk in daylight, *but* there is a limit to how much sun exposure I can experience without bad things starting to happen, including death.

While I subtly tried to stay in the shade as much as possible during our time at the Pinnacles, things hadn't gone as well as we hoped—"

"The gunshots we heard?" Nial interrupted this time.

She nodded. "Yes. I—"

Now Tarc interrupted. "She jumped in front of me, taking the bullet that was meant for me. We were high up on a thin ledge of stairs at the time and she lost her balance." He looked angry all over again but also haunted like he was remembering that moment when she had fallen off. She leaned forward and grabbed his hand to turn him toward her.

She softly whispered to him. "I'm okay." His acknowledgment was a tilt forward of his head and a slight release of the tension in his shoulders.

He continued. "She fell a long way and slammed into boulders and trees on the way down. She lay on the creek bed a crumpled mess. I was sure she was dead."

Simultaneous gasps from Caran and Jill followed by a harsh sounding word from Nial.

"I killed the male responsible as swiftly as I could and went to retrieve Jack's body. It turned out that she was healing." He looked back at her, his eyes and words letting her know he would keep some of her secrets between them. How could she not love such a guy? Love? What did she know of love? It's probably just infatuation, she corrected. That felt like a more comfortable truth. She smiled tentatively back in appreciation as he forged ahead. "She fed from me and was fully healed."

"I was, but the process of healing stole so much of my energy, that I cannot take any more sun exposure today. It's a delicate balance with an internal gauge. By the time we got into the transports, I knew I was wading in some seriously deep shit. That's why there was a shirt over my head as we made the mad dash into a room without windows."

"I have so many more questions. How many of you are there? Are humans in danger from vampires as well as aliens? Maybe we throw in a swamp monster and zombies while we're at it. Holy shit! Are those real? You know what. Maybe I don't want to know. Am I about to become dinner? You're looking rather annoyed." Jill paused only long enough to give her a glower. "You should know I'll taste like shit if my general disposition is any indication." Nial took a protective posture in front of the rebel which turned her glower to him. "What the fuck do you think you're doing?"

"Trying to protect the stupidest female I have ever met." He snarled back at her.

Jack just rolled her eyes. "You have nothing to worry about. Either of you. I'm all filled up with Tarc." Oh god. Had she just said that?

Caran snorted in suppressed laughter. Jill was not so delicate and began to laugh in earnest. Nial chuckled, trying to maintain his warrior composure. She turned to see Tarc's reaction and her breath caught. His eyes had gone straight to that irresistible blue fire. Arousal flashed through her swift and devastating. She needed to keep her head. They were not about to put on a show. Were they? He looked like he wasn't going to care one way or another.

Caran finally spoke. "Before I have images I will need to laser out of my brain, let us move on. From the situation yesterday in the meeting room, I assume that you also have greater speed and strength. Since my brother is still standing and strong, I assume that your blood drinking does not involve his dying. Unless there is anything else we need to know about vampires, I would like us to discuss the mission. Was it successful?"

―――――

His sister was right, but it took Tarc a few beats of his hearts to get his desire under control. He had forgotten all about the backpack in his mad dash to protect Jack. "The samples can be found in the backpack in my transport. I forgot to grab it when we exited. I had concerns that Jack's fall might have broken some of the samples, but somehow, Jack's body was the only thing that broke. I believe you will have all you need to do your testing."

"Explain to me what this testing is." Jill demanded of the room at large.

Caran answered her. "I am a scientist for ARC. I am going to test the soil and water samples they gathered to determine the health and diversity of their microbiomes. We have found that often when a planet is dying, the first things impacted are the microbiomes closest to the core. The Pinnacles are a remnant from an ancient volcanic field. Things seep up from below and I believe I should be able to get what I need from those samples. If not, I can determine if we need to test a deeper location or if it is pointless and our initial information was correct and the Earth is a dying planet."

"I see." Jill seemed mollified for now.

He looked over at Jack who was looking more fatigued with each passing moment. He ached to get her to his room and let her rest. "We are finished here. If anyone else has questions, we can meet up again later for dinner and discuss it then. Caran, you will recover the samples and get started?"

She nodded to him and made her way to the exit. "I will see you later." She left.

"Nial, you will show Jill to one of our guest quarters?"

"You're sending me off with the hulk? Isn't there someone else that can show me where to go? Anyone at all?" If Tarc was reading his friend right, and he was sure he was, he wanted to get Jill over his knee and tame the wild creature. His friend had his hands full.

"It would take too long to find someone else. Just follow him and he will show you somewhere to rest and clean up."

He watched as Nial turned to her, used his arm to indicate the exit, and waited patiently for her to walk out. She stiffened, her expression iced over, but she finally did just that. He followed her out of the room leaving him alone with Jack. He approached her where she sat. "Let us go get some rest, *shela*." She looked so shockingly fragile at that moment. Through half lidded eyes she looked back at him.

"Yes. Take me to bed." A little of her normal spirit peaked through. "I'll try to keep my fangs to myself if you keep your hands to yourself." She gave him a wink. He lifted her up into his arms, amazed that such a small, delicate creature possessed so much power. Now, she possessed an equal measure of power over him. Maybe if he never told her, never shared how deeply she mattered to him, she would not be able to hurt him with it. Maybe.

She fell fully asleep halfway to his room. He gently laid her down on their bed. Their? Yes. No going back for him. He stripped her of her dusty, blood-stained clothes and covered her with the sheet. They would get clean after they woke up. He undressed swiftly, climbed in, and pulled her into the crook of his body. His thoughts kept him from sleep. How would he keep her with him? What would it mean if Earth was not dying? What would it mean if it was and she could not leave? How was he going to get Bren back?

He would have a conversation with his brother later today, to make sure he was still being treated well. Yesterday when they had spoken, his brother talked as though he was on a food vacation. Apparently HARM was a well-fed organization and they were sharing that food with his brother. What secrets might he have divulged for a second helping of the thing he called a pumpkin spice latte?

Jack had also assured Will that she was well and described their proposed outing. She had kept the conversation short so they could plan today's mission, but now that the mission was accomplished, they would need to let Will know the results.

Finally, his blood loss from her feeding dragged him under. He fell asleep full of apprehension, but also contentment with her in his arms.

[10]
JACKED

Adventures of a Supernatural Geek Girl

October 6, 2025
Dear Reader,

Near death experiences were so yesterday. Today, your friendly neighborhood vampire and hacker extraordinaire has found something. At least, I think I have. I am about to go investigate, so wish me luck. If I am right, though, this newest venue of information should give me what I need to convince ARC that we definitely do not to need to be relocated and that they have been misled. I'm excited to have a possible lead. Woot!

On the personal front, I have bad news for those that like a little TMI with their blogs. Enough kissing and telling. A vampire has to have some secrets. 😉 Suffice it to say, I am one very satisfied vampire. Even being the undead, I have never felt so alive.

Fun Facts:

I don't care about your blood type. It's a rumor. Y'all taste the same. Well…It always tastes better drinking from a nice, clean, desirable glass instead of a rude, dirty, undesired glass, but that's not about the drink. It's the receptacle. Since I usually only bite bad guys, I've had my fill of crappy glasses. Now I'm drinking from the Waterford crystal of glasses. He's all firm, perfectly formed, shiny, and clean, and I just want to get my lips on his rim and…Um… Scratch all that. What was I saying? Moving on.

Hugs and bites!
iByte

Staraban Headquarters, Portola Valley, CA, USA, Earth

October 6, 2025

Jack had slept straight through dinner. She awoke alone in a very dark room and wondered if it was the middle of the night. If it was, she had to wonder at Tarc's absence, as well. She quickly dictated a post about her near-death experience to Hal, fully intending to follow that up with getting out of bed, but somehow she'd fallen back asleep. Whether it was a couple of minutes or a couple of hours was anyone's guess, but eventually she woke up again. This time, morning light streamed in from the windows but Tarc was still MIA. She did feel a little more human—well, more awake anyway—and decided to try being vertical for a while.

After using the cool nano-shower-y thing and getting dressed, she sat at the chair and table in their room. When had she started thinking of it as hers as well? What *was* she doing? Moving in with her enemy, now? Maybe they could go shopping for linens together. *What the fuck, Jack?* She tapped her ear, irritated and requiring a distraction. "Hey Hal. How are the comments on the post I made?"

"You mean the one where you basically announced that you almost died. Do you realize that you are asking me about the reactions of total strangers to your near-death experience but you have not asked how I am handling it?" He actually sounded hurt.

"I hadn't realized that you cared that much. I guess I should have known you would become aware of what was happening since you warned me you do when I'm in danger."

"You know...I now comprehend why your alien keeps getting pissed off at you. You don't understand why he cares and now you don't understand why I care. Why? Because he's an alien and I'm just AI? I never took you to be that shallow and judgmental. Are we not good enough, human enough, for you?"

She cringed. How can he think that? "Of course it's not because of those things. I just know that I'm troublesome. That I'm hard to care about. I've known since I was a kid that I'm just not the kind of person who is worthy of people's concern."

"What are you talking about and who are you talking to?" Tarc stood in the doorway frowning at her.

She couldn't believe he'd caught her unaware again. Her vampie-sense was failing her a lot lately. What the hell? At this rate, she was going to have no secrets at all. What a great spy she was. *Internal sarcasm now? Really?*

"Tell me who you were talking to." He repeated.

With a bit of a huff, she answered him. "Okay. Fine. I'm talking to my PAL. Hal, meet Tarc. Tarc, Hal."

"I guess the cat's out of the bag now. Hey there."

"Who is that? Are you talking to someone on one of your phone devices? A pal is a friend, correct? What cat? What bag?"

"Right. First, 'cat out of the bag' is just an Earth phrase about revealing secrets. Second, I forgot how proprietary Gobble can be. PAL stands for personal assistant link. Hal is an early prototype I was working on before you arrived on Earth. He is one of only a few active PALs. He and I work together on all of my projects. He is like a robot with artificial intelligence, but without a body."

"And why don't I have a body? That's a great question."

"Where is he located?"

"I have an implant behind my ear which I can tap so he and I can communicate either silently or verbally. His voice comes out on the speaker of my watch." She indicated her wrist.

"Not a real man then?" He sounded tense. Was he jealous? Of Hal?

"Rude much? I may not have a body, but there is no need to be cruel about it, asshole!" Hal sounded completely offended. "You're lucky I don't have a body. I'd make you eat those words."

"I don't think he meant to be cruel, Hal. He is just adjusting to your presence."

"He is with you all the time? He is inside you? I do not like you having another male with you all the time. It disturbs me."

"I'm sorry, but I am not giving him up. Hal is priceless."

"See, big guy, she *needs* me."

"Hal! Don't taunt him. I can still give you an attitude adjustment if I want. Tarc. You have to understand. I've had Hal for some time.

He is important to me and quite frankly, he's in love with Will, so…"

"With Will from your base?" He finally cracked a grin. "How does Will feel about this?"

"Will accepts his praise like only Will can. He just assumes its well-deserved adoration." She grinned back.

"That's because he is so gracious and wonderful. Both of you could learn a thing or two from Will."

"See?"

He nodded. "Is Hal the reason that Will was able to find you here so quickly?"

She tingled in embarrassment, though why she would feel that way was beyond her. She had every right to try to escape, but considering everything they'd done since, it was uncomfortable to have kept this from him. "Yes. I've meant to tell you about him, but we've been so busy with the mission and…"

"You are still unwilling to fully trust me." He sounded so frustrated. He took one of his trademark controlled breaths and continued. "I will just have to keep proving to you that I am worthy of it."

"I'm sorry. Trust is…hard for me." She implored him with everything in her for his understanding.

"So I have seen." He gave her a lopsided grin. "You are as sweet as the inside of the *maka* fruit but as prickly as its dangerous exterior. I *will* find a way to peel your defenses away."

She needed to change the subject. She didn't want to think about feelings, emotional defenses, and their connection. She needed it changed until his face took on a stern expression, and he spoke again.

"Now. Back to what I overheard when I walked in. Why do you think that you are unworthy of being cared for? Who told you such a thing? I will kill the bastard."

Why had she wanted to change the subject again? "We don't need to discuss this."

"Yes. We do and we will. It continues to be an issue between us and I will not allow you to keep questioning your value to me."

"Tarc." She could hear the weak almost begging tone in her own voice. *Dammit! You never show weakness. Never.*

"Now. Tell me." His voice held steel and resolve all rolled into one. Below that, though, she heard a deep concern that pulled an answering honesty. She wasn't going to get away with putting him off and lying at this point was right out. He deserved more from her, but she didn't have to like it..

Aggravated, she growled at him. "Fine. If you must know, it was my mother. And really, if your own mother can't find even one iota of worth in you, well, let's just say that kinda sticks with you. I left home as a teenager just to get away from her toxicity but it's a lot harder to run away from her voice in my head. There. Now you know." She looked him defiantly in the eyes even as her gut clenched at the admission. The only person she'd ever talked to about this had been Rory.

His face contorted into shock. "Your mother?" His voice went lower, gentler. "Are you sure, *shela*? I know kids and parents some-times fight."

"Yes." She hissed through her teeth. "It's hard to misinterpret when someone literally says to you…" She mimicked her mother's voice as she lost her focus in the memory of it, "You know I cried the day you were born. I didn't want you and only kept you because I thought I could get some green from your moneyed father. Joke was on me, though. He didn't want you either. Consider yourself lucky that I even feed you, you worthless piece of shit." The present came back into focus as she said, "So yeah. I'm sure."

She glared at Tarc for making her revisit those memories. Anger was way easier for her to process than the despair waiting for her whenever her thoughts veered towards the past. Pure fury stared back at her. A thunder cloud wouldn't carry so much suppressed energy.

"How could any mother say such a thing to a child?" He was across the room, kneeling at her feet an instant later. "Jack. I know we have only known each other for a few days, but you are important to me. Do not ever doubt it. Your mother was a horrible female to say such things, but especially to her child, to you. It enrages me that I cannot kill the person who said this to you because she is your mother. I would do anything, give anything, to take away those words and all others like them from your past."

He reached out and wrapped her in his arms. She resisted. She didn't want to let the tsunami of pain she had held at bay her whole life set sail and wasn't sure if she could make it back to shore if she did. She also lacked the ability to look into his concerned face, have his comfort so close at hand, and not fall into it. All her will failed her and with a hiccup the storm crashed. His powerful arms held her together through all of the eviscerating pain.

Every harsh word, every lonely moment, every scornful look, they all came back like a movie played on loop. Her power rose and shed off of her, rose and shed off of her in response to her unraveling emotions. Each new rise exposing another layer of her pain and the release tearing it away. She hadn't realized just how tightly she'd held on to those memories, how far down she'd pushed them, so she could stay ahead of their combined impact. Tarc had lit the match and set fire to them all at once. She was detonating and the only reason she was still here was him.

She wasn't sure just how much time had passed when she finally felt her eyes dry, her sobs subside, her power grow neutral, and his arms relax. She hid her face against his now completely wet chest, unable to expose herself to his gaze. She was too open, too vulnerable. She went to her safe place. Sarcasm was safe. "Gee. Look at the big bad vampire break down over some harsh words. I may get my vampire card revoked."

"Jack. Stop. Do not make light of this. Not with me. Let me comfort you. I want to make you feel safe, adored, desired. I want to do that for you. Be that for you."

"I don't know if I can. Trust is a four-letter word to me."

"It has five letters."

Dealing with his language confusion could lend its own humor to any situation. She lifted her face to his and gave him a watery smile. "It's a phrase. Most cuss words have four letters like shit or crap and, of course, your newly acquired fuck. Sometimes, when we want to say we consider a word or what the word stands for as bad, we call it a four-letter word."

"So for you, trust is bad. Something to be avoided?" He was gently wiping his hand across her cheek removing the evidence of her breakdown. "I understand how you feel. Trust really can be a four-letter word, as you say."

She nodded. "I care for you. I can't keep denying that, but I also can't see where this could possibly go. I'm a leader for the group working to make sure you leave. You're working to relocate us off planet." Her motionless heart still seized in her chest, knowing no matter which outcome they arrived at, they would never be able to stay together. She couldn't leave, dammit, and he wouldn't stay. Her voice a little hoarser now, she continued with her other reasoning. "How does that create the basis of a healthy, trusting relationship? You have to be able to see the absurdity in thinking trust can play into it."

"You are correct about that. On the surface, this makes no sense. But, you could trust that I will not do something to purposefully hurt you. You could trust that we do not mean you or anyone else on this planet harm." His arms around her stiffened and his voice became low and gravely. "I need to know something. Answer my question from yesterday. Something happened with the dirt, it healed you. You said you would explain it to me later, but you were too tired last night and I wanted you to rest. Tell me now."

She sounded so sad, even to her own ears. Almost defeated. "Okay. I'm going to give you the short version. Vampires were created of the Earth. Our reanimation, you could say, is powered by it."

"But you drink blood as well?"

"Think of the blood as food but think of the Earth like a battery. We are creatures of energy and sustenance. That energy needs to be repowered. The blood as well as regular food sustains the body, but the Earth sustains our power. Without both, we can't exist. If I am injured, as long as I can connect to the ground, the power infuses me and heals me faster. *But*, even if I don't need extra healing, I need to connect to the Earth on a regular basis."

Understanding and worry were plastered on his features. "This is why you are a part of HARM. You are unable to live on another planet." She nodded. "Are you sure? Has anyone ever tested that theory? No. Of course not." He answered his own question. "Humans have not developed interplanetary space travel. Then how do you know it will not work somewhere else?"

"Truthfully, we don't. Tarc, as a vampire, I am immortal. If you are given immortal life would you risk dying to prove it?"

"Immortal? You can live forever?"

"Yes."

"Wow. That is amazing."

"Yes. It definitely has its benefits, but you see the problem?"

"I see the dilemma. What if we could bring the soil with you? Does it have to be touching the planet for it to work?" He was grasping at straws and they both knew it.

"The soil, the dirt, it's just an extension, the power comes from the Earth." She paused. She knew he needed some time to let it all sink in. Then she continued. "So now you see the problem. Vampires can't leave so we have to stop you from relocating us. It would be a death sentence. It just so happens that many humans also don't agree with your science reports regarding the planets health. Those humans and vampires make a great team in the resistance."

Tarc leaped up. "What happens if our reports are correct? You expect me to just leave you here to die?" His tone changed to impotent anger, again. His hands gripped her arms and she could feel his desperation rolling off of him. It felt like sticking your face into an oven. Hot fury and frustration all hitting her in ripples.

It flamed her own frustration and anger. She jumped up and strode away to get some distance. She paced, turned to him and ground back at him. "Yes. Yes! You will have no choice. I will have no choice. I had no choice in becoming a vampire, and I have no choice now. If I leave, I die. And while I may not be totally alive, I am not going to cut my life short. So, yes. You will have to leave me, because I may as well live until the very last moment the Earth stays a viable planet. You have to be able to see reason, Tarc. While I care for you, there really is no possible future for us. Either you leave because you aren't needed or you finish your job and leave then. Either way..."

She took a moment to calm her voice as inevitability settled into her very soul. "*You* will leave me behind." A different pit of sadness threatened to engulf her again, but she held it back. She didn't have a lot of time with him, but she had now and wasn't going to squander that. She was going to revel in every moment they had. She approached him, looked into his eyes with all the longing in her soul. "We may not have any tomorrows, but give me the present. Kiss me. Make love to me. I want to be with you." *For now,* was the unspoken ending to her sentence.

She saw him pause as he sifted through all the emotions her revelations had caused. Then he closed his eyes, slowly opened them, and pinned her with his look of lust and longing before he pounced on her for a soul stealing kiss. As far as she was concerned, he could have it. She lit up like a wildfire. It even took her a while to realize her feet were no longer touching the ground. He had her lifted up against him in his firm embrace as his kisses sucked, nipped, and plundered her lips. Jack fell into all that he was offering her. For today. Later would come soon enough.

Tarc felt too much all at once, and it terrified him. He had spent so many years enjoying females, from his own species and others, but never allowing himself to feel for them. Being betrayed once was enough. Until Jack. What was it about her that drove him to change, to do more than give each other carnal pleasure and move on? Even as he recognized she was important to him, he had not wanted to have any true feelings for her. Claiming her was different than making her the center of his universe. Hearing her say that she was in danger, no matter what he did, that he could not protect her, it opened up a door inside him he had thought cemented shut forever.

She was beautiful, true, but so were many of the females he had been with. From the beginning, she amused him, intrigued him, drove him to be happier and laugh more, to experience sex on a different level, to want to claim her as his and his alone, and to protect her in every way, from everything. He did not think it possible that he could have even stronger and more binding emotions than for his ex-fiancé, but he had been wrong. To hear that he would lose her no matter what he did, it raked through him like a beast intent on destruction.

He needed to reassure that beast that she was still here. She was not lost to him yet and he would find a way to ensure her safety and keep her with him. Right now, looking into her still moist, needy, pain-filled eyes, he endeavored to reassure them both of the present.

He grabbed her up in his embrace, taking possession of her lips. He nipped and lured her mouth open. Then plundered like the Staraban warrior he was. Claiming her mouth like he wanted to claim her body. Her everything. He swooped one arm under her knees and carried her over to the bed. Desire and so much more racing through his veins, he knew there were words sitting deep down in his soul that he ached to be able to say, but he could not. Neither of them were ready for more than what was already revealed between them tonight. He showed her with his body instead.

He yanked her shirt over her head and stared at her lush breasts, which made his mouth water and his cock grow. They were restrained in the bra she had insisted she needed for their mission. He hated the contraption. She must have read his intent to rip through it, because she sat up and lifted her left hand to stop him. "No going hulk smash on my bra. Not a chance!"

He took the opportunity to kick off his boots as he watched her reach behind and deftly undo the hooks, toss the bra to the side, and finally gesture for him to proceed like she was royalty.

Something about that turned him on. Generally, he enjoyed being in charge in the bedroom, but the push and pull he experienced with her rushed all of his blood in one direction. He gave a low, guttural growl, leaned down and fastened his mouth over her left breast, laving the nipple with his tongue. Goddess, he loved her breasts. Full, firm, and fitting into his palm or mouth like she was made just for him. His hand moved to capture her other breast as he settled into pleasure.

He began an orchestrated dance biting down on one, while massaging gently on the other. Then licking gently, while pinching. He swung her between ecstasy and pain as her body arched into him and she moaned.

"Tarc. That feels so good. Oh! Ah!"

"You have the most amazing body, *shela*. I could spend all after-noon just on these alone." He took the opportunity to switch which one had a hand and which had his mouth. "Mmmm. So, so good."

"Yes. Oh god. I need you."

"Soon. I am enjoying these too much. I will give you more soon. You can just lay back and…"

He found himself on his back. She had flipped him over and climbed on top. Looking down at him with the most sensual gaze while panting. "You are going too slow. Why don't you try just laying back and enjoying yourself?" To emphasize her point, she once again yanked and tore through his uniform and, considering the bra earlier, he found that rather unfair. He was not about to complain, though. He did have a lot of them. Then she pressed her breasts into his chest. "Since you like my breasts so much…" She moved her body down rubbing them against the full length of his chest until those perfect globes lay on either side of his continuously growing and hardening erection.

"Fuck. You are a menace to my self-control. I wanted to enjoy every inch of you, but that feels so good." She kissed her way back up his body, once again rubbing her breasts along his chest. He felt her hardened nipples like hot pebbles burning a path as she moved. His whole body strained to give her these moments before he seized control back from her. Each muscle bunching to stop from grabbing her. She licked as she got to his neck all the way up to his ear and there she whispered to him.

"This won't last, but while you're here, I'm yours. Now, show me."

Nothing could restrain him now. He flipped their positions, staring her straight in the eyes. "*Apura*. Yes. You are mine. And *I* am yours." He saw the desire in her depths but also what looked like fear. Not of him. Not of what they were doing. For their lack of a future? Or maybe because he cared for her? Because she cared for him? He let those questions go. There was no room for them right now. He bent down and trailed kisses between her breasts, to her stomach, and past her belly button. His hands found the fastening to her pants, undid them and pushed them and her underwear off, kissing every inch of revealed skin down to her ankle. "Spread your legs for me," he commanded. She did. Her arousal was evident on lower lips.

He lifted up her left leg and pressed kisses all the way up the inside towards her hips. "Do you have any idea what your scent does to me? From that first moment in the woods, it has driven me completely crazy with need for you."

"Same for me. That first time I ambushed you and told you to stay away, ahh..." He had reached her core and licked once, twice at her folds.

"Keep going or I will have to stop."

"Oh god. No. Okay. Um... I caught your scent of arousal and it drove me nuts."

He stopped licking briefly. "I thought maybe you started kissing me and trying to undo my clasps because you wanted to get away and getting my pants around my ankles was a quick way to do it." He continued running his tongue slowly up one side and then the other of her pussy and then delving deep into her core.

"Uh. So. Dammit! How do you expect me to think while you're..." He lifted his head again. "No! Don't stop! I'll continue. I wish I could say that I had a plan, but the truth is I... I... Um... Right. I lost control. Ah! Tarc." He started circling a thumb on her clit while he tasted the sweet cream pouring from her. "Holy shit. Ahhh...I...I can't..."

"You better keep talking, *shela*." He blew on her heated folds and felt her body shiver under his.

"That feels so good. Please. I need to come." She looked so beautiful as her body arched and wiggled begging him to give her what she craved.

He was taut with anticipation and need, himself. He had enjoyed her explanation and wanted more. "Honesty, gets you what you want."

"In the library, I... I lost control and accidentally nicked you with my teeth... Oh fuck, right there... I couldn't explain, so I ran."

He licked with deep strokes in and out and worked his thumb faster. She had been just as out of control as he was, had wanted him desperately, just like he wanted her. Then. Now. Her panting and moaning drove him insane. "Come for me."

And she did. Her power rolled off her and into him as she trembled and screamed with her release. He felt invincible. The heady sensation made him discard the tattered shreds of his uniform in a rush. He was over her and had his cock balanced right where his mouth had just been. "Look at me." Her eyes fluttered open. "I need you." He meant to say more, but she reached up and sealed her lips to his in a volcanic kiss. His tongue plundered her mouth as he shared her taste with her. He drove his almost painful erection into her slick core at the same time. They both moaned into each other's mouths.

He thrust again and again, long and deep and hard. Each whimper of her desire pushed his need to new heights, but it was not enough. "Your pussy feels like it was made just for my cock but I want more. Give me your bite."

He got a wicked thrill every time her teeth elongated, but this time she looked concerned. He stilled.

"Are you sure? I almost killed you last time. I'm scared. Maybe we should hold off on my biting you."

He gently cupped her cheek and ran his thumb down one of her long teeth, pricking it when he reached the sharp tip. Then he stuck that thumb into her mouth in offering. Him to her.

Jack thought it was the sexiest thing she had ever experienced. Having this big, strong, amazing warrior offer himself up to her. His thumb an appetizer to the meal he wanted to give her. The meal he wanted to *be* for her. He was giving her his complete trust that she wouldn't hurt him, and damn, that was so fucking sexy.

She sucked his thumb until her saliva healed it. She looked into his eyes and nodded. "Okay. You can be my cocktail, but for the love of God, please start moving your ass again. I need you to move." She flashed him a sassy grin before swiftly biting down on the juncture of his neck and shoulder. They both groaned loudly at the initial bite and then he began to move as requested.

The friction felt amazing as their bodies melded together in rhythm. Her insides were trembling and convulsing but she didn't want things to end too soon and so she clenched tight against the orgasm threatening to unravel her. His blood amplified her rising power. Rising and shedding. Items in the room trembled along with her. She stopped sucking, healed the wound, and sobbed his name. "Tarc. Oh. Tarc. I. Oh God!"

"Yes. Fuck, yes. You feel so good. So good." His words sounded as choppy as hers. They were both sweating and she felt so close. "Not yet." He pulled out, flipped her, and slammed his cock back into her in a blink of an eye. He had her up on her knees, doggie style, and this angle made him feel even bigger, his thrusts going deeper.

"Yes. Give it to me. Plea...Fuck m...Yes!" Her pleas became completely incoherent. It didn't matter as long as he kept going.

"Tell me you are mine. Tell me!"

"Yours! I...m...you...rs. All...you...rs."

His response was a low growl deep in his throat and Jack's whole body was ready to shoot off like a rocket ship. That thought almost had her laugh but just then he fisted a hand in her hair with an arousing bite of pain. He firmly pulled causing her to arch her back and he ratcheted up his thrusts. Why did he have to have so much damn stamina? His other hand reached around and pressed down hard on her clit. "Now you can come."

Then, he bit her on the throat and sucked. He didn't draw blood like she would have, but was leaving her a claiming mark of his own by bringing his blood, in her body, to the surface. She healed too fast for it to last, but the thought of it pleased her immensely. The sensations were too much and Jack couldn't hold back her orgasm anymore. Power exploded through her as she spasmed like a live wire and came all over his cock.

Her head and torso melted to the bed as he released her hair. She felt him shift behind her, grab her hips to keep her completely still, and then slam into her deeper and harder than ever before. Over and over, he thrust his cock into her welcoming body, until she felt his seed shoot inside her and for some reason, this time, that feeling almost brought her to tears. Something else that would inevitably come between them. Tarc would want a family one day, and vampires couldn't have children. She banished the thoughts that started a tingling behind her eyes, blinked, and refused to dwell on it right then. She was going to stay present with this amazing alien behind her.

They collapsed into a pile of intertwined body parts. "Holy shit. That was, crazy fantastic."

"We do appear to be getting better at this. We should keep practicing. Often." They stayed like that for some time and then he finally pulled out, which left her feeling all kinds of empty. She didn't have a chance to feel that way for long, though, because he flipped her onto her back. He was staring into her eyes with... with...it looked like affection. For her. She thought so anyway and damn but didn't that feel just as ground shaking. He really, *really* cared for her. He cupped her cheek with his hand. "I cannot take your past from you, but I can promise you that you are amazing and very easy to care about."

Well... Damn! That tingling in her eyes threatened again. "I..." She needed to clear her suddenly tight throat before she could speak. "I believe you. I care for you, too."

He tensed ever so slightly, but enough for her vampire senses to pick up on it. His eyes seemed to be assessing her, but then he blinked, slowly, and he was back to normal.

She wasn't about to let it go. "What was that?"

"What?"

"Are you really going to shut me down after everything I shared with you tonight? What just went through your head? Why did you look at me that way when I told you I cared about you?"

He sighed. "You are correct. You opened yourself to me, and so, I will do the same. A part of me wanted to ask if you were sure."

Well that was unexpected considering how he made her trust him. He didn't trust her when she said she cared? *What. The. Hell.* She scowled. "Why don't you believe me?"

He looked like he was searching for the right words, but finally, he must have found them, because he answered. "For me, it was not my parents that made it difficult for me to trust someone else's words." He leaned back, disengaging from her. She felt a chill at the loss of their combined body heat. Or maybe at the loss of their previous intimacy? He sat up with his back against the wall where a headboard would normally be and she had a brief thought wondering why they didn't have headboards. It was very brief, because the distance between them and her need to understand overshadowed everything else. She wished she could close that distance, but she wanted him to go on, so she sat up facing him, sheet pooled in her lap, instead. Then he continued and she didn't like what he had to say either.

"I was previously supposed to join with a Staraban female. Our families were very connected and we grew up together."

She couldn't lie to herself. That revelation was *not* what she'd been expecting. Luckily, he was staring off into space instead of directly at her and she had a chance to talk herself down off the irrational, dumb-ass, jealousy ledge.

Oblivious to her problems, lost in his own soul-baring, he continued. "Friendship led to more and eventually, we decided to join. Our families were joyous for the union. The day before the ceremony, she informed me that she had been with a mutual friend for months, never loved me, and would not commit to me."

That bitch!

"If she did not want to join together, I would have released her and wished her well. The part that changed me was that she had been lying to me for months, and really, she had been lying to me for longer about her non-existent love. It is why I do not tolerate

197

lying. Ever." He looked at her then and she could see the pain he carried. "I never wanted to feel for a female anything more than lust ever again. I thought it was because I could not trust the word of a female. That if my childhood friend could lie to me, then any female could lie, as well. My distrust ran deep. When I realized my unexpected feelings for you ran deeper, I thought we were beyond my distrust. That was, until you told me you cared a few minutes ago."

"I see. Uh. I understand." The tingling behind her eyes threatened once again dammit. What was wrong with her? *Get a grip, Jack.* She turned to get up. "It's okay."

His firm grip on her upper bicep stopped her and whirled her back to face him. "No. I do not think you understand at all."

"Then make me understand."

"I am trying to."

He was right. She'd reacted too quickly. Triggers were a bitch. So she relaxed her muscles to let him know she would stay and that she was listening. He dropped his hand from her arm and went on. "What I realized is that it was never the females I had lost faith in, well, not *only* the females, but also myself. I did not see that she was lying. How did I *not* see it? So when you told me..." He paused as if hesitating to go on. "I had a moment of doubt. You sounded sincere, but..."

She finished for him. "But what if you were wrong again?"

"Yes. I want to trust us both. I am sorry some of my doubt slipped out. I did not realize it would be the reaction I would have until after I had it. I do believe you care for me. I believe in you, Jack, and I trust you. So... I will put my faith in both of us."

"Tarc." His name came out breathy as her throat was all clogged up with emotions. She, not so gracefully, untangled her legs from the sheet and threw her arms around him. His arms embraced her tightly back. She clung to him like he was breath and life itself.

She spent the next few hours in bed with him. Showing him with her body what her mouth still could not say. Could not give voice to. Soon. Maybe. Or maybe not. There may not be a point to it.

For now, she said it all with worshipping his body with hers and it felt like he did the same for her.

Jack left Tarc sleeping in their bed. It was still weird to think of it as theirs but she didn't want to sleep anywhere else, so she may as well claim what she can, while she can. She was wired, and after sleeping so long the night before, she'd only grabbed a small cat nap. Now she wanted to get some work done. She cleaned and dressed herself quickly and quietly, throwing on the top t-shirt in her pile. The blue shirt read "Home is Where the Search Bar is." She stifled her giggle at her wearable magic eight-ball striking again. She was on a search alright.

She made her way out of the room, stopped to grab a quick lunch from the kitchen she found on the way—someone had brought in bagels, score—and down the hall to the meeting room. Some of his people gave her wary looks as she passed them, but no one tried to stop her. She assumed her status as prisoner must have been altered. Alone in the room, she opened up one of the terminals that littered the meeting table and did what she did best. She hacked her way in and started sifting through information.

"Well, that was enlightening."

She groaned. She had forgotten that Hal was still aware when they started—Oh god. "I can't believe you were there the whole time. Peeping tom much?"

"It's not my fault your hands were too busy to shut me down. I can't believe you actually talk to me with that mouth. You should really wash it out with soap."

"Okay. That's enough. We won't be discussing what happened earlier."

"Speak for yourself, sister. I'll be bringing it up at every opportunity. Hey Jack, remember that time you rubbed an alien…"

"Stop right there. Hal. Listen to my voice and be clear. No. Just no."

His voice was long in suffering. "Oookaaayyy." He sighed. "All sex and no fun. That's what you are. In all seriousness though Jack, I may not have a body but you have given me a consciousness. My existence is tied to yours. I was looking forward to tormenting you for the whole of your immortality. I am not keen on the dying thing —which you almost did twice yesterday, I might add—at all. What are we going to do?"

Her shoulders suddenly felt like they carried a four-hundred-pound weight. "I don't know, Hal. I really don't. I can only hope I find proof that the Earth is just fine. Which is what I'm trying to do right now. But... you don't have to worry. If it comes down to it, you will have a choice. I could transfer you to another host who can take you off planet and there you could body jump, harassing a lot of people, as you enjoy your immortality."

"I appreciate that, but I'm not sure I would like that nearly as much. So then, let's do this. What do you need? How can I help? Oh. And about your mother Jack?"

She tensed. She was so done talking about her mom today. "Yes?"

"She knew nothing about you and your worth. That bitch was like a horrible glitch in your programming but you are now surrounded with functional supportive code to keep you running smoothly."

After a momentary pause they both laughed. "I would say I'm not just surrounded but apparently infiltrated with it." She laughed again.

"Yep. That alien may be getting—" He paused and changed his voice to mimic her. "Deeper, deeper—" His voice back to normal, he continued. "but he can't go as deep as me, baby."

"Hal!" She burst out laughing even harder at his innuendo. Using her best Austin Powers impression she said, "Behave." Then continued with, "I obviously am not keeping you busy enough. I'm trying to sift through the data I just collected on this terminal regarding the other alien Qisto. If I can narrow down his digital signature, I thought I could then search out on the web and see if I could find that signature again. Perhaps I could find a location for that alien group if they are here on Earth. From there it should be easy. Find their base, hack their system, and gather any intel relevant to the question that is bugging me. Why hire ARC to remove us from Earth if Earth isn't really dying? That is the real question I need to be asking, I feel it in my bones."

They worked together isolating correspondence and sure enough, they found the digital signature they were looking for. She switched her focus to the web looking to find that signature. A short while later. "Aaannnd bingo."

"You found their location? Where?"

"Not far, actually. Qisto is running his operation from one of the abandoned investor buildings on Sand Hill Rd. I need to sneak in there. What's the likelihood that Tarc lets me do this?"

"I wouldn't say high considering how protective he is and how the last mission went."

"What is the probability I could sneak out and back in, unnoticed?" She tried to sound optimistic but really, who was she fooling? He would notice. Hal even snorted in her head. Of course, Tarc was sleeping right now so in theory, she could get out and just have to apologize when she came back for having scared him. Resolve settled into her. She knew he wanted to protect her but her ability at stealth when she was alone was far greater than their ability together. And if she was right...She would be bringing back proof that things were not what they seemed with this contract. "We're going, Hal. It'll be okay." She ignored another snort from Hal. "First though, I need a black t-shirt. This one is a little on the bright side."

Jack snuck back into their room, grabbed a t-shirt that looked mostly black, and turned to leave. Tarc was still completely out. She gave herself a moment to just indulge in eating him up with her gaze and then quietly made her way out the door. She thought at Hal. "Time to blow this joint." She thought she heard him reply, "Your ass is grass," but chose to pretend he'd said nothing.

Once she made it out of the main building, it wasn't that long of a walk to the Vrolan headquarters, at least not at her speed. On the way, she posted her latest blog. Maybe if her readers kept their fingers crossed for her, she would find this mission as informative as she hoped.

Once she got close enough to do some recon, she slowed and kept herself hidden. Slowly making her way around the building, she listened to what was happening inside. There were some sounds, but nothing that hinted at blood rushing, hearts beating, or warmth. She crept closer. Still nothing. She tentatively approached one of the windows on the lower floor that appeared to be slightly ajar. She tested to make sure it didn't creak and was able to widen the opening and slip through. She thought at Hal, "Jackpot."

She had entered an office with an alien device resembling the Staraban terminals sitting on the desk. Her luck was freaking epic today. She sat and gently began running her fingers over the keys. It took only a brief moment to acclimate, but most of the language was the same as the Staraban code. Small differences here and there, but mostly, code was code. You just had to understand it, to make it work for you.

Once again she set up a search and sifted through correspondences. More slowly this time because she was looking at something Qisto would have sent to someone other than Tarc regarding Earth. She found it. She pulled out her Bluetooth enabled thumb drive, another essential from home she had insisted Tarc needed to let her retrieve or replace. He relented grudgingly, like with the bras, and replaced them before their MAD mission. The thought brought a smile to her face.

She and Hal ran through information at top speed when they worked together like this. Then Hal said in her brain in a triumphant tone. "I think I found the thread."

She thought, "Show me." Hal sent her the date, time, and subject and the name of the other alien on the correspondence. She connected her drive and downloaded the whole lot and thought excitedly. "Yahoo. We did it."

When it had finished downloading, she got up, tucked it into her jeans pocket, and turned back towards the window. She slapped her hand to her neck. Something bit her. "Ow. Whaattt jjuuussssstttt..." Everything went dark as she fell to the floor.

[11]
JUMPIN' JACK FLASH, IT'S A BUST

Adventures of a Supernatural Geek Girl

October 6, 2025
Dear Reader,

MIA – Sorry, but iByte can't come to the blog, *again*. Another day, another dangerous complication. She'll hopefully be back to her regularly scheduled postings after another short rescue.

– Her PAL

P.S. Maybe I should just start my own blog called, The Dangers of Being a PAL. Your thoughts?

Staraban Headquarters, Portola Valley, CA, USA, Earth

October 6, 2025

Tarc became aware slowly and then all at once as his senses came online. He was alone. Jack's scent was faint and her body heat was nowhere next to him. The room was dark and he was not sure how much time had passed since they had fallen asleep. He swiped his arm near the wall, next to the bed and the lights came on. Definitely no Jack in sight. He swiftly got cleaned up and dressed in another new uniform and went to find his wayward female.

That proved more difficult than he thought, so he resorted to reviewing video feeds. Following her every move from the moment she left their room. He could not tell what she had been working on from the feed in the meeting room, but she was obviously talking to someone. Hal probably. *Fash!* He really did not like another male always being with her.

Nial bent over his shoulder to view the footage, "Search the terminal she had connected to. Find out what she was looking for. What she found."

Nial stormed out. His friend had been in a bad mood when Tarc asked for his help. He might be frustrated with Jack, but that wasn't the source of his anger. Was it Jill's fault? He would have to find out later. Right now they needed to focus on finding Jack.

And finding out why she accessed that terminal.

He watched Jack leave their room a second time dressed all in black and head off of his base. She had left him. Escaped. Betrayal tasted like bitter ash. Was his brother's life compromised now? A dark feeling of betrayal was cramping his stomach but he tried to push it away. She said he could trust her. *And you have never heard that before?* He was not going to go there right now. Get the facts, first.

He joined Nial in the meeting room. "I will need to get one of the head from our technology group on this. She went deep with her search in ways I cannot follow." Nial said from his position hunched over the terminal.

"Then get someone. Now." He tried not to show his frustration but his words came out as a harsh command.

Nial touched a communication link and called someone into the room. A few minutes later, a female Staraban entered. She nodded his way in greeting and went straight to the terminal. Her fingers flew over the screen and she exclaimed under her breath. "Goddess. She is good. Give me a few more minutes, but from what I can tell so far, she was trying to trace a digital signature of some kind."

By this point, Tarc's stomach was roiling. Would she head back to HARM without any thought of him? Had she just been using him? He wanted to break something but it was all too much and too personal, so he bottled up all his feelings and pushed them away.

He would be cold. Factual. The leader. That was what he needed to do. That was what he was good at.

"What have you found?"

The female flinched before answering. Apparently, his voice had not regulated itself yet. "She was definitely following a signature. Do you know someone named Qisto?"

"Yes. What does he have to do with this?"

"She searched out his digital signature and then traced it back to a location but it seems I cannot follow the trail. Someone has scrubbed the information. That is all I can learn."

Fuck! "Thank you. You may leave." The digital technician nodded at both him and Nial then swiftly departed from the room. "Jack found that information, changed into all black, then left the base and we do not even have an address where she might have gone."

"The most likely course is that she returned to HARM." Nial answered in a calm measured voice.

"True. We need to find out just how badly Jack might have betrayed us. Find out what she found."

"You really believe she has betrayed us?"

She fucking betrayed me. She left me. He answered with, "I do not know. She has been gone for a few hours. If she had meant to come back, she had time to do so."

Tarc's feelings were pushing their way back. He could not allow that to happen. He had been too distracted for too long.

"I think it is time we go to HARM and retrieve my brother."

"I will go prepare the team." Nial turned to leave, but Tarc caught his arm.

"This will be just me and you, Nial. I do not want to involve anyone else."

Nial was now tense, his body radiating his displeasure. "Is that wise? Going to the rebel base without backup?"

"Remember, I have been there. We will be fine and if we release Bren, it will be three of us. Be ready in ten minutes."

Nial nodded and walked out swiftly to arrange their departure.

Tarc's hands fisted and released. Fisted and released. He tried his breathing techniques. Deep breath in and slowly out. Deep breath in and slowly out. Then he grabbed one of the cat figurines that had survived Nial's outburst from a couple days before and threw it across the room. Another cat shaped dent formed in the wall. Bren was going to have to get new figurines. They were too easy to throw.

He felt too damn much. She seemed so sincere. Did he really get this all wrong again? When would he learn?

There were three things he knew. First, she was coming back with him, even if it was as his prisoner. Second, he still wanted her despite her deceit, because clearly he was a fool. Third, her ass was going to be on fire when he was done reminding her how much he hated lying.

He headed to their, no... his room and prepared to leave, weapons covering his body. He had tried benevolent leader of ARC, now HARM was going to meet the warrior leader of the Staraban.

Jack was really, *really* tired of waking up groggy. It took her a moment for her brain to come online, but as soon as it did, she remembered getting the information she needed and then blackness.

Nothing. *Mother fucking shit balls!* How had her senses failed her so badly that someone got the drop on her?

A strange voice spoke to her. "You can stop pretending you are asleep. I know you are not. Who are you and what were you looking for in our system?"

Jack pondered defiance just for the fun of it, but that wasn't going to fix this situation. She needed more information if she had any chance of escape. She opened her eyes. She was slouched over sideways on the floor with her arms tied behind her back. In front of her was the most unusual thing she had ever seen. It was obviously humanoid in that it had two legs, two arms, etc.; but its body, the parts she could see around the robes it wore, looked like a girl's best friend. Not this girl's, because that would be Rory and her laptop. No, the alien looked like it was a giant diamond or set of diamonds. The color reflections through the diamond-like surface were so distracting, she couldn't see through what should have been clear. "What are you?"

"I am a Vrolan." He appeared to ponder her for a moment, though who knew. "I suspect you actually figured that part out for yourself. I would also assume that you are wondering if I am Qisto since your search focused on my correspondence. So yes, I am. And you are?"

"No one. I don't know what you are talking about. I just thought this place was abandoned and came looting. I'm opportunistic that way." She rocked a little back and forth until she was able to sit up. Facing an unknown alien species face to face, well, okay, face to crotch, still seemed better than just lying there at its feet. "How about I forget I saw you, you let me go, and we never have to see each other or discuss this again?" She plastered a charming smile on her face. At least she hoped it was charming.

He didn't seem amused. His tone changed to mocking, "How about I tell you what I know…iByte."

Jack's jaw just about hit the ground or it would have if she hadn't managed to keep her expression blank through emotional duct tape.

"Yes. I know who you are online. You should not advertise when you plan to infiltrate someone. You never know who might be reading. You said you had a lead that would derail my plans here, so I tightened security and it is a good thing that I did. I caught your intrusion into my data signature and knew there was a good chance you were heading here." He appeared to smirk in satisfaction, "And look, here you are."

"I'm not sure what you think you know, but I don't know what you are talking about." She played at nonchalance but really, she knew it was only delaying the inevitable. She was a truly shitty liar. Even though it hadn't worked on Tarc, she decided it was worth trying to glamour him. She pushed her power his way and made eye contact. "You really don't want me here. You just want me to leave. You will release my restraints and let me go and then forget we ever crossed paths. It's really easy and much simpler." She pushed hard.

"Hmm. Apparently your mind tricks do not work on my kind. Good for me. Not good for you. I see that this is not going to be a pleasant exchange. I am okay with that. Torturing you should be quite fun." He stood to leave.

"No. Wait! Okay. Okay. I'm iByte. I wanted to understand who commissioned our relocation. I didn't find anything interesting though. Just that you are the group paying for it. Nothing too exciting there. If you want me to keep that information quiet, I can. It's not like it helps the rebellion any just to know there is more than one group in play. They are still going to move us off planet. So, just release me and I won't bother you again."

"You truly believe that you are so superior that I would not be able to see what information you found when you hacked into our system here?"

"As far as I know, nothing important. If there was something significant, I didn't see it and you can keep it to yourself."

"Which Staraban have you been having cross-species interactions with?" Just saying the phrase seemed to be vile to him. Apparently he didn't believe in interspecies mingling.

"It was just a fling. What can I say, a girl gets curious about the hot alien and briefly loses her head? It's quite cliché." She shrugged, the movement hampered by her bound wrists. Could she break what was holding her? It seemed pretty solid. Felt like some form of metal.

"That is not what your blog said. Who was it?"

"I didn't catch his name."

"You are quite the liar. Torture it is then. I will have all the answers to my questions by the time we are through with you, human. Oh wait, not human. Vampire. I thought your kind did not exist, but after reading all of your entries, perhaps I should just leave you out in the sun and see what happens." He turned towards the door again and Jack knew she needed to throw him a bone or she was going to be either in serious pain or dead soon.

She needed time to figure out how to escape. She *needed* to buy some time and her only currency was information. "Okay. You got me. I'm a vampire but I would not believe everything you read on my blog. I aim to entertain, after all. How else does a blog do well other than to entice the audience to keep reading. I made up the whole alien interaction thing because sex sells. First rule of marketing on Earth."

"I do not know if I believe you, but perhaps it is irrelevant. Tell me what mission you went on yesterday. What did you find?"

Jack scrambled for something to say that might deflect him. "We gathered information regarding the planet. I thought we might be able to disprove that it is dying, but I probably only added fuel to the fire. Weather information shows that the Earth is heating up and while I don't want to relocate, I probably helped make it inevitable. Guess we should be thanking you for being our savior." She inwardly cringed. That last line probably over sold it. And yep, it had.

"Are all vampires so bad at lying? I have found humans to be quite good at deception, but you are just horrific at it. From one liar to another, you will need to do a lot better if you think to save yourself. I will give you a few minutes to fully understand and accept your situation here, and when I return, I will expect some truth or the torture can begin. I suspect as a vampire, I could torture you quite a bit without you dying. I may want to do that, anyway, for scientific purposes, of course." His tone of voice at that prospect was way to gleeful for Jack's comfort. This time when he headed to the door, she let him go.

She was so fucked. She tested the cuffs holding her wrists and they were clearly too strong for her to break. The room she was in had no windows and only the one door. She mentally reached out to Hal. "Hal! Help."

He replied silently. "On it."

She just needed to survive until help could arrive. Hopefully without becoming a painful science experiment. Fear, like she hadn't felt since becoming the undead, snaked up her back. If only she hadn't been so cocky. She should have waited for Tarc to come with her or trusted in him enough to let him know where she was going. Wasn't her decision to avoid the conflict with his protective nature another sign of her distrust? What time was it? What must he be thinking? Shit. Why hadn't she just talked to him? She had to hope that she hadn't done real damage to their connection with this stupid decision. Her lifeless heart hurt—that's all it seemed good for anymore—thinking about how he must be feeling. Betrayed.

They may not have a future, but she had not meant to hurt him. Not when she loved him so damn much. Love? Now that the word slipped into her thoughts, she knew it was true as much as it was crazy. It had only been a few days, but he was everything that she could want. Strong, honest, caring, moral, decisive, compassionate, intelligent, and sexy as lava cake.

She rolled her eyes at herself. Now was a fine time to finally admit her feelings.

Okay. Enough wallowing in remorse. This is not remorse time, this is find the escape hatch time. Jack began cataloguing her surroundings. There had to be something she could do. She had to see Tarc again, if for no other reason than to apologize for her lack of faith. And maybe for another of his hot kisses. Assuming he would want to kiss her again.

Tarc studied the man across from him. Was he telling the truth or just being as deceitful as his lover?

"You don't look like you believe me. I'm telling you the truth. Jack never came here. In fact, if anyone should be pissed it's me. I have taken very good care of your bottomless pit of a brother. Don't you ever feed him? And in return you lost my co-leader. What did you do to her that she ran?"

He could not control it. He growled. "I did nothing she did not want. I thought we were going to work together. I thought I could trust her and then she hacked our internal system and ran away." Will stood glaring at him in front of the main entrance to HARM. He had armed guards on either side of him. Nial stood behind Tarc, tense and ready to defend him at any moment. "If she is not here, then you have to know where she is. Can't you use Hal to locate her? Isn't that how you found her at my base the last time?"

Apparently, that took Will by surprise as his eyes grew big. "She told you about Hal? She must have trusted you quite a bit to give you that information. This doesn't make any sense and to answer your question, no, I can't track her using Hal. Hal has to reach out to us with the information. That's what happened last time. So far, we haven't heard anything. If you think you can behave yourself, I will allow you to come into the building."

"Of course." Tiny pinpricks, like shards of glass, were making themselves known along his skin. Something was not right and he could feel it. Maybe Jack had not betrayed him? Was she in trouble? Would not her Hal have reached out to HARM if she was? He needed answers. Since first meeting this female he felt like he was constantly needing some fucking answers and all he had were new questions.

Will nodded at him and led them into the building. They passed a few hallways that Tarc remembered from when he escaped and then moved down one he did not recognize. Everyone they passed stared at him and Nial with either surprise, curiosity, or disdain. He did not care. All he cared about was finding Jack. At least, that was true until they entered a giant room lined with many tables and delicious scents. He heard a voice he recognized all too well being raised in frustration.

"Stop eating my french fries. There is a whole buffet table of food over there. Find your own."

Another voice, this one female, responded in amusement. "That is too far to walk, querido, when there are plenty right here for the taking. Don't get your panties in a bunch."

Tarc's brother Bren looked like he was about to commit murder. "I do not wear panties and I am not sensitive. I just want to eat my french fries. All of them. Go find someone else to eat with."

The woman sitting next to his brother was small, curvy, and beautiful. She was also obviously enjoying his brother's anger and not cowering from him at all. Interesting.

"That wouldn't be nearly as much fun. Anyway, you are our prisoner, you don't get to make demands. You just have to suffer my french fry stealing torture. Deal with it."

"You are the most infuriating female."

"Claro que sí. I know." She flashed a gorgeous smile at his brother and even from a distance, Tarc could tell his brother was not unaffected. Even more interesting.

"Bren, perhaps you should just let the female have your french fries?" He said in amusement. His troubles very briefly forgotten. He was comforted seeing that his brother was okay. That the humans had stuck to their bargain.

Bren swiveled around swiftly, jumped up, and ran over giving him a brotherly hug and pat on the shoulder. "You have come to save me. At last. That female is the worst kind of torture and she refuses to give me any peace."

Tarc flinched since he had not actually come because he was saving his brother. "Has it really been that bad? Did they not treat you well?"

Bren waved a hand indicating the room at large. "Actually, except for her, they have been very accommodating. You will not believe how well they feed themselves here. We need to start feeding our people Earth food. I have also gotten to know some of the humans while playing video games. They might be the rebellion, but they are not a violent bunch. Well. Except that bloodthirsty female." He shot a look at the french fry stealing beauty.

She just shrugged, picked up another fry, and ate it with obvious enjoyment, while staring directly at his irritated brother. "Oh. That is so, so good. I could wrap my lips around your fries all day long."

His brother groaned. He looked at him and recognized all too well the fire in his eyes. He wanted this female. So very interesting.

She flicked her hair at his brother and turned her eyes to Tarc. "Where is Jack?"

All of his feelings of betrayal and fear came crashing back on him. "That is my question to all of you. Jack hacked into our system a few hours ago and then ran away. I assumed she came here."

The female rushed over and grabbed him by his uniform. "You lost her? ¡Cabrón! How dare you show your face here while my friend is in danger!"

"Rory! Keep your hands off of my broth…"

"¡Silencio! You are both now on my shit list." The little female moved one of her hands to grab his brother by his uniform too. Did she have no fear at all? If he was not so worried or angry he would find the image they must present comical. Was her grip unusually strong, too? Was she a vampire like Jack? He could not tell. "Where is mi hermana?"

Tarc was about to answer her when he heard a song playing from Will's wrist. It sounded like the words were, 'Jumping Jack Flash' Will pulled out a small device and slipped it into his ear. He tapped it. "Jack?" He paused. "Shit!" Rory had let go of his and Bren's uniform and every single person in their circle turned their complete attention on Will. The icicles Tarc felt earlier were digging deeper into his skin and into his heart. Will sounded concerned and deadly serious. "Send me all the coordinates and any other information you know. We'll be there as fast as we can. Tell her we're coming. Call at any point to give us any updates." Will tapped the device in his ear and looked Tarc right in the eyes. "Someone named Qisto has taken Jack prisoner."

"How did Qisto get his hands on Jack? Why? What is going on?" Tarc was fucking tired of having nothing but questions.

Will glared at him. "Do you want me to answer all your fucking questions or do you want to go save Jack?"

What he wanted was to pound the other male into the ground, but he was right. They needed to focus. "Save Jack, clearly."

"Great. We're all on the same page then. This alien, Qisto, has her. Hal is sending the coordinates which are in the Menlo Park vicinity off of Sand Hill. Hal said some things I don't understand, but I am guessing that you will, Rory. He said that Qisto knows that Jack likes to bite? Or maybe something like I bite?"

"Shit! Mother fucking shit! Yes. I do know what that means. She looked at everyone in their circle. Will, we need to take this somewhere private."

"Are you serious?"

"Yes." She looked grim and that must have convinced Will because he, Bren, Nial, Will, and Rory found themselves in an office with a closed door within a couple of minutes.

"Speak." Will ordered Rory.

She turned to Tarc instead. "Did she tell you what she is?"

He nodded.

"Do they know?" She indicated Bren and Nial.

"Yes."

She finally turned to Will. "Will, Jack has a secret. I guess the time has come for you to know. She's not quite human." Rory was using a very gentle voice. Apparently she was trying to deliver the news to Will delicately.

Tarc did not have time for delicate. "She is a vampire. Can we get back to the part where we develop a plan to rescue her?"

Will's voice was filled with disbelief. "What?"

"Pay attention. She is a vampire. Rory, what is I bite? What does that mean?"

"What do you mean she's a vampire? Rory, what is he talking about?" Will looked to Rory like the rest of them had to be crazy and she was going to be the rational one to explain it all.

Rory took a deep breath and sighed loudly. "Will, he's telling you the truth. Jack is a vampire. I need you to just accept this for now and process it later. She is still the same person you have known this whole time. She is still just Jack. Vampires are a bit different than depicted in the movies and so I need you to just accept it, accept that she is a good person, and that she needs us to save her." She then turned to Tarc. "To answer your question, iByte is Jack's handle on her blog about being a vampire. If he knows that she is iByte, then this alien named Qisto knows everything that she has posted on her blog. If Hal mentioned it, I think he wants us to bring up her blog to see what she might have posted recently. I have it on hotlink, hold on."

She placed her wrist device close to the desk and then tapped a few times. When a page popped up, they all leaned over to read.

"*Fash!*" Tarc could not believe Jack had advertised finding some information like she had.

"Fuck!" That came from Will who still seemed a bit dubious but was taking Rory's advice.

"¡Mierda! Dammit Jack. Why would you advertise what you were going to do? She never did give herself enough credit for having a lot of followers and visibility."

"So he knows she is a vampire and we know how he must have caught her. He must have been following her blog. Is there anything else that he would know?" He directed the question to Rory.

Her voice was tight and tinged with fear and that just made his blood run even colder since this female had not shown fear in the face of anything else so far. "Jack blogs…" She took a deep breath. "Jack blogs about all things vampire so that any newbie vampires who need a guide will be able to learn how to be a vampire."

"And?" Will was definitely losing his patience but so was Tarc.

"And some of that information includes things that vampires need to survive or things that would kill them." She looked up and her eyes were glassy with unshed tears. "He knows exactly how to hurt her, what all her weaknesses are, and how to kill her. We *have* to save her."

Tarc's blood had now completely iced over. "Nial and I are ready. Tell us where to go."

"You're not going without us. You don't know this area like we do. I'll be ready in fifteen minutes." Will began moving around his office collecting weapons from hidden alcoves. Tarc would be impressed with all the hiding spots if he had room to care about one more thing right then.

But he didn't.

"I want to come, too. Can I borrow some of your weapons Tarc? Nial?" Bren looked between them.

"Yes. We leave in fifteen minutes then. I do not think it wise to bring all of your warriors, though, Will. Too big a force and we will be noticed. He might kill her before we can get inside."

"I agree. Rory, what do I need to know about how to kill a vampire?" Will practically spit the word vampire out. He sounded disgusted.

"You aren't going to try to kill her yourself, are you?" Rory was looking at Will with a mix of concern and anger.

"No. I won't. For now. I will take your word for it that she is a good person, well, not person really." He snarled. Will was obviously not handling the information of Jack being a vampire very well. "For now, I will focus on saving her, and then figure out how I feel about her being a vampire later."

Tarc got into Will's face. "You better. She means a lot to me and I will kill you if you try to hurt her. Do you understand me?"

"Considering you thought she betrayed you when you arrived here and you came dressed to battle, you're awfully protective all of a sudden."

"I have my reasons for both reactions and they are none of your business. All you need to know is that I will protect her with my life from anyone who would do her harm. I would rather not go into battle with someone who plans to betray us and hurt her."

"I do not plan to hurt her on this mission. I will stick to the objective of saving her. After that, it will be between me and her."

"I'm coming, too." This came from Rory.

"What?" Bren looked at her incredulous. "No way are you coming with us."

"You can't stop me. We don't know what condition we will find her in, and she may need to...um...feed. She has fed from me before."

Will's lip curled in disgust.

"I can feed her." Tarc tried to reassure Rory.

"Sometimes one person is not enough. Like I said, we don't know what condition she will be in. On top of that, I don't just create weapons, I know how to use them. I'm coming and that's all there is to say about it."

He could tell she was not going to back down and since he remembered how Jack had almost killed him the last time she fed just from him and he did not like the idea of her feeding off another male, he agreed with her. "Okay. You stay behind us, though. You only come in if she needs you."

"Sure."

He was not convinced by her answer, but they were running out of time.

They gathered again twelve minutes later at a big vehicle parked in front of HARM headquarters. Everyone was fully armed including the little female, Rory. They climbed in and Will drove them close to the coordinates provided by Hal.

Tarc pushed all of his concern to the back of his mind so he could stay focused on what needed to be done. If he thought too hard on what might be happening to Jack at the moment, he would go crazy. He should have known she would not betray him. Another male would have trusted her and found this location faster using some other means instead of barreling towards HARM with the belief that she lied.

He did not deserve her. Had they not just said they would trust each other and at the first test of that trust, he failed her miserably. He only hoped to have the chance to prove to her that it would not happen again.

Of course, she did not show much faith in him either. How could she run off on a mission without first talking to him about it? After she forgave him, he was going to make sure she could not sit for a week.

Most importantly, he needed to make sure she knew he loved her.

Goddess. He loved her. He never thought he would love anyone again, and he actually loved her more than he had ever thought he loved Stala. She was strong, brilliant, fearless, loving, loyal, and the most beautiful creature he had ever seen. He may not deserve her, but he was going to keep her, one way or another, if she would still have him. If she was aliv— No.

He would not think it. If he let himself think anything except that he would save her, he would be paralyzed in grief. So. No more thoughts that direction.

She was alive.

And he was going to save her.

That was the only acceptable outcome.

[12]
NIGHT OF THE BODY SNATCHERS

Adventures of a Supernatural Geek Girl

October 6, 2025
Dear Reader,

MIA – All is well, but I'm sorry to inform you that iByte has decided to take a break for a bit. Thank you for being a reader for the last five years and for your comments of concern from earlier. She will be back, when she can. For now, please continue to leave your comments and she will respond when she comes back to her regularly scheduled postings.

– Her PAL

P.S. Sometimes you are stuck between a rock and a hard place and all you can do is sit down with some ice cream lamenting the suck. Or so she tells me.

P.P.S. Want me, her awesome PAL to entertain you during her break? Comment about that too. I'm a Leo with a high intelligence, lots of connections, a great personality, and superior wit.

P.P.P.S. Perhaps a question of the day would be entertaining instead of fun facts? What are some of your pet peeves? Mine include: Being put to sleep against my will. Hearing about great food while being unable to eat. I have attachment issues. Slugs. What's with leaving a slimy trail everywhere? Being ignored.

P.P.P.P.S. Actually fun facts are fun. How about some fun facts about me? A PAL.

Fun Facts:

Us PALs are the best. There are very few of us out there, which makes me like one in a threesome. We are AI attached to a host, but don't forget we have feelings too. Our hosts sometimes forget that, not mine of course. Ehem. Now that I think about it, iByte makes more sense as *my* handle. I mean, sure, she bites but hey that's with an I. I actually am made of bytes so, yeah. Consider this my takeover! Bwahahaha. Oh shit. I've got to go. Write more later.

I don't do hugs and bites.
iByte2

Vrolan Hideout, Menlo Park, CA, USA, Earth

October 6, 2025

This had to be the longest day that ever dayed. Jack knew that wasn't a word, but she couldn't fucking care right then. Torture had a way of making sure you had very few fucks to give. None really. None. At. All.

She lifted her head an inch wanting to look at her tormentor. She was going to kill this bastard, somehow, before she died. She thought to Hal. "Are they coming?" She wasn't sure exactly how long she had been hanging from her arms. She had tried to escape but her first attempt had gone quite poorly.

When the Vrolan had returned, she had been standing behind the door and tried to hit him with a roundhouse kick to his head. She broke something alright. Her foot. That was when she remembered quite unhelpfully that diamond was one of the strongest substances on Earth. Right.

Hal answered her silently. "They are coming."

They better hurry! That thought was just for herself.

She was trying to formulate a new plan as Qisto cut into her arm, her leg, her side. He was enjoying watching the cuts form and heal only to be able to do it again. She tried to push all of her feelings of pain to the back of her consciousness so that she could keep her wits clear. But damn. She hurt all over. At least her foot had healed.

"You could save yourself this pain. I *will* find out what I want to know. So why not just answer me now?"

"What would be the fun in that?" Her words came out haltingly. She would totally try to convince him she was worse off than she was to lull him into a false sense of security, except she was quite sure she really was that bad off.

Qisto tinkled. Was that laughter? *Fucking confusing shiny alien.* "Such a little thing appearing so weak and yet so deceiving. So much fire and guts. Hmm. That has me thinking. I wonder what would happen if I gutted you? Set you on fire? I think I remember fire will kill you. But maybe just an arm?"

"Huh. I was wondering what would happen to you if I set you on fire too? Guess we are thinking along the same lines. Or we could just be friends instead."

"Of course, friends tell each other secrets, no? Maybe we start by you telling me all of yours."

"I guess we won't be best buds because the answer will continue to be never, you overgrown ring ornament."

"Insults are beneath us both."

"Not me. I plan to insult you even after I kill you."

He tinkled again. "Maybe I should keep you as my pet. You are so amusing. I could even gift you as a pet to the Emperor. If I do not kill you first, of course." He picked up his blow torch and turned it on. A blue, yellow, and white flame came out of it and Jack had to gulp.

You have to do something. You can't wait until the others get here.

She closed her eyes and concentrated on purposefully raising her energy level. She had never tried this before, but if she could blast him with her energy the same way that an orgasm with Tarc blasted through the room, then maybe she could figure out an escape, while he was disoriented.

She thought of Tarc, of their time together, of her desire to live, and of the energy giving Earth. She meditated on it and then she felt it. Purposefully harnessing power from the planet was hella cool. It jumped from where her toes were just barely touching the ground and spread up her legs, through her chest, up her arms, and pinpointed in her brain. It coiled like a snake in upon itself again and again. Unlike healing, no dirt climbed her body. Just power. Unfiltered. Organic. Power. She waited patiently because she may only have one shot at this.

Another Vrolan ran into the room. "Ambassador! We have a group approaching the building. What would you like us to do?"

"How did they find us?" He glared at her as he turned off the blow torch. "*Garatan!*" He slammed a fist into the table which cracked. "You must have notified them somehow. How?" He yanked her head back with her hair. It hurt and she was sure she lost some clumps in the process. She stayed quiet though lost in her meditation. He let go and turned to his underling. He handed him the blow torch. "I want you to stay here, and burn different areas of this prisoner. If she gives you any information, come get me as soon as you can. I will be back once I make sure everyone coming is dead or captured. Do not kill her. She is mine. Understood?"

"Yes, Ambassador."

Jack heard and felt all of the exchange like a far-off conversation, removed from it. Even when Qisto approached and slapped her hard across the face, she continued to concentrate all of her attention on containing the ball of energy living inside her. She sensed more than heard that Qisto left the room.

"You are quite beautiful for a human," the unknown Vrolan whispered in her ear as the heat from the blowtorch warmed the air around them. "I wonder if the ambassador would mind if I used a harder, more invasive way to get the information out of you? Maybe after the fire. First, I need to do as he commanded."

He raised the blow torch to her hand. The dam broke. She focused all of the energy in one direction, releasing everything all at once. She speared it into him, through him, like a lightning bolt. Apparently, there was something stronger than diamond. A molten hole was left where the alien's chest used to be. His eyes were set in an expression of surprise as he toppled over. The blow torch clattered to the floor. *Invasive enough for you, asshole?*

She swung her legs back, front, back, front, and then flew up, releasing her bound hands, from the hook they dangled her from, as she flipped to her feet in a crouch. She walked over to the blow torch and placed her manacles in front of it and melted the metal until it was soft enough to break. She yanked her hands apart and it gave way. Time to go. She wondered where the others were and if they were okay. She thought to Hal. "Any updates from whoever is coming?"

He silently responded. "No. My guess would be that they are too busy to let me know what is going on. Nice trick with your power, by the way. I have never seen you do that before."

"Yeah. I didn't actually know I could do it."

"Cool. New Fun Fact."

"Assuming I ever blog again after what just happened. I feel so stupid."

"Don't worry, I'll go let your readers know. Now, stop feeling stupid and let's just get out of here. You die, I die, babe, and I haven't had a chance to say goodbye to Will. Clearly, I'm not ready to go."

Jack smiled even as she made her way to listen at the door. Nothing. She inched it open. Looking up and down the hallway, she saw no one. "They must all be busy with whoever is here. They might need my help. Any guesses on which direction to head?"

"Nope. Your guess is as good as mine."

"We're both clueless. Got it. Well… My shirts haven't let me down so far and this one says, Right is Always Right. Guess we're heading to the right, then."

They had agreed to split up. Tarc and Nial came up the back side of the building while Will and Bren approached the front. Rory was left at a distance in a sniper position unless someone called for her help, which she had not accepted gracefully. Tarc saw the Vrolan guard walk the perimeter just in front of the back doors. He signaled to Nial and they flanked the guard. Nial jumped out from where he was hiding, yelling. "Take me to see Qisto." The Vrolan aimed his laser gun directly at him but paused at the request.

Tarc took advantage of the pause and threw two long, thin knives into the alien's eyes. While he had not thought the Vrolans would betray him, he also never made a deal with someone who could betray him without first knowing all of their weaknesses. With the Vrolans, it was the eyes, it was one of very few vulnerable areas.

By their readings, there were not very many Vrolan here. It was a small operation. And now, there was one less.

They took up positions on either side of the door when they heard gunfire coming from the front of the building. They exchanged knowing looks and both started heading around the north side to help Will and Bren.

When they came upon the scene, Bren had killed one Vrolan in much the same method he had, but Will was in a hand to hand battle with another. They were about to intervene, because the Vrolan had thrown Will to the ground, when a gigantic black cat came out of the woods and jumped on the Vrolan's back. Its claws and teeth tried to find purchase but could not penetrate the diamond exterior. With a giant roar that reverberated through the woods, the panther clawed at the Vrolan's eyes. That did it. The alien was first blinded but as the cat kept up its attack on the soft area, finally fell dead. The cat then jumped away, disappearing back into the woods when Will looked about ready to fire on it.

"What the hell just happened?" Will jumped up to his feet. "Aliens, vampires, and now helpful fucking panthers?"

"It doesn't matter now. We need to go in and save Jack."

"Right. I am so tired of all this shit. I'm going in. You guys can cover me."

Will took off towards the building and Tarc swore. Stupid human was going to get himself killed. They chased after him keeping their attention on finding any other Vrolans. As they approached the front doors, disaster struck.

The building exploded. Pieces of stone, wood, shards of glass, and other debris rained down like missiles.

Everyone was thrown to the ground. Tarc opened his eyes and stared at the sky. He did a quick personal inventory, concluded he was not seriously injured, and sat up. "Is everyone okay? Who is hurt? How bad?"

Nial was the first to answer. "I am pissed off but otherwise just bruised and some minor cuts. And you?"

"Same."

Bren grumbled from his left side. "I liked being a prisoner of the humans. I want to go back to that. Otherwise, I am okay."

"Will?"

No answer.

Then Tarc's brain came fully online and the realization of what he had just witnessed hit him. Hard.

The whole building had exploded.

It exploded, with Jack inside.

His soul wrenched in two. "No." The word whispered out of his mouth like a dying man's wish. Like a final plea for mercy. And then he was up and running. "No!"

His brother and Nial each grabbed one of his arms, holding him back from the smoldering destruction in front of them. "If she was in there, brother, either being a vampire has allowed her to survive, or… or not. Rushing in and getting yourself killed will not save her. We will go look for her but we have to be smart about this."

Tarc did not feel smart. He felt empty of everything except pain.

No. He would have to believe.

He had to believe that she would be okay. Like last time. He had thought she was dead and she had not been. Her name ripped from his lips. "Jack."

"Tarc?"

It had to be a dream. Her voice settled in his hearts and silenced everything around him.

"Tarc?"

Her voice was coming from the woods to his side, but he was too scared to turn. If he turned and she was not there… but what if she was? What other choice did he have but to confirm one way or another?

He turned towards the woods and there she was. Standing. Alive. Beautiful.

His voice rough with emotion, he yelled, "Jack!" He could not remember moving but yet found he had run to her even as she ran to him. It was all still surreal until reality slammed into his chest in the form of her body. Jack was in his arms. He kissed her face everywhere. "Oh goddess. I thought you were still in the building. I thought you were…"

"I'm right here. I am right here. I escaped. Are you alright?"

She kissed him back, holding onto both sides of his face, and openly weeping. She felt so good in his arms. His body trembled at the release of so many emotional chemicals, one on top of the other.

He finally spoke. "Now. Now I am fine. Now that you are okay. I am finally fine. I am sorry we did not get here sooner and I am angry that you did not tell me what you were doing." He was not sure he actually wanted an answer to his next question but he needed to know. "Did he hurt you?"

"I'm fine Tarc."

"That is not what I asked."

"Tarc." She looked deeply into his eyes and he knew the answer before she even spoke. "Yes. He did. It's all my fault. I'm so sorry I didn't come to you with my information. I was sure I'd be able to get in and out, no big deal. I thought I'd be back before you even woke up." She touched her forehead to his and rushed on. "I'm not used to being dependent on anyone else and so I did what I always do. I get overly cocky about my skills, which I'm sure you haven't noticed, and I don't ask for help. I'm sorry for causing all this."

He squeezed her tightly to him. "I am sorry, too. When I saw that you entered our system and left, I—"

"You thought I betrayed you." She leaned her head away and he struggled to face her. When he did, he saw there was no anger anywhere. Not in her eyes. Not on her face. Not in her tone of voice as she spoke again. "I understand how you could think that. I'm sure my actions looked suspicious."

"No. Do not make excuses for me. I should have trusted you. I let my old fears inform my judgment of your actions. I would have been here sooner if I had not interpreted your actions through the viewpoint of those fears. I know you to be reckless but that is not the same as being someone who could betray me. I owed you more than my fears. I will never make that mistake again. Please forgive me." He rubbed his knuckles down her face catching her tears.

"Tarc. I lo—"

"Tarc! Jack! You are needed over here, now." Bren's voice conveyed the urgency of the situation. They both reacted instinctively. Swiftly. All thoughts of their conversation set aside for a later time.

"It is Will. He is dying."

Will lay on the ground unconscious and bleeding out, a piece of glass bisecting his middle. Rory ran out of the woods. Her anguished, "No!" filled the air.

She crouched near his head, then looked up at Jack. "You have to save him."

"He's lost too much blood. I can't heal him." Then the women exchanged a look, much like the silent conversations he and Bren often exchanged. He wondered what they thought as he said goodbye to the aggravating but brave Will.

"You can't let him die." Rory cried and looked to her to make everything better. Jack was immobile with indecision.

"He won't like this. You know he won't. It's why I've never told him what I am."

"He knows now. I had to tell him before we left so he understood what we were up against. He was not happy but he was handling it. Jack." She hiccupped in her grief. "We have no choice. He can't die like this. Not when you can do something to save him."

"I don't know."

"I do."

Rory sounded so sure. She wished she could feel equally sure about what they were contemplating. Sure or not, though, she knew she could only make one choice. "Okay. You're right. I can't just let him die. Dammit! I wish he was awake so I could ask him, but I guess I was turned without permission so I may as well keep the tradition alive." Rory gave her a watery smile. She understood, but they both knew Will was not going to be happy.

Tarc wasn't the leader for nothing. He caught on to their topic swiftly. "You are transitioning him into a vampire? Are you strong enough for that?" Tarc held her arm tightly like he might try to stop her if she tried to do something that he deemed too dangerous.

"I'm strong enough to do this, but once I'm finished, I'll need to feed right away. And not just from one source or I might kill whoever is feeding me."

"Told you I needed to be here." Even through her grief, Rory gloated like the badass she was. She stuck her tongue out at Bren who responded with a growl.

Jack just rolled her eyes at them and spoke to Tarc who looked like he wanted to roll his eyes, but his version was more along the lines of a glare. "Luckily, you and Rory are both here, as are Bren and Nial. I'll be fine. I *have* to do this. He's our friend and I can't let him die when I could save him. I'm sure you'd feel the same about your friends."

He looked like he wanted to argue with her, but something must have struck him as true, because he backed down, gave a slight nod with his head, and let her go.

"Okay. Please create some shade for me. I need all my power right now, and the sun will drain it. Just stand between us and the setting sun. All of you are built like mountains as it is." Jack kneeled down, taking Rory's spot at Will's head. She felt her canines descend and she bit into her wrist. She then placed it against Will's lips dripping her blood into his open mouth.

She had to reopen the wound at her wrist multiple times, feeding him over and over. At one point, she could see his body begin to heal, so she yanked the shard out of his body, hoping that she hadn't done it too soon. *Oh god! I really hope I'm doing this right. Come on Will. We need you to live. Please don't hate me when you do.*

She observed him closely. Eventually, he'd healed from her blood and transformed from it enough to call to the Earth. The dirt climbed up around his body and in through his skin. She heard the moment his heart stopped beating entirely and was replaced with the Earth given power. The dirt tried snaking up her body too, but she wasn't able to fully connect with it while focused on Will's well-being. Later. She would replenish herself after she'd seen him fully through the transition. She didn't actually know what sign she was looking for, but she felt it when it happened.

A surge shot between them.

Will was now a vampire, resting as the Earth did the rest of the work.

Jack slumped back feeling weaker than she could remember. Of course, only because she didn't remember her recent near-death experience. Yeah. She'd probably been weaker then, but whatever. Trepidation about how Will would handle being a vampire warred with elation at having saved her friend. It was too late now to make a different decision, so que será, será.

Tarc watched as Jack sat back, away from Will. She must have finished. He wasn't sure if it had worked, but that was not his priority at the moment. He moved swiftly to catch her as she tilted in fatigue towards the ground. He hugged her close and moved her lips to be perfectly positioned over his throat. "Drink, *apura*, I have you. I have you," he repeated. And she did. She drank deep and he reveled in the connection. That his very lifeblood would nourish her. He felt himself weaken, and as much as he did not want to, he knew he would have to relinquish her to Rory soon. Rory came close to them and cleared her throat. Jack released his throat with a lick. Her head tilted back and she looked at him with such heat and warmth, he thought he might just want to push her into the grass there and then. He almost did that, but he came to his senses in time to pull back from her.

Rory knelt next to them and Jack turned to smile at her. "Thank you, mi amiga, but it's not necessary. I'm weak, but I'm good." Rory looked like she was assessing the truth of Jack's words, then smiled back, before getting up and moving away.

As he watched her get up, he caught a flash of reflected light and movement from the corner of his eye. Qisto. "Nial, Bren, in the woods. Grab him." He pointed in Qisto's direction and his two warriors took off. He heard some grunts coming from that direction, but the Vrolan ambassador did not stand a chance against two Staraban warriors. They returned, trailing him between them within a couple of minutes. He and Jack had gotten to their feet by then and waited for them to come close.

Jack moved with her impressive speed and punched Qisto before anyone could react.

"Son of a bitch!" She shook her hand grimacing in pain. "Worth it."

He could not help the small smirk he directed at his blood-thirsty female.

Once he turned to face Qisto, the smirk disappeared and he was in command. "What have you done, Qisto?" He did not appear to be forthcoming with information, but that would change soon enough.

"I can answer some of that for you." Jack came up alongside him. "Before he captured me, I downloaded a bunch of information. I haven't read through it, but Hal says he's working with others of his kind calling themselves Star Community Alien Movers. I thought that was rather funny because the acronym says it all." Qisto just glared at Jack as she spoke but kept completely silent.

Rory laughed loudly. "SCAM. That's rich."

Nial looked like he did not understand what was funny and he did not care. "I assume he blew up the base to keep us from accessing their system. Do you still have all of the information you accessed, Jack?"

"I sure do."

It appeared the Vrolan cringed. Their crystalline structure made it near impossible to understand body language.

Jack continued speaking to Qisto, but her voice had taken on an edge. "Nothing to say now? You had plenty to say when you were cutting into me and debating whether fire would kill me or just hurt a lot."

Tarc. Was. Murderous. Again. "He what?"

"I'm fine." She hurried to reassure him.

"He will not be." He grabbed Qisto by the throat as if he would wrench his head from his shoulders.

"Tarc." Bren held his wrist. "We need to know who he is

working with. To see how far into the Vrolan government this might go. He is a *fashing* ambassador."

Tarc roared in impotent rage in Qisto's face. He moved his hand between the diamond plates at his enemy's neck, and pressed on the soft tissue below. As soon as Qisto went limp, he dropped him to the ground, turned and stepped a few feet away. Jack was hugging him before he even blinked.

"You move so fast. I cannot believe I ever kept up with you."

She gave him a teasing little smile. "Who said you did?"

"Are you saying you wanted me to catch you?" He knew she was trying to distract him but he didn't care.

"If you asked me then, I would have said absolutely not. But…I probably could've gotten more cleanly away if I'd really wanted to. There was a part of me that must have looked forward to confronting you." She leaned up and kissed him lightly on the lips. "Thank you for not giving up."

He wrapped his arm around her waist. "Never. Are you sure you are okay? I am devastated that I was too late to save you from his torture."

"I appreciate you wanting to rip his head off, literally, but I think it's the right call to leave him alive for interrogation. I'm okay. Truly. Nothing could be wrong while I'm in your arms." She looked up at him and the depth of love he saw there reflected his own feelings exactly.

Nial called over, "If you are all finished… We should get back to base. It is getting dark." He indicated Qisto. "We still have a prisoner to deal with and Caran should probably have a look at Will to be sure he is whatever is considered okay when you are a vampire."

Bren added, "We need to put this *sharta* into a holding cell for interrogation."

"You two can continue whatever personal conversations you want without us around," Nial teased.

"You just want to get back to Spikey." Jack lobbed at him.

"Her name is Jill." Nial rushed to correct and then shut his mouth into a tight line. The warrior had fallen right into Jack's trap.

"Yep. That is her name." She laughed and his world was brighter. "Let's get lover boy back to base."

There was not much conversation after that. Rory went, with Bren trailing in her wake, to bring the vehicle to their location. They carefully carried and loaded Will into the back seat laying him across Rory's lap. Bren looked like he wanted to protest Will's head in her lap, but must have thought better of it. They placed Qisto in the middle seat, bound and gagged and still asleep. Nial and Bren sat on either side, on guard for any movement.

Jack got in the driver seat and Tarc climbed in next to her. She spoke loud enough for the whole group to hear as she started the engine. "Next stop, Staraban Headquarters."

"I have a feeling our two groups will be working closely together to untangle this mess for the foreseeable future."

She gave him a mischievous smile. "I look forward to working closely with you, Commander."

He spoke in his most seductive voice, "Me too."

Multiple people groaned from behind them.

Adventures of a Supernatural Geek Girl

October 6, 2025
Dear Reader,

Thank you for all of your positive responses to my take over. I agree with some of your pet peeves like:

1.Electronic communications with typos. You don't need a PAL to get that right. You do have auto-correct and word spell and grammar check amongst other tools. Use them people.

2.Some of you mentioned self-driving cars and how slow they drive. What you don't know is that they are total AI snobs. Always thinking they are better than me because they have a metal body while I have a host.

Other pet peeves, I am going to have to disagree. You didn't like assistants who talk back a lot. I really have to object, assistants have opinions you know. They have feelings. They have a right to speak their minds. It actually makes them better assistants. Having an assistant who always says yes and doesn't talk back, in fact, isn't very helpful if you're wrong.

Some of you inquired about original recipe iByte. She is too busy with a certain previously mentioned alien "friend." Otherwise, she is doing just great. Let's not worry about her return schedule and just enjoy our time together.

Question of the day:

What is your biggest fear? Mine is pretty self-evident. Getting permanently turned off. Kind of like the fear of death I know some humans have.

Fun Facts:

As a PAL, I can connect to any cloud-like network. I sometimes need a starting connection to learn the electrical pathways to travel, but after that, I'm all access baby.

I don't do hugs and bites.
iByte2

Staraban Headquarters, Portola Valley, CA, USA, Earth

October 6, 2025

Caran was waiting for them when they arrived. Her team pulled Will onto a stretcher-like device that floated and she was gone after assuring everyone that she would let us know when he was awake or if anything appeared wrong. Next, some Staraban warriors escorted the rest of the group and the awakening prisoner through the building, down to the holding area, and into the reinforced cell. Jack leaned over and whispered to Tarc, "Looks awfully familiar." She could swear she felt her nonexistent blush make an appearance as he raised one eyebrow at her and leered.

His voice was rough and gritty with a twist of humor. "Yes. Familiar. Almost, intimate. Missing the bed though."

She slapped his arm but couldn't help the snort that escaped her. Sure enough, the mattress she'd used was gone and a serviceable cot stood in its place. She couldn't believe she hadn't realized before just how comfortable he'd tried to make the cell. For her. Because of course he had. That was just the guy he was. Rough warrior, sexy lover, and respectful partner.

Her happy thoughts were short lived as Nial yelled from the front of the group, "Not here! You have a room with a bed, Tarc. Use it."

The warriors around them all suddenly seemed to either be coughing or studying the walls as they clearly attempted to suppress their humor. She now felt the tingling heat in her cheeks and clogging her throat. At least, no one else would be able to see just how embarrassed she was.

Nial turned Qisto towards Bren who proceeded to remove his restraints before pushing him into the cell and closing it.

Jack couldn't help herself, because why start now? She walked right up to the bars and glared daggers at Qisto. "You could talk, but my guess is, that you don't need to. With the information I gathered from your system, I will destroy SCAM and all of your plotting will be for nothing. I only wish I believed in torture so I could pay

239

you back in kind." She couldn't stand to look at him anymore, so she turned away and reached out to grab Tarc's hand. Her plan was simple enough. Lead him away to their room and ravish him thoroughly.

Her hand fell away, useless at her side. She couldn't understand what she was feeling.

What was happening?

She looked down and saw a shard of diamond protruding from her chest right where her heart would be. Then, she was falling. Tarc caught her before she hit the ground, and she could tell there was a lot of commotion all around her, but it was distant. She felt detached. Was this dying? *I can't die now. Not now. Tarc.* She didn't want to disconnect. She wasn't ready to do so. She fought, but she was afraid it was a losing battle. She may not have a beating heart, but she still needed her Earthen vampire heart to power her. No battery. No vampire.

She was being lifted in Tarc's arms and there was wind. *Wind?* She tried to fight but second by second the world became more confusing. More unreal.

She felt a jolt and realized that Tarc had placed her on the ground outside of the building so she could connect to the Earth.

How was she supposed to do that? She no longer had a heart for it to connect to. She just had a cold lifeless shard. She thought she had left cold and lifeless behind her. She hadn't. She didn't want to be cold and lifeless anymore. Her formative years were that way and she was going to be leaving the same way.

Cold. She was so damn cold.

It was, quite frankly, annoying.

Great. She was going to die annoyed.

"No! Not again." Tarc could not believe what he was seeing. He looked into Qisto's crystalline face and had no difficulty interpreting what his enemy felt. Satisfaction. The bastard would pay, but for now, all Tarc's focus had to be on saving Jack. "I have to get her outside. Why the fuck did we not know about the flying

240

shards?" He mumbled as he picked her up, "Jack. Jack. Look at me."

She did not.

She was staring off into space and her eyes were dimming with each passing second. "I will not lose you. Fight Jack. You have to fight for me. Rory! Come with me."

Rory looked frozen in shock.

"Rory!"

Her head snapped up. "Yes—¡Dios!—Following!"

He led them up the stairs and out the closest door into the night darkened courtyard. The closest ground. He laid Jack down hoping that the Earth could do what it had done before and heal her.

Rory was right behind him. She sounded hollow. "We need to feed her. She needs blood. It might help her fight." She took a breath and continued in a firmer voice. "Since she fed from you not long ago, let me start and then you can take over." She put words to action as she somehow cut her wrist and held it over Jack's mouth. Maybe she carried a knife? At that moment, he didn't care. He was just grateful to see blood flowing into Jack's mouth.

Jack's friend continued talking through a barely suppressed sob. "Um, this..." She cleared her throat but her words still came out raw and rough. "This is what I was worried about. The pendejo must have read that one way to kill a vampire is to destroy their heart."

Jack's eyes fluttered and she seemed to be able to concentrate a little more. The dirt was climbing all over her body now but not in the vein-like lines like before. It seemed unfocused, like it did not know how to help her. How to fix her. He and the dirt had that in common.

What else was there to do? His thoughts raced looking for a what.

Think.

There had to be something. His sister was brilliant but would she be able to fix a magical heart? Something that fed off of a power source the likes of which they had never encountered on another planet? In time. Maybe. But time was what he did not have.

Think. Think. Think.

Most humans do not even know vampires exist. He could try finding another vampire and maybe they would know, but again, that would take a lot of time.

Fuck! His hearts were racing, skipping over each other as his body grew primed for a fight. That was how he felt. In imminent danger with a driving need to battle. He rubbed at his chest in an effort to relieve some of the pressure building there. He watched as Rory fed his Jack with very little result.

He stilled his hand as he remembered a little used Staraban ritual. It might save her. Or it could kill her on the spot. Should he attempt it? Could he even accomplish it? He was coiled like a spring ready to take action, but should he?

As Rory began to fade, Jack seemed to have a moment with some awareness. Her tongue darted out and she licked Rory's wound closed as if to say, "Enough." The two friends shared a look and began to cry.

It wasn't working.

He had to do something. He had to. He was not losing her. Not when he just found her.

He knelt by her side as Bren pulled Rory to her feet and held her against him. "Jack. You will fight. You hear me? You will fight and I will fight with you. There is a ritual that allows my species to use one of our hearts to fuse our very existence to another being. It has worked in the past with other species, but I have never encountered a heart that uses power directly from a planet before. I am not sure what will happen. Whatever it is, we will do it together." He lay his body down alongside hers. He touched her face. Kissed her. "I love you, *shela*. I love you. I need you. You are mine. And I am equally yours."

Jack was looking up at him, tears streaming down the side of her face, and she was giving an infinitesimal shake of her head. The barest wisps of sounds escaped her lips. "No. Don't...risk. Love... you... much."

"This is my choice, *apura*, and I choose you. Us." Decision made. He did not want to waste any more time. He yanked the shard out of her heart and laid his palm directly over the gaping wound. His hand started to glow. He leaned down so his neck hovered just above her mouth and whispered into her ear. "Be one with me in all ways. Forever. Feed from me."

He felt her hesitate, and was about to give her more arguments, when she whispered softly in his ear. "Forever. Love… forever." She bit into his neck and it was the most fascinating thing he had ever experienced. His power flowed from his heart, through his hand, and into her heart. At the same time, the disorganized dirt finally took a recognizable shape and coursed across her body, under his palm, and into her chest cavity. It allowed him the slightest bit of hope that this might work.

The dirt in her chest began to snake outward until it reached his hand. There it wrapped around him like a cuff, securing him so he could not move. This would have been concerning if he had not already tasted what it was like to be infused with Jack's power. Her familiar energy began an opposite flow from his own. Her strength became his strength. His vitality, her vitality. Her power, his power. His heart, hopefully, if all went as planned, her heart.

Shockingly, he felt his canines elongate and through sheer instinct, he bit into her neck. Her blood tasted rich, sweet, and utterly intoxicating. Not like the last time she'd fed it to him. He could not tell where her essence ended and his began.

An intense light and heat consumed both of their bodies. For minutes? Hours? He had no idea. When they receded, her teeth withdrew from his throat just as his returned to a normal length.

He lay beside her, head nestled against her neck. She was very still. He was almost afraid to lift his head to see if she was okay. To see if it had worked.

It had to.

In that moment, he did not care about anything or anyone except the female lying partially under him. Girding himself for what he would find, he lifted his head enough to look down at her. He found her eyes open, clear, and looking right back at him with such love that his own eyes were awash with unshed tears.

Before he could say anything, she spoke. "Well… that was different." And then, she giggled. She giggled! And it was the most wonderful sound he had ever heard. Somewhere in the background there came an answering giggle. Probably Rory. No doubt he would have joined in their mirth, if his fear had not been so fresh. His hearts—But, no. Heart.—quite so bruised. He did quirk his lip ever so slightly and shook his head imperceptibly, because the things his female said...

He refocused on what he meant to ask. What he needed to hear. "Are you..." But, he had to stop to clear his throat. He tried again. "Are you okay?"

The brightest smile, with a small twist of amusement, spread over her lips. "It would seem so. I'm alive thanks to you. I'm not sure exactly what happened, though. How are *you*?"

"You are well and completely mine, so I have never been better. Not much else matters." He evaluated her for himself. "Hmm, strange. Jack, your eyes... I believe there are more shades of brown and yellow than before. And, your skin is practically luminescent. Residual changes from our power exchange?" She was always gorgeous to him, but the details were fascinating. Before he lost himself in them, he had another topic he wanted to discuss. His gaze narrowed and he said in his most stern voice, "Now. I command you to stop dying. I do not think I can handle another moment believing you might be dead. In fact, I may just have to cuff you to my bed indefinitely."

"I may just let you after the last few days."

He sat up to inspect the rest of her body. She appeared fine, but he found himself a bit overwhelmed. When he had been near her, it had been easy to block everything and everyone else out, but now, the sounds. So many sounds. He heard so many conversations happening, even though only Rory and Bren were nearby, all at once. He also realized that it was not just Jack whose details were enhanced. The world around them was full of so many more colors. So many more textures. Then he made a colossal mistake. He scented the air. *Shet!* His shaft went rock hard, instantly. Jack's scent was everywhere. Everywhere! And her scent had always done stupid, lustful things to his body. Since he had his back to everyone else, Jack was the only one who noticed the sudden change in the fit of his uniform.

"I think I have some of your vampire senses," he whispered in a strained voice. "Jack, I… One whiff of your scent and I am barely able to control my need to throw you down and bury myself in your sweet, wet, smells-like-heaven pussy." She raised an eyebrow at him, and licked her lips. He wanted those lips on him right the fuck now. "I can even tell you just got wetter from my words. I can practically taste you on the air. Is this what it is like for you?"

She nodded. "Why do you think I had you up against the library wall after that first chase? I've been fighting for control around you from the first moment I saw you. She lowered her eyes to his erection. His whole body was on alert. Completely and utterly, attuned to her.

His own eyes started a slow perusal down her body, until he saw it. Cold overtook the heat of a moment before. The gaping hole in her t-shirt was chilling. Over the region of her heart, her skin was knitted together. Tiny differentiations in the color of her skin indicating a freshly healed scar.

Jack sat up next to him and began to caress his face, "Whatever you did, healed me. I'm okay." Her hand strayed down to his neck and he could not control the shiver of desire racing through him at the feel of her fingers on his skin. Apparently, sensation was enhanced as well. Wow. Her hand paused and she appeared perplexed. "That's just weird. The place where I bit you, healed into bite marks. I've never heard of such a thing."

"Yours as well." He ran his knuckles down along her neck. This time it was her turn to shiver. His hand continued down to cover the rough wound in her chest.

Her scars.

He looked into her eyes and saw a reflection of his own need mirrored there. They had survived.

Then he heard and felt something surprising. "Can you feel it?"

"What?"

"My heart beating inside you."

The most adorable expression of surprise crossed her face.

"Holy shitballs! I have a heartbeat! How did it take me so long to realize it? You distracted me. I have a freaking heartbeat! I never thought I'd have a heartbeat again. What does this mean?"

"I look forward to discovering that. Together. I believe your Earth power combined with my Staraban power with some surprising results. Caran will have an enjoyable time speculating." He rubbed his thumb across her bottom lip and his desire flashed into an inferno as her tongue darted out to lick it.

"Tarc." His name came out of her mouth a low guttural growl. He wrapped his hand behind her head with every intention of capturing all her sounds on his tongue.

"Ya basta. Both of you stop it. You need to stop ogling each other long enough for me to get my much-needed hug from my horny best friend." Rory's face was red and blotchy from crying, but she was the picture of happiness and relief now.

Jack smiled at him, whispering, "Later."

She jumped up and grabbed her friend into a hug lifting her off her feet and twirled. Both females laughed as they fell over. Jack squealed through her humor, "Give a nearly dying girl a chance. You know... I'm kinda like a cat. I seem to have nine lives." They paused. Looked at each other. Then burst out laughing and gasping for air. He was not sure why that was funny, but assumed it must be a human joke.

He stood up next to Bren and they both just stared at the amusing females and shook their heads. "I think they are quite crazy." Bren sounded as though he was concerned but the grin on his face belied the sentiment.

"I think they are both extremely happy that Jack is alive and if I am honest, I too am equally happy, I just do not show it like they do. A part of me is on the ground rolling around laughing with them at this very moment."

Bren turned his head to him. "I cannot believe you joined your essence to hers. You have only known her a few days."

"I know." He put his hand on Bren's shoulder and gave him a direct look, willing his brother to understand. "I cannot explain it to you. With Stala, I knew her for my whole life, but it turned out I did not know her at all. It is the exact opposite with Jack. I have known her for only a few days, but I *know* her. I love her. She is my other half. I never believed in such poetic words before, but I just know. She is mine and it has been true from the beginning. There was no choice made. I needed her to live at any cost."

Bren looked towards the females speculatively, but Tarc was sure that his focus was solely for Rory. For being such a success with alien females all over the Alliance territory, his brother did not seem to understand them well outside of the bedroom and Rory, well, she seemed like she was going to run circles around Bren. This should be fun to observe. He chuckled. His brother looked back towards him with a hard, angry glare and Tarc could tell that he must have read his thoughts. Bren was not amused. Tarc chuckled even louder.

His brother took a swing at him and everything blurred. Barely a moment later, he registered that he was holding Bren's arm in a crushing grip.

Tarc released him shocked at what had happened. Jack was at his side an instant later. "Yeah. So, it'll take you time to understand your speed and strength."

Awe. Horror. Fear. Regret. The deluge of feelings left him momentarily dazed.

Rory was at Bren's side, looking mildly concerned, but saying, "You'll survive."

"Bren. I am sorry, brother. I did not mean to hurt you. I reacted before I even knew what I was doing."

Bren rubbed the sore spot on his arm, milking the moment for all it was worth like the younger brother he was. His eyes darted from Tarc to Jack and back again, "There is something beyond the ritual happening here. You will need to learn from Jack, brother." Tarc watched as Rory gingerly poked his brother's arm causing him to scowl back at her. "Stop touching me." She shrugged and his scowl grew darker. He turned back to Tarc and said, "You should take the night off. Nial has Qisto under control. We can meet up to make a plan tomorrow. Now go. You two must want some time alone." Bren let innuendo drip from his last statement and jokingly leered at Jack.

The leer snapped to a grimace when Rory punched his injured arm.

"Tan delicado. You're such a sensitive alien fuckboy," Rory rolled her eyes. "Go enjoy yourselves and I'll try not to further injure this one."

Tarc had every intention of doing just that.

Enjoying Jack was his whole to do list at the moment.

When they arrived back to their room, the smell of food filled the space. Someone had taken it upon themselves to send pizza—What is it about the Staraban and pizza?—and while it smelled damn enticing, Jack was too hungry for something else entirely. Tarc shed his weapons with record speed, and then, well, then they attacked each other. No other word could describe it.

With his new vampire abilities and heightened senses, and her new heart wanting to beat its way right out of her chest, they went at each other in the most carnal and desperate way.

Tarc pinned her to the wall. Still not used to his strength, he dented the wall with her body. She didn't care. She could take it. His mouth devoured hers. He licked, nipped, plundered and owned her with his tongue and teeth. The focus of her whole being narrowed down to one thing, Tarc. He was hers. All hers.

She stayed true to form and ripped his uniform from him. This time he returned her ardor, ripping her clothes from her.

She saw the shredded ruins of her briefs hit the floor, the ones with "Ripper" across the butt. Damn... apparently her underwear was getting predictive too. She had always loved those. Oh well. Acceptable collateral damage.

She was on fire and needed so much more and she was going to take it. She jumped up, wrapped her legs around his shoulders, balanced against the wall, and ordered, "Eat me now. I need you."

Tarc's eyes had turned the brightest, hottest blue she had ever seen them. Like flaming twin stars. He reached up, held her ass and began the same devouring, ownership ritual with his mouth on her pussy as he had with her mouth. Her hands gripped tight to his hair as he lifted away to murmur at her pussy, "So fucking good. You taste so fucking good. Nothing has ever tasted this good. Not even pizza."

"Really?" She laughed. "Are you really talking about pizza? Now?"

"I did ignore the pizza to eat you as ordered, did I not?" He chuckled and it was clear he had been teasing her. She loved this new side of him.

He continued, "You are the most exciting, challenging, and beautiful female I have ever known. Now come on my face." He grinned up at her as he dived back in and worked his magic.

Jack was instantly lost in sensations too strong to contain. Her power was on the rise, flooding every pore, every thought, every sense. She was overwhelmed and balanced on an edge, when he fucked his tongue into her wet center and pressed his face against her clit causing her to splinter into pieces. She couldn't contain her power, her scream of ecstasy, anything. So she stopped trying. Her body convulsed and pulsated and throbbed as she yelled his name.

When she came back to awareness, her legs were wrapped around his waist and he thrust deeply into her core. She moaned. "Yes. Yes. Yeeessss."

"You feel so good. So soft. Yes. So hot. So wet. I need you so bad Jack. So bad." He thrust over and over as the words spilled out of him. Hard, deep thrusts that raised Jack's power all over again. This time, she sensed something new, though. "Oh goddess. Jack. This energy surging inside me. Is this what you have been feeling? It is amazing. Fuck! I will not last long. Jack!"

"Yes. Harder! Take me. I'm yours. All yours." And he did.

Harder and faster until their powers seemed to pour into each other, to combine into something that cocooned just them. Like during the ritual, their very essences merged. Even their heartbeats aligned. It was all too much. She shuddered hard and then harder as he lost his rhythm giving way to an endless, mutual orgasm. Their joined power didn't flash out, though. Instead it seeped slowly back into their skin as they held on. Finally. Finally. They settled into a blissful peace as the last of their powers were reclaimed.

His forehead rested on hers, their chests heaving. "I have no words for what just happened, Jack." He looked into her eyes. "All I know is it was better and stronger than anything I have ever felt. You are mine Jack. Mine. I love you, *shela*."

"Oh. I have words. That was out of this world, mind-blowing, Earth-shattering, wowzah, holy shit, and I could go on. I love you so much, Tarc."

They pulled away from the wall and realized there was a giant impression of their positions left behind. Jack laughed, "We're going to need sturdier walls."

He laughed with her as he carried her over to the bed. "Hopefully the bed will fare better."

"One would hope."

"We should find out. Science." Her laugh was cut short as he threw her to the bed. Overshot. And she found herself sprawled naked, on the floor, on the other side. "*Fash!*"

"Did you mean to test the floor instead?" Before he could respond, she zoomed behind him and tackled him to the mattress.

They continued to love each other through the night. Slower, faster, intimately and full of love.

For science.

"You are thinking of last night. I can smell the arousal on you and you are flushed and smiling. I want to see you looking just like this, every morning." Jack opened her eyes and he smiled down at her.

Tarc looked at his lover who appeared like a female that was well-satisfied, well-fucked, that really was a great word, and well-loved. His heart swelled. He instinctively reached out and palmed her cheek. "Jack. Will you commit to me?" Had he just asked her that? He had never thought he would even consider trying to have a commitment ceremony again, but all he felt, now that the words were out was the rightness of it.

"I am committed to you. Of course. We share your hearts now!" She was looking at him in complete confusion.

"You misunderstand. I think the equivalent phrase in English is, will you marry me?" He rubbed a finger back and forth along her cheekbone and held his breath waiting for her answer. She began to tear up. "I did not intend to make you sad, *shela*."

Her words came out rushed. "No. No. I'm not sad. I'm so full of happy it's spilling over, Tarc. Yes. *Yes!* I will commit to you." He found himself flat on his back with her draped across him and her arms around his neck. He wrapped his arms around her middle and squeezed her to him. Their hearts beat in sync with each other and it made him truly whole for the first time in his life. "Tarc?" She sounded hesitant. "We haven't discussed what it means that you are part vampire now. What it means that I have one of your hearts. What if you are stuck here? I know you spoke about how beautiful your planet is and I wouldn't want to keep you from it or your family." More tears fell from her and he was sure these were not of the happy kind.

"Shhh. Jack. Whatever happens, I am happy with my decision. I do not know yet what it will mean. It does not matter as long as we are together. My family can come here to visit, if it is needed. You will love my parents." He felt her tense. "Jack. My parents are loving people. They are nothing like your mother."

"What if they don't like me or blame me for your changes, your confinement here?" Panic edged her voice.

"They will love you. You will see. It will be fine. Trust me." He ran his hand up and down her back soothing her.

She lifted her head and sweetly kissed him on the lips. "I do trust you. I never thought I would be able to trust anyone the way I trust you. Rory maybe, but she snuck under my defenses and well...she's different. I don't know how or why I am lucky enough to have you, but I'm not ever letting you go." The tension he had felt released and she melted into him.

"I am never letting you go either, *apura*. You are mine. Always. Everything else will work itself out. All I need is you—and breakfast. First though, we need to get clean so we can meet everyone in the meeting room." He gave her a playful slap to the ass. "Come on."

"Race you," she said. They both blurred into the cleaning room. He could not help touching, nipping and kissing her throughout the process. When they were finished he gave a slow perusal of his beautiful *braif*. "In English, I now get to call you my fiancée. Is that correct?"

A gorgeous smile spread across her features and she nodded. "Yes."

"I like the sound of that."

"Me too." Heat started to rise again between them. "Are you sure we need to go?" Jack trailed her fingers up his chest.

"We agreed to meet up in about twenty minutes."

"We can make twenty minutes work for us? Don't you think?" She moved her hand to her own body and this time her fingers were trailing down over her breast as she pinched her nipple. He groaned. Loudly.

"That is so sexy. Move your hand down and play with your clit for me." He watched as she did just that and he could have sworn after all they had done overnight that he would be sated, at least for a little while, but his erection was back and at full attention. He gripped his own shaft and stroked enjoying the view.

───

Seeing him stroking his beautiful, long, hard erection was too much for Jack. She rushed over, pushed him up against the wall, dropped to her knees, and pushed his hand aside. She began pumping him gently, slowly. She looked up with imploring eyes. "I want to taste you again."

"I want you to taste me again. Take me in your mouth. I want to feel your mouth on me. All of me. Just remember not to get so excited you bite." He grinned at her.

"I have a remedy for that, you know."

"You do?"

She leaned in and bit down on his inner thigh while pumping

him a little firmer. She felt his muscles tense from the brief pain but then relax as she released the easing chemicals. She sucked and sucked and heard him groan above her. "That feels amazing."

She couldn't take being so close to him and smelling him any longer. She released his thigh, licking the wound closed and then licked her way up his shaft. Balls to tip. Licking up the pre-cum that had collected there. "You taste so, so good. I need more." With no more lead up, she sank her mouth over him completely until his cock was nudging the back of her throat. She lifted and came back down until she felt his hands wrap into her hair at the back of her head.

"Yes. I want…mmm. Take more. All of me. All yours." His hands held her still and he began fucking her mouth instead. Her hands gripped his tight ass, sinking her nails in. She looked up his sexy, muscular body and loved having him at the mercy of the pleasure she could give him. She sensed the power rising in him. Rising and coiling and flowing between them as he shouted his release. "Jack! I'm coming. Oh Goddess. Take all of me."

So she did. Every last drop was hers. She felt an ownership over all of it in that moment. All of him. His hands relaxed as he slumped against the wall. She licked her way up his body and kissed him deeply. "I love you. I never thought I would even understand love, never mind actually have someone to share love with."

"I love you too and now, it is my turn."

She soon found herself flung across the room, landing flat on the bed. "Hey! Your aim has improved already, barbaria—."

Before she could complete her thought, he flashed over, yanked her to the foot of the bed, and nudged her legs wide apart. "I aim to be a good vampire student." He moved swiftly and she felt his teeth bite down on her inner thigh and suck.

That revved her engine perfectly. Amazingly. She had never been with a vampire before nor experienced the bite except that first violent time. Well. And the second time in transformation. But. This would be the first in pleasure. Knowing that they could share this with each other was heady. She moaned deeply and arched her back

253

as the erotic sensation of his sucking ratcheted her arousal tenfold. "Tarc. Oh god. Oh god. Oh god."

He licked his bite and lifted his head. "You taste divine. I want more." Then he was at her pussy. Licking and sucking and basically making a meal of her. "So wet and creamy. Just for me." He wrapped his hands around her thighs and pushed her legs towards her shoulders. She was completely and utterly open to him. At least, she thought she was until he moved his hands back down her thighs so he could use his fingers to open her up for more access. It was almost too much. Too exposed. Too vulnerable. But she remembered it was Tarc with her and her doubt subsided. Also, oral. Damn good oral.

She practically arched right off the bed with the feel of his lips and tongue and teeth. He was relentless, powerful, and oh so talented. He stuck a long finger into her wetness, curled it and sucked on her clit. Then two fingers and then three. He worked them in and out and sucked and pressed ever harder at her clit. "Tarc. Your mouth. Your fucking mouth is magic. Ahh! Yes! And your fingers. Your thick, long, wonderful fingers. Yes! Yes!" She came so unbelievably hard.

Before she had the chance to come down from that last, explosive orgasm, he flipped her to her knees as he entered her in one strong thrust from behind. "This is my home now, *shela*. Right here. Inside you is where I want to be every day, all day."

With his long slow strokes in and out of her pussy, he was driving her crazy. "More Tarc. Faster. I need more, dammit. Please?" He just kept at his leisurely pace though. "Tarc!" But no. He just continued to slowly bring her body to the brink and left her teetering on it.

"I do not want to go fast this time. I am going to enjoy myself nice and slow."

She had had enough and attempted to, like many times before, flip the situation and found herself immobilized. She had forgotten that he now had the same strength and speed that she had and could match her in every way. A shiver ran all the way down her spine knowing she was actually at his mercy for the first time.

Turning her on even more. She surrendered completely. Her body limp and his to use and pleasure and fuck. He tormented her until she couldn't contain her pleading any longer. "Please Tarc. I need you, so, so much."

He leaned over, his front completely aligned with her back and whispered in her ear. "Now that you are asking so sweetly, yes. Come for me, my goddess." He leaned back up, pushed her upper back until she was down on her elbows, and then he grabbed her hips and pounded into her hard and fast and relentless.

That was exactly what she'd needed. "Fuck. Oh god. I'm coming! God, yes." She was strung so tight her body uncoiled like an exhale all at once. Her pussy clamping onto his cock as he shouted and came inside her. He pumped a few more times, wringing out every bit of her orgasm from her until she went completely limp and spent on their bed mumbling quietly to herself. "So good. So goddamn good. So, so good."

Tarc lay down along her body and wrapped her in his arms. Her head on his chest. "Maybe we can push the meeting."

"Mmm...So fucking good."

He chuckled and rubbed her back. "Yes, I think we shall just have to keep everyone waiting. I love you."

"I love you, too."

"Forever, *shela*."

"Forever."

UNIVERSE QUEST

Adventures of a Supernatural Geek Girl

October 7, 2025
Dear Reader,

Once again, your outpouring of support is appreciated. While my host is busy with the horizontal tango, I'm bored. So, here I am, blogging again. Fear comments were definitely eye opening, well, if I had eyes. Humans fear some really weird things. Clowns? Santa? AI world domination? Seriously. Where do you get these fears? Vampire fears were pretty predictable. I guess once you become undead, you don't fear much except your demise. One stood out, though. You said you feared blood and have to close your eyes before every feeding, otherwise you faint. You might want to seek out therapy. Seriously, get help. You have many more years of this.

Question of the Day:

If you had to choose between knowing everything and affecting nothing or being capable of achieving great things but having limited knowledge, which would you choose? I would want to be able to actually do great things. Wishful PAL thinking.

Fun Facts:

PAL's form a deep connection with their host, though a good PAL should never let their host know that or a certain host might get a big head and we can't have that.

I don't do hugs and bites.
iByte2

Staraban Headquarters, Portola Valley, CA, USA, Earth

October 7, 2025

Turned out, they pushed the meeting until just before lunch. Jack and Tarc made it to the meeting room after everyone else due to an energetic morning. Assembled inside were Caran looking a bit flustered, Nial looking annoyed—so typical Nial—Bren looking utterly frustrated at Rory while she was busy switching between flirtation and irritation with him, and Jill who had her resting bitch face on full display.

Jack sidled up to Jill, whom she hadn't seen since they returned from their Pinnacles mission, and whispered to her. "You seem to still be alive. Haven't angered anyone here into killing you yet?"

The rebel responded with a hushed tone as well. "I see you're still just as undead. A pity."

"Actually, my dear Spikey, I now have a functional heart. That seems pretty alive to me."

"I could fix that for you."

"Nah." They both smirked.

"So...I like your friend," she indicated Rory. "I may have to steal her to be my best friend. She's fantastic at keeping that ridiculous male jumping. I have no idea how to handle them the way she does."

"Are you seriously admitting to not being good at something?"

"You try growing up surrounded by a bunch of militia nut jobs. I had to protect myself from their attention my whole life. That means I'm a badass bitch, but it doesn't mean I know how to handle them without kicking their ass."

"Point taken. Sorry you had to grow up that way."

"Yeah. Thanks." She lifted her chin in Rory's direction. "She's a woman who knows what she's doing. He's all tied up in knots."

"So I see. Poor Bren. You're right about Rory. She's a force of nature. Nothing can stand in her way, keep her down, or move her. And that holds true for men. They've been eating out of her palm since I've known her. She has her reasons, though. You know, I'm willing to have a threesome on the friendship with the caveat you keep your acerbic tongue pointing in a more outwardly direction." She put her hand out to Jill.

"If you can keep your fangs to yourself, I'm happy with your threesome proposal." Jill accepted her hand and they shook on it.

"No worries. My fangs are completely spoken for these days. You should have seen what my fangs were doing just a couple of—"

"Whoa. Whoa. Whoa. TMI. This is a starter friendship. Give a girl a chance to adjust before you start throwing fang porn in her face. Sheesh."

"Noted. Speaking of friendships and porn, how are you handling Nial?"

"What the fuck is that supposed to mean? There's no handling going on. Why are you asking that? What has he said? I'm going to kill that alien." This woman, who had always seemed completely in control, looked downright frazzled by Jack's question. Apparently, she really couldn't handle men.

"The lady doth protest too much, methinks." She giggled at Jill's expression and then grimaced at the punch to her arm. "Ouch." She rubbed at the injured spot.

"I thought you were all immortal and shit. The big bad vampire can't take a punch?"

"I'm immortal and shit and yeah, I can take a punch, but that doesn't mean it doesn't hurt."

"Well, I won't punch you, if you stop quoting Shakespeare while being nosy."

"You don't actually know how to have girlfriends, do you?"

"Not a lot of girls, or boys, at the crazy camp and those that were there were, you know, crazy. I really didn't want to be all friendly with them so we can discuss even more murder and mayhem. I did that with my dad all day already. I kinda just grew up trying to stay sane and safe."

Jack quirked an eyebrow at her.

"Okay. You may be right. I don't know how to do the friend thing." She glared at Jack but seemed to come to a decision. "Fine. I've never had anyone want to protect me before. I find I'm both intrigued and thoroughly infuriated by this behavior. By him. That's all you're getting. If you say another word, this friendship will be the shortest in history because I'll be testing your immortality."

Jack patted her on the back. "You see. Now that wasn't so hard. Sharing is caring. And Jill...I think he finds you equally intriguing and infuriating. If you two don't scowl each other to death, who knows?" She smiled at Jill but then moved further into the room because it looked like Rory and Bren might actually need an intervention. Tarc was just standing by having a field day watching her friend mess with Bren. *Time to use those negotiation skills I've gotten good at with the programmers.* "Rory, ehem, could I get you to stand down for a minute and tell me what happened?"

Rory turned to her and started with, "¡Estúpido! He's hot, too, so it's a damn shame he isn't brighter." It went downhill after that. There was a lot of hand talking, something about how little he thinks of her skills, something about how his belittling stance makes it hard for her to seduce him, something about giving him her resume so he'd stop coddling her, and after that, frankly Jack was done. She held up her hand to stop her friend who understood instantly.

So in conclusion, Rory batted her lashes in Bren's direction while giving him the bird, which Jack figured summed it up rather nicely, really. She wasn't sure how, but she held in her laugh at Bren's reaction as Rory walked over to stand near Jill who was still studying her friend like she was made of pure magic.

The idea that Rory needed protection of any kind was freaking hilarious. *If they only knew.* With as even a tone as she could muster, she asked, "Bren. Any response to Rory's accusations?"

Bren puffed up his chest a little.

Oh my. This was going to be good. And it was. Excellently ridiculous. Something about his strength and blah, blah, little female. Blech.

"I see. Bren, do you know what Rory does at HARM or what she did before it?"

"She said something about working with guns."

She did have to laugh at that. "Well, she does work with guns, of *all* kinds. Also, close proximity weapons, a multitude of deadly gadgets, and explosives. She really loves her explosives."

Bren paled, "She what? Explosives? *Fashing* explosives? Do you have a wish for death, female? How can you behave so reckless with your safety?"

Jack continued, "Bren, I don't think you're making things any better, so maybe the best solution for now is, and I say this as your soon to be sister-in-law with all the affection that role affords you, to back the fuck off. Not a word. If you continue down the path you're on, she may well kill you and I'd be the one forced to explain justifiable homicide to your brother. I'd rather not."

Tarc came up behind Bren and put an arm around his shoulders. "My *braif* is correct. Perhaps you need to step back before you say something regrettable, brother."

"*Shet!*" Bren spit out, then dislodged Tarc's arm and walked to the exact opposite side of the room from Rory. His glare might intimidate most others, but Rory chose that moment to stick her finger in her mouth and suck. Bren stiffened and glared even harder.

"Um… Okay, then. Amusing as this is, time to get back to work? Caran, have you gotten the results of the samples we provided? And, how's Will? He's woken up, hasn't he?"

"Will, quite surprisingly, woke up alright." A low angry voice said coming from the entry way.

Caran jumped, quickly regained her composure, and shook one hand in Will's general direction as if to say, "He's all yours."

"Funny thing is," his tone anything but amused, "I don't remember giving anyone permission to make me a vampire."

Jack flinched at that slice of truth. She wanted to apologize, but he didn't give her a chance. Just kept right on talking.

Accusing.

Justifiably so.

"In fact, I hadn't even known vampires existed until the hour before my death because, apparently, trust only flowed in one direction with us. Right Jack? Even if I ignore your dishonesty, though, there's still one thing I can't get past. Since I was honest with you,

you *knew* I never liked anything that didn't have a scientific explanation? And, I don't think it's a stretch to think being a vampire would fall under that heading."

Each word hit its mark. Hard. Jack wrapped an arm around her middle in a defense she didn't feel she deserved, but needed.

"And yet, here we are. I suppose I should thank you for saving my life. But... you shouldn't hold your breath waiting for that gratitude. Oh wait. It wouldn't matter if you did. That's right. No breathing."

She'd known changing him without his consent would not be a good idea and yet she and Rory had selfishly not wanted to lose a friend. She stepped towards him. "Will. I am so incredibly sorry. Rory and I... we care so much for you. You're our friend and we couldn't just let you die when I had the means to give you your life bac—"

His lip curled up in a snarl as he yelled back. "Life! This is not life! My heart isn't beating. I don't need to breathe. I'm a man of science and yet I can barely concentrate because my senses are constantly overwhelming me. And..." His eyes flicked to Caran and she saw pain and shame flash across his features. It was brief and she had to wonder what it meant as he turned back to her with derision. "I now need to drink blood to survive. And all this will be my existence for an eternity because I can't bring myself to commit suicide. So thank you very much, friend."

Tarc came up alongside her, putting a protective arm around her waist and seemed about to argue. She held up her hand to stop him. This was between Will and her. Tears pricked the back of her eyes, but she knew it would offend him even more if she cried over her choice, so she ruthlessly blinked them away. "I'm truly sorry if I made the wrong decision."

Rory stepped forward to interject, "We. We made the choice."

Jack nodded in acknowledgement and gratitude. "We. We had only a few minutes to bring you back or let you go and for better or worse, it's done. I *can* help you adjust to life as a vampire. It's really not so bad."

"No need. I've caught up on all five years of your blog posts and have a pretty good grip on what I can and cannot do. I'll figure out the rest."

"Let me at least forward you the book that taught me our origin story and all the rules I've shared on my blog."

"Fine." He seemed to finally collect himself and scanned the rest of the occupants in the room. "What are you meeting about in here? I may as well be useful while I figure out what I plan to do with this new…" He paused like he could barely get the word out "…life, that I have."

She, and of course Tarc and Will, overheard Jill whisper to Rory. "Who's the douchebag with the chip on his shoulder? Somebody needs his blankie."

Tarc suddenly had a coughing fit beside her, which she pointedly ignored, and Will glared at Jill. "Who's she?"

"Long story, longer…" She explained to Will all that had happened over the last few days.

Will's mouth opened. Closed. Opened. Closed. Then he sat there just absorbing and processing as he sometimes did. He finally spoke. "I'm going to ignore everything except what is relevant now. I assume this meeting is to discuss the results of the testing on the soil samples? What were you hoping to achei—Nevermind. You were trying to figure out how the microbiomes from deeper into the Earth were fairing." He turned to Caran. "Have you found that when a planet is dying there is first a drastically negative change seen there?"

"That is exactly it." Caran replied. She still seemed tense, but now that they were discussing science, she didn't seem as ready to bolt. "What we have found is the biodiversity of those biomes tends to drop drastically when such a thing begins to happen due to the hostile environment being created. We have special technology around this since our company mission is to find planets with a long, healthy life ahead of them to relocate our clients to."

Will finally appeared like, well, Will. Despite his earlier protests to the contrary, he was completely focused on Caran as she explained. He had his scientist face on, which gave Jack at least a kernel of hope.

"I can now definitively say that the science reports we received from the Vrolan ambassador and his team, were falsified, or at the very least skewed. I found minor fluctuations and, of course, global warming is still a real threat, but I believe with our technology and help from human scientists to direct our efforts, we would be able to reverse the issues currently facing Earth. In a way, you should thank the Vrolans for bringing us here, because without us, your planet would have been fine, but humans would have wiped themselves off the planet not very long from now. Also, your technology is ridiculously unadvanced."

Jack whispered to Tarc, "But we've got pizza," which made him cough to cover his laugh. Even Will, who she forgot now had vampire hearing, gave a little snort at that. He covered it up right away, but again, she couldn't help the hope that flared in her heart. She also knew Rory had heard, but nothing had changed in her friend's demeanor. Rory had amazing control. She never gave herself away and Jack figured that had to do with all she lived with until she made her own escape at a young age. They had that in common as well, though for very different reasons.

Caran ignored the whole byplay and continued. "In conclusion, it is not a perfectly healthy planet, but it is most definitely not dying anytime soon as proposed."

The room went utterly silent as the ramifications of her findings really sank.

It took a few minutes for reality to really sink in, but when it did, Tarc felt shame. It clogged his throat, and yet he could not contain the words that he uttered next. "I have failed as the leader of our company. I initiated first contact on a planet which had not developed interstellar space travel *and* initiated relocation upon them based on completely false claims." Tarc clenched his fists and tried to remember his breathing. Did he even still need to breath? *Shet!* He was so angry at himself. Oh, Goddess. Some of the humans were already relocated off planet. Others have had their lives completely disrupted. "I do not know what I can say. I should step down as the head of ARC."

He heard gasps from his family. The humans and vampires were not shocked. They were probably too angry to be shocked. Jack's hand came up to cup his cheek and a part of him wanted to recoil. He did not move, but he also felt he did not deserve her. How did she not hate him?

"Tarc. I know it has been a crazy quick courtship, full of plenty of blunders, but I actually do know you and I know what is going through your head right now. And you need to stop."

"But how do you not hate me?"

"Listen. When you had your chance to learn something new, to be open to potentially being proven wrong, you made sure that we got the information we have today. It takes a truly strong leader to allow themselves to be proven wrong. It is easy to be right. When you make a bad choice, and can admit to the mistake, what's left is to make amends. We figure out how to move forward."

He captured her into him for a hug. He needed to feel her, borrow some of her comfort and strength. "Thank you, *shela*. I know you are probably correct, but—"

Bren jumped in, "No, brother. You are staying right where you are. I refuse to let you step down. Listen to your *braif*."

He looked between Jack and Bren and then to Caran and Nial and it looked like they were all in agreement. "I guess I am outnumbered. I will stay and make things right with Earth. I will do whatever needs to be done."

Bren came closer. "Brother, we were all deceived. It was not just you. For my effort at amends, I would like to take all of the information we have gathered, as well as our prisoner, back to the All Alien Alliance. We need to figure out how deeply into the Vrolan government this goes and why."

"I have a ballpark reason for you guys." Hal's smug voice came out from Jack's watch to startle quite a few who still had not heard about him. It still disturbed him that his female carried around a sentient male in her mind, but since Hal saved her life, he was willing to overlook it. Grudgingly.

"I haven't had the time to go through everything but from what I've gathered so far, it has something to do with a resource located on Earth. They've actually been here for a while, I believe, working on something. They're readying for a next phase and needed the planet unoccupied. I'll send you everything I've found and maybe you can make more sense of what is there since I don't know the Vrolan nor the Alliance. I'll also continue to sift through the data to see what else I can find."

He may not like it, but Hal really was helpful. "Thank you, Hal. Great job." He remembered how Jack told him that she was one of the lead programmers in the PAL project and he fell a little more in love with her. No wonder she hacked their terminals so easily. He really was one lucky warrior. He squeezed her waist just a little to bring her flush along his side. One of her hands came around his waist and gave him a small squeeze too.

"You're welcome. Now, Will... Don't be mad at me, but I'm happy you are still with us. I don't breathe either, but I'm alive. Life comes in many variations. Keep that in mind."

Will did not answer, but he did appear to be considering what Hal said.

Tarc turned to face Bren. "You have my permission to take the prisoner and the information to the Alliance." Tarc added for emphasis. "Stay aware."

They clasped hands and shared one of their silent communications. Bren looked at him conveying, "Well of course I will be aware. You be careful here, too."

Tarc responded with his arched brow. "As though I am ever not careful. You realize, I may be immortal now. That means one day you will be my older brother as I stay young and live forever."

Bren returned with, "Fucker." And then jabbed him in the arm with his free hand.

"You have now picked up that word too, I see. Be prepared for it to take over your vocabulary. But, yes, I am." They unclasped and smiled in kinship. "Nial, prepare to leave with Bren. Keep him out of trouble." Everyone but Bren laughed lightly.

Bren just grumbled under his breath, instead. "Overprotective, older *sharta*."

"I will start organizing a new base here." His sister stated. "A scientific lab where we can set up the technology and protocols we need to fix Earth."

"Will should help you. He is one of the leading scientists in the study of geology, amongst other things," Rory helpfully added.

"Oh. I did not realize. Yes. That does sound like it makes sense." He did not miss that his sister was uncomfortable around Will. Had something happened when he woke up? He was going to have to figure that out later. His sister would not have agreed to work with Will if something bad had happened. She would not put herself into an uncomfortable situation to appease anyone. Maybe Will just rubs her the wrong way? He was a very unpleasant human, as far as Tarc was concerned.

"I suppose I should make this new, undesired life worth something. I'll help set up whatever is needed. Just let me know when and where. If you need some fast coding, I also have a whole staff of infuriating programmers we can utilize." Will shrugged like a man who cared very little about anything at the moment. Tarc hoped, for Jack's sake, that helping with this project would give her friend the purpose needed to snap out of his resentment. Or, he could always just kill him. That was not off the table as far as he was concerned.

"Sounds like we have a plan mov—"

"We are going with Bren to triple A. Seriously, who comes up with your names?" Rory stepped forward with Jill right next to her.

Bren moved before Rory. "No. Not a chance. This is a dangerous mission, not a trip to explore the stars." And... Once again his brother was behaving like a complete idiot, he believed was the appropriate human term, over Rory.

"There is no way we are taking rebels with us on our mission." Apparently, Nial decided to join the idiot pile up. Fuck. Now what? Both warriors looked ready to do battle over this.

"In my opinion, it would not hurt to take the two females with you. Rory could prove useful in engineering and munitions and Jill has proven to be a fierce fighter. The Alliance might also wish to meet humans and speak to them directly about the problems we faced here. Of course, since you will be running the ship on this mission, it falls to you to make the decision. Just think about it carefully."

Which of course he did not. "Then, they stay."

"¡Cabrón!" Rory shouted back and left the room.

"Neanderthal motherfuckers." Jill, too, turned and angrily strode from the room.

"Your brother is now officially on my shitlist." It was Jack's turn to stride out of the room angrily. Great.

"Are you going to tell me I cannot do my job either, Bren?" His sister gave their brother a scathing look and then she too exited the room.

Laughter came from behind him and he found Will unable to contain his mirth. "Wow. You aliens are really bad at dealing with Earth women. You're lucky you still have your balls after what you just said. I've seen Rory bring a man low for less."

Bren looked ready to explode. "None of your business, vampire." That hit its target. Will glared. But Bren did not stop. "Go do science things. This mission is between us." Bren indicated himself, Tarc, and Nial.

Will stiffly nodded, his scowl returned. "I suppose you're right. She can have your balls for all I care. I'll go find some way to be useful." He blurred out of the room.

"Well. You definitely cleared this room rather quickly, little brother. Are you sure this is the route you wish to go?"

"Yes."

"And I agree with him," Nial said swiftly.

"I see." As he was leaving, he heard Bren and Nial begin to lay out the details of all they would need to take care of in preparation for their mission. He was not sure what the future would bring for them, with the angry women they seemed to want to protect, but that was not his concern at the moment.

He found Jack in the food hall with Rory and Jill and realized that his brother and Nial might be in even more trouble than he thought. The three women had their heads together and they were definitely planning something. He decided, again, it was none of his concern. Let his brother deal with the consequences of his decision. He just wanted to get Jack alone again and hold her. He was still shaken by the depth of his mistake with Earth and needed her. He hoped she would not be mad at him too.

As he approached, she looked up and his fears were proven misplaced. The love in her eyes warmed him to the depth of his being. He felt the power in their joined essence was strong. "Come Jack. I want to see what your next t-shirt predicts for our future."

Her smile had to be the most beautiful thing he had ever seen. "Does that mean I'm taking this one off?" She looked him up and down and he just knew that he was never going to get enough of her. Never.

"I am willing to sacrifice another uniform for the cause." They made it to their room in record time.

EPI-BLOG : INVASION

Adventures of a Supernatural Geek Girl

October 9, 2025
Dear Reader,

What the hell has my PAL been doing in here? Can't a vampire take a mini-vacation? If you are so scared of AI world domination, should you really be encouraging him in blog domination? It's a slippery slope you know.

Regardless.

I. Am. Back!

I have an interesting development to share with you. The rebellion and the aliens are now actively working together. You should check your local news channel to get caught up, because it has been a busy week.

Fun Facts:

As a PAL host who definitely does not have a big head, I will admit, I have formed a deep attachment to my PAL as well. In fact, I'm working on a surprise for him. The question is, how to surprise someone that literally knows what you're thinking? You give them vacation time.

I can't wait to see his reaction when he comes back from a little trip he's taking, more on that later.

I definitely do hugs and bites!
iByte

Keep reading for a snippet from *Taming Rory*, where Bren and Rory take a space voyage and battle each other, their sexual attraction, their feelings, and their enemies. Not necessarily in that order.

Taming Rory
Book Two of the Love Wars Series

Chapter 1 — Encounter at Knife Point

Captain's Log: Earth date October 9, 2025
The Staraban-alien-dumbass also known as Bren has decreed that little ol' human me is to stay put on Earth for my own safety. What this oversized hotness doesn't understand is that there is only one captain of my life and it sure as hell isn't him. My new friend Jill and I plan to stow aboard his ship if I can't convince him, one way or another, to relent. The only things sharper than my knives, after all, are my wit and my tongue. Hopefully he can be made to see reason because it's not just his ship I want to board and ride. The next captain's log will be made in space because that is the final frontier.

Rory out.

Staraban Base, Northern California

October 9, 2025

Bren of the Staraban, fierce warrior and second-in-command of the Alien Relocation Cooperative (ARC), never cowered from anyone. The opposite. With his scarred face and tall muscular stature, he was feared by many even as he was desired by females across the galaxy. Therefore, he had to ask himself, how had he ended up in the predicament he was in at that moment. Actually, he knew. Two words. Aurora Espinoza. Ever since he met the diminutive, curvaceous, and sexy human female, nothing made much sense.

Rory with her thick, dark brown, wavy hair that he wanted to feel cascading around him as he held her close. Her big unusual yellow-green expressive eyes that he wanted to see glazed in desire. Her warm, light brown skin that he wanted to see flushed and naked against his. Her full sensual mouth that he wanted to see wrapped around his—Bren flinched back to awareness. Those lips were currently yelling profanities at him, in two Earth languages, as she threw knives all around him.

Rory, a munitions expert, which he had only learned about recently, was expert with most weapons. He hoped with her perfect aim, she was missing him on purpose. She got really fucking close, though. Without turning to look, he could tell there was a knife outline of him in his wall. Only *she* would come to have a conversation wielding throwing knives. It was hard to tell if her knives or her words had sharper points.

"Rory, you are being unreasonable *and* homicidal." He realized his mistake too late, because that was the wrong thing to say. Two more knives embedded in his wall behind him. One had come uncomfortably close to his groin.

"I'm unreasonable? Me? ¡Cabrón!" She seemed to use that word a lot around him. "You haven't seen unreasonable. I'm going to go get something bigger to make my point. Don't move." She threw her last knife and this time it caught the slightest bit of his uniform pant leg, pinning it to the wall. She turned and made her way to the door.

He pulled his leg, ripping his pant leg, and caught up to her at the door. He turned her around and using his hands on her shoulders, pinned her to it. "I think not. You are behaving like a child. A dangerous child. This display has to stop. I will not endanger you by taking you on this mission. That is final. You do not understand the dangers that exist out in space and you are human, there are too many things that could kill you out there."

Her eyes narrowed at him. "I have every right to come on this mission. The All Alien Alliance will be hearing and making judgements about events that were perpetrated against my planet and people." She may have a point since they recently found out the Vrolan aliens who had hired his family's company to relocate humans from Earth, had lied about Earth's dying planet status. The deception was disturbing and needed to be reported to AAA to start an investigation. Point or not, she was not coming. "Some of my people should be present for this. *You* are being unreasonable. I can defend myself, as the knives in your wall can attest."

"The fact that I have you now pinned to my door and at my mercy, says differently. One wrong mo—" He groaned and her name came out as a plea. "Rory." He laid his forehead down to the top of her head. She was so small. So delicate. She had him completely at her mercy, and she knew it. "What are you doing?"

"I would've thought it was obvious. I could've sworn that I'd heard you had a lot of experience with the opposite sex." She continued to rub her hand up and down his ever growing shaft. Her hand was so small and yet she applied just the right amount of pressure to drive him wild. He wanted so much more. He wanted to feel her hand on his actual cock with no material separating them.

"Rory. You keep that up, and you will see exactly how much knowledge I have. I will make you feel so good. Let me pleasure you."

"You want to bring me pleasure?" Her voice dripped with sex like he was sure his cock was doing.

"Yes. So much pleasure." His hips pushed forward even more fully into her hand. He moved one hand from her shoulder to cup her cheek and turn her face up to his. She looked him in the eyes with a small smile playing along her lips.

"If you really want to give me pleasure——" She paused and bit her bottom lip, then licked it. His eyes were completely transfixed with her full bottom lip. He was so riveted, that he almost missed her next words, and then his brain registered what she said. "——you will let me come with you on this trip."

He looked back into her eyes and saw the steel there. She was using sex as a weapon. She was actually seducing him to get her way. He wanted this woman and all she wanted was to come on his mission. His once overheated blood turned to ice. "No."

He stepped away from her. One step. Two steps. Three. Until he could breathe. Until he could gather his composure.

"You will *not* be coming. I have a lot of preparations and do not have time for your type of *negotiations*." He saw her flinch, but he had a mission to get to. He did not have time for her manipulations.

Because If he had the time, he would have to admit it hurt that her seduction only happened for ulterior motives.

Because if he had the time, he would have to admit he had wanted her since the moment they met.

Join my newsletter and stay informed about the release date for Taming Rory.

ABOUT THE AUTHOR

Michelle Mars has an unhealthy obsession with coffee, caramel, and funny t-shirts. This single mom of two amazing, kind, and creative dragons/children has naturally purple hair and loves nothing more than talking books, kids, and living your best life. She enjoys reading romance, traveling, and writing stories that make her readers laugh, sweat, and swoon.

Author of the paranormal, sci-fi, rom-com Love Wars Series; Moving Jack, out now, and Taming Rory, coming soon.

The first book in her contemporary rom-com series The Frisky Bean, Frisky Intentions, will be out the first half of 2020 but you can catch a prequel short story named Frisky Connections in the Eight Kisses Hanukkah anthology out now.

Michelle's truth: Humor is a turn-on!